"Then why are you going home?" he asked.

"Oh, I can't get a job here."

"They won't keep you?" he remarked, intuitively.

"They can't," said Carrie.

"I'll tell you what you do," he said. "You come with me. I'll take care of you."

Carrie listened, but did not answer. It seemed like a way out of her difficulty. Drouet seemed to share her way of looking at things. He was clean, handsome, well dressed, and sympathetic. His voice was the voice of a friend.

A Background Note about *Sister Carrie*

When Theodore Dreiser was born, in 1871, America was becoming an industrialized country. In many cities, factories were being built, and people moved from rural areas into the cities to find work. Many immigrants, looking for better job opportunities, also came to American cities. But factory work was brutal. People worked long hours, under harsh conditions, and for little pay. Some workers resorted to strikes, trying to force businesses to improve working conditions.

Most people were poor. Fighting their way out of poverty was difficult, and few succeeded. When workers lost their jobs because their companies went bankrupt or because they became ill, there were few agencies to help them find housing, food, or work. Suddenly, people could lose everything—their homes, their money, and even their hope.

At the time, there were many "self-made men," who started out with nothing in life and later made a fortune. There were also a few "independent" women. These were single women, who made their own living without the support of families or husbands. Today many people take women's independence for granted. But in Dreiser's time such a lifestyle was unusual, daring, and often dangerous.

SISTER Carrie

Theodore Dreiser

Edited, and with an Afterword,
by Lisa Barsky

TP THE TOWNSEND LIBRARY

SISTER CARRIE

TP THE TOWNSEND LIBRARY

For more titles in the Townsend Library,
visit our website: **www.townsendpress.com**

All new material in this edition is
copyright © 2005 by Townsend Press.
Printed in the United States of America

0 9 8 7 6 5 4 3 2 1

Townsend Press, Inc.
1038 Industrial Drive
West Berlin, New Jersey 08091

ISBN 1-59194-011-7

Library of Congress Control Number:
2004117937

CONTENTS

CHAPTER 1

The Lure of the City

When Caroline Meeber boarded the afternoon train for Chicago, she carried with her only a small suitcase, a handbag made out of cheap imitation alligator skin, a small lunch in a paper bag, a scrap of paper with her sister's address, and four dollars in cash. It was August, 1889. She was eighteen years old, eager, and timid. And because she was young and inexperienced, she was also full of illusions about the world. She had a moment of sadness as she left behind her family, her village, and her childhood. But it was easy to break ties with them, since they could never offer her anything important.

Of course, she could always come back. Every day there were many trains that came to Chicago. And Columbia City, her childhood home, was only a few hours away. She looked at the little slip of paper with her sister's address on it and wondered. As she watched the familiar green countryside pass by her, she quickly turned her thoughts to Chicago and imagined what it might be like.

When a young woman leaves her home at eighteen, she does one of two things. Either she falls into the hands of someone who can save her, and her life becomes better. Or she takes on the moral values of the city, and her life becomes worse. There is nothing in between. Like a powerful magnet, the city shrewdly, powerfully attracts human souls. With its thousand lights, sounds, and activities, the city can fascinate and seduce. And it can easily trick or corrupt an innocent woman, especially if she has no one to guide her.

Caroline, who was called Sister Carrie by her family, was guided mostly by self-interest. She was a typical American girl—of average intelligence, though not well educated. She was pretty, though not yet able to flirt like a woman. But she was eager to develop her charms, to own more things, to conquer the city.

"That," said a voice in her ear, "is one of the prettiest little resorts in Wisconsin."

"Is it?" she answered nervously.

For some time she had been aware that the man sitting behind her had been looking her over. She knew that she ought to ignore him. But previous conquests had made him daring. His magnetic appeal was stronger than her timidity. And so she answered.

He leaned forward, putting his elbows on the back of her seat.

"Yes," he pursued smoothly. "That is a great resort for Chicago people. The hotels are swell.

You aren't familiar with this area, are you?"

"Oh, yes, I am," answered Carrie. "That is, I live in Columbia City. I have never been through here, though."

"So, this is your first visit to Chicago," he observed.

All this time, she had been looking at him out of the corner of her eye. He had bright red cheeks and a light moustache. He was wearing a stylish gray felt hat. Torn between wanting to protect herself and wanting to flirt with this attractive man, she now looked directly at him.

"I didn't say that," she said.

"Oh," he answered pleasantly, pretending that he had made a mistake. "I thought you did."

He was a traveling salesman. And he dressed and acted with one goal in mind—seducing young women. His type was called a "masher." Without good clothes, of course, such a man was nothing. This one wore a flashy, tight-fitting brown suit, highly polished tan shoes, a pink-striped shirt with gold-plated buttons set with jewel-like stones, and several heavy rings. Whenever he saw a single woman, he approached her in a slick, familiar manner. But he used a special technique with young women who looked vulnerable. First he would be attentive to them, offering to help them in all kinds of little ways. Then he would gradually move in closer and win them over.

As Carrie looked at this man's fashionable clothing, she became self-conscious about her own plain, blue dress and worn-out shoes.

"Let's see," he went on. "I know lots of people in your town—Morgenroth, who owns the clothing store, and Gibson, the dry goods man."

"Oh, do you?" she interrupted. She remembered how much she had longed for the things in their store windows. And so she became more interested in the conversation.

Having found a way to capture her attention, the man now came around and sat beside her. He talked about clothing sales, his travels, Chicago, and things to do in the city.

"If you are going there, you'll really enjoy it. Do you have any relatives?"

"I am going to visit my sister," she explained.

"There's so much to see—theaters, crowds, tall buildings, fine houses. Oh, you'll really like that."

She realized that she would never be able to afford such a lifestyle. And that made her feel even less important. And yet, the possibility of so much wealth also appealed to her. She could not help smiling when he told her she reminded him of a popular actress.

"You'll be staying in Chicago for a little while, won't you?" he asked, now that they were having such an easy conversation.

"I don't know," said Carrie vaguely, worried for a moment that she might not find a job.

"Several weeks, anyhow," he said, looking steadily into her eyes.

She realized that he was interested in her for the one reason that a woman both enjoys and fears. If she had been more experienced, however, she would have known how to keep her true feelings secret. And she would never have looked a man so steadily in the eyes.

"Why do you ask?" she said.

"Well, I'm going to be there several weeks. I could show you around."

"I don't know whether you can or not. I mean, I don't know whether I can. I shall be living with my sister, and . . ."

"Well, if she minds, we'll fix that." He took out his pencil and a little notebook as if it were all settled. "What is your address there?"

She fumbled in her bag for the address slip.

He reached into his hip pocket and pulled out a fat wallet. It was filled with slips of paper, some mileage books, a roll of dollar bills. She had never before met anyone so impressive. She imagined that he was at the center of a world of fortune. And so she had a positive attitude toward everything he might do.

He handed her a neat business card, which read, "Bartlett, Caryoe & Company." He touched the corner where his name was engraved, "Charles H. Drouet."

"That's me," he said. "It's pronounced 'Drew-eh.' Our family was French, on my father's side."

Then he showed her a letter with a picture on it. "This is the company I work for, at the corner of State and Lake." He was proud to be connected with such a company, and he made her feel the same way.

"What is your address?" he began again, ready to write it down.

She looked at his hand.

"Carrie Meeber," she said slowly. "Three hundred and fifty-four West Van Buren Street, in care of S.C. Hanson."

He wrote it down and asked, "You'll be at home if I stop by Monday night?"

"I think so," she answered.

But their casual words did not express their true feelings. When he took her address, she felt that she had given up something to him. And he felt that he had gained a victory over her. Already they felt that they were somehow associated. Already he took control in directing the conversation. His words were easy. Her manner was relaxed.

As they approached Chicago, it was almost night. And night promises pleasure and freedom for people that work hard during the day.

"This is the Chicago River," said Drouet, pointing enthusiastically to a little muddy creek. "Chicago is getting to be a great town. It's wonderful. You'll find lots to see here."

But she felt only fear—fear that she was alone, away from home, and rushing into the city. For the city seemed to her like a huge sea of life and work.

"Chicago! Chicago!" called the conductor,

slamming the door open. Carrie picked up her poor little suitcase and closed her hand firmly on her bag.

Drouet stood up, straightening his pants. "I suppose your relatives will be here to meet you? Let me carry your suitcase."

"Oh, no," she said. "I'd rather you wouldn't. I'd rather you wouldn't be with me when I meet my sister."

"All right," he said kindly. "I'll be near, though, in case she isn't here. And then I can take you out there safely."

"You're so kind," said Carrie. She appreciated his taking care of her in this unfamiliar situation.

"Chi-ca-go!" called the conductor, stretching out the word. Carrie watched the glow of the streetlights passing by. The train was slowing down, and people were crowding in front of the door.

"Well, here we are," said Drouet, leading the way to the door. "Goodbye, till I see you Monday." He held out his hand.

"Goodbye," she answered, taking his hand.

"Remember, I'll be looking till you find your sister."

She smiled into his eyes.

They got off the train, and he pretended not to be watching her. A thin-faced, ordinary looking woman recognized Carrie and hurried over toward her.

"Why, Sister Carrie!" she began, as they hugged each other.

Suddenly Carrie felt a cold reality closing in on her. Looking at her sister, she was reminded that the world of work was hard and grim. At that moment, the wonderful city world of lights, sounds, and excitement seemed to disappear.

"So, how are all the folks at home?" she began. "How is father, and mother?"

Carrie answered, but she was looking the other way, toward Drouet. He was looking back. He saw that she saw him, and that she was safe with her sister. He gave her a faint smile and turned to go. As he left her, Carrie felt that she was losing something. With her sister she felt alone, a lone figure in a tossing, thoughtless sea.

CHAPTER 2

Poverty and Power

Carrie gazed out the front window onto the street below her sister's small third-floor apartment. She marveled at the lights, sounds, movements, and murmur of the vast city, which stretched for miles and miles in every direction. Inside, the apartment was a hastily put-together mixture of ugly wallpaper, thin rag carpeting, and cheap furniture. Minnie Hanson briefly introduced Carrie to her husband. Then she let Carrie hold the baby so that she could prepare dinner. Minnie's husband asked a few questions and sat down to read the evening paper. He was a silent man, who at this time earned his living cleaning train cars. He was concerned about making monthly payments on a property that he wanted to own. His ambition was someday to be able to build a house on it. Naturally, Carrie was expected to find a job and pay for her own room and meals. He couldn't care less about Carrie; he was interested only in how quickly she could earn some money.

"It's a big place," he said. "You can get a job

somewhere in a few days. Everybody does."

At one point, when the baby's crying disturbed his reading, Hanson came over and held it. Carrie then saw another, more pleasant side to him. He was patient. And he was very involved with his child.

"Now, now," he said, walking. "There, there." He had a faint accent that he had picked up from his father, a Swedish immigrant.

"You'll want to see the city first, won't you?" said Minnie, when they were eating. "Well, we'll go out Sunday and see Lincoln Park."

Carrie noticed that Hanson said nothing to this. He seemed to be thinking of something else.

"Well," Carrie said, "I think I'll look around tomorrow. I've got Friday and Saturday, and it won't be any trouble. Which way is the business district?"

Before Minnie could explain, her husband suddenly started telling Carrie about the big manufacturing businesses in Chicago.

"Lots of girls work there. You could get home easy, too. It isn't very far."

Then Hanson jumped up and handed the child to his wife. "I've got to get up early in the morning, so I'll go to bed."

Minnie explained, "He's got to get up at five-thirty."

"And what time do you get up to fix breakfast for him?" asked Carrie.

"At about twenty minutes of five."

Minnie and her husband had become conditioned to constant hard work. In fact, the whole tone of the apartment shut out everything except a narrow life of drudgery. Carrie could see that she would have to give up her relationship with Drouet. Hanson spent every evening sitting in the front room, reading his paper. He and Minnie went to bed around nine. Her brief flirtation with Drouet now seemed remote. She first needed to find a job and pay her own way. Only then could she even think about having anyone visit her at the apartment.

"No," she said to herself, "he can't come here."

She asked Minnie for ink and paper, got out Drouet's card, and wrote him a note.

"I cannot have you visit me here. You will have to wait until you hear from me again. My sister's place is so small."

Carrie wanted to add something else about their relationship, but she was too timid. So she simply thanked him awkwardly for his kindness. Then she couldn't figure out how to close the letter. She ended up deciding to write "Very truly." But then it seemed so cold that she changed it to "Sincerely."

Carrie then went to the little corner of the front room, where she would be sleeping. Before she went to bed, she pulled the small rocking chair over to the open window and sat looking out upon the night and streets in silent wonder.

When she awoke at eight the next morning, Hanson was long gone, and her sister was already busy sewing. Carrie observed that Minnie had changed into a thin, hardened, twenty-seven-year-old woman. When she was younger, her parents had limited her pleasures and sharpened her sense of duty. Now that she was married, her husband had restricted her life even further. Minnie had invited her sister to live there only because Carrie wasn't satisfied at home, not because she wanted to be with her. She expected Carrie to get a job and pay her own way. Any job would be good enough—as long as it paid at least five dollars a week to start. She assumed that Carrie would end up in the workshop of a large manufacturing company. There she would do well enough until . . . well, until something happened. Neither of them knew exactly what that might be. They did not expect her to be promoted. They did not exactly count on her becoming married, either. They simply thought that this dull life would go on and on until eventually Carrie would be rewarded for coming to the city and working hard.

As she started out that morning, Carrie joined the many other people who had come to Chicago either because they were eager to make money or because they had lost money elsewhere. Indeed, the entire downtown business district was designed to impress and intimidate job seekers. The towering buildings were supposed to make them give up trying to cross the barrier from poverty to wealth.

As they looked through the large plate glass windows, job applicants could see polished office lamps, hard-working clerks, and well-dressed businessmen sitting around in small groups. Carrie entered this business district timidly. She was eager to find a job, but intimidated by so much wealth and power. She was fascinated by this world, but she did not understand it. And she felt helpless before its power and force. The walls that lined the streets of the business district seemed to keep her out. The vast offices were like mysterious mazes that only distant and important people understood. She could picture them only as counting their money, wearing magnificent clothing, and riding in luxurious carriages. She had very little idea about what they really did, how they worked, and what it all meant. But all of it was wonderful, vast, and far removed from her own little world. Her hopes sank, but her ambition stirred as she thought of entering any one of these mighty businesses and asking for something to do—something that she could do—anything.

CHAPTER 3

A Small Fortune
in the Big City

Once Carrie crossed the river into the wholesale district, she looked around for a door that might open onto a job. As she looked at the wide windows and impressive signs, she became self-conscious and ashamed about being seen as someone who was unemployed. So she hurried along as though she were simply running an errand, and passed by several blocks of businesses without even looking at them. Then a large door decorated with a brass sign attracted her attention. Inside were six or seven floors of bustling activity.

"Perhaps," she thought, "they may want someone."

As she was about to enter the building, Carrie looked through a window. There she saw a young man in a gray checked suit, who happened to be glancing in her direction. Afraid that he might have noticed her, she felt overcome by shame and hurried by without entering.

Across the street was a magnificent six-story building that displayed the name "Storm and King." This was a wholesale dry goods business.

With rising hope, she noticed women moving around on the upper floors. She decided to enter this place, no matter what. She crossed the street and walked directly toward the door. But just then, two men came out of the building and stopped at the entrance. A messenger dashed by her, climbed the few steps up to the entrance, and disappeared into the building. Several pedestrians hurried past, as she paused, hesitating, on the sidewalk. She looked helplessly around, and then, seeing herself observed, retreated. It was too difficult a task. She could not go past those two men.

After that, Carrie's feet carried her forward. But instead of making progress, she was really just running away from her defeat. Block after block passed by. Although her feet were getting tired, she was pleased at least that the streets were bright and clean. Finally, she began to admit to herself that she was a coward. So she turned around and made up her mind to find Storm and King. And this time, she would enter.

On the way, she ran into a huge wholesale shoe company. Through the wide plate glass windows, she saw a gray-haired gentleman sitting at a small table between the street entrance and the executive offices. After walking past the building and hesitating several times, she finally entered, unseen. She stood in front of the desk and waited humbly.

"Well, young lady," asked the old gentleman, looking up at her somewhat kindly, "what is it you wish?"

"I am, that is, do you—I mean, do you need any help?" she stammered.

"Not right now," he answered, smiling. "Not right now. Come in sometime next week. Occasionally we need someone."

She backed out awkwardly, without saying anything. She was astonished at how pleasantly she had been treated. She had expected it to be more difficult, that something cold and harsh would be said, though she didn't know what. It was remarkable that she had not been made to feel poor and ashamed.

Somewhat encouraged, she now tried entering another large building. It was a clothing company. She noticed several well-dressed, middle-aged businessmen, who were talking together. They were surrounded by brass railings.

An office clerk approached her.

"Who is it you wish to see?" he asked.

"I want to see the manager," she said.

He spoke to one of the men, who then came toward her.

"Well?" he demanded coldly. His harsh tone destroyed her courage.

"Do—do you need any help?" she stammered.

"No," he replied abruptly, and turned briskly away from her.

Humiliated and with a sinking heart, she left the building and hid in the crowd on the street.

Carrie spent the rest of the morning walking aimlessly, not daring to ask about any other positions. Hungry, she entered what looked like an inexpensive restaurant. But the prices were far too high for her limited savings. The only thing that she could afford was a bowl of soup. She ate it quickly and returned to her job search.

Once again she saw the Storm and King building. But this time she managed to go inside. She stood for a few minutes, nervously looking down at the floor. Nearby, there were several gentlemen talking together, but no one paid attention to her. Just as she was about to give up, a man sitting just inside the railing called her over to his desk.

"Who is it you wish to see?" he demanded.

"Why, anyone, please," she answered. "I am looking for work."

"Oh, then you should see Mr. McManus," he responded. "Sit down," he told her, pointing to a chair against the wall. He returned to his paperwork. Eventually a short, fat gentleman came in from the street.

"Mr. McManus," called the man at the desk, "this young woman wants to see you."

The short gentleman turned toward Carrie. She stood up and came forward.

"What can I do for you, Miss?" he asked, looking her over with interest.

"I want to know if I can get a position," she replied.

"As what?" he asked.

"Not as anything in particular," she answered, stumbling over her words.

"Have you ever had any experience in the wholesale dry goods business?" he questioned.

"No, sir," she replied.

"Do you take dictation? Do you know how to use office machines?"

"No, sir."

"Well, then, we haven't anything here," he said. "We employ only experienced help."

Carrie began to step backward toward the door. But something about her sorrowful face attracted him.

"Have you ever worked at anything before?" he asked.

"No, sir," she said.

"Well, then, you probably won't find work in a wholesale house of this kind. Have you tried the department stores?"

She admitted that she had not.

"Well, if I were you," he said, looking at her rather pleasantly, "I would try the department stores. They often need young women as clerks."

"Thank you," she said, relieved by this spark of friendly interest.

"Yes," he said, as she moved toward the door, "you try the department stores." And off he went.

Carrie entered the first department store that she saw, a store called The Fair. Each counter that she passed was a showplace of dazzling interest and attraction. Each item—no matter how cheap or expensive—caught her attention. And yet she did not stop. She could have used every single thing in the store: the dainty shoes and stockings, the frilly skirts and petticoats, the laces, the ribbons, the jewelry, the purses. She longed to own them all. And she was sharply aware that she could not afford a single one. She was unemployed, an outcast, a lowly job seeker. The wealthy ladies elbowed her and brushed by her. Carrie realized painfully that they were too busy shopping to notice her. Carrie compared herself with the pretty, young saleswomen. She envied their air of independence and sharp indifference to her. She knew that they could tell at a glance that she was poor and out of work. With all her heart, she was beginning to long for the wealth, fashion, and luxuries that the city had to offer.

She made her way to the managers' offices, where she waited in line for three-quarters of an hour. Ahead of her were other job applicants, young women like herself. But city life had given them a self-satisfied, independent look. They eyed Carrie in a way that was painful to her.

Finally, one of the managers called her sharply to his desk.

"Have you ever worked in any other store?" he asked briskly.

"No, sir," said Carrie.

"Oh, you haven't," he said, looking her over closely.

"No, sir," she replied.

"Well, right now we prefer young women with some experience. I guess we can't use you."

Carrie stood waiting a moment, not quite sure whether the interview was over.

"Don't just stand there!" he exclaimed. "We are very busy here."

Carrie began to move quickly to the door.

"Just a moment," he said, calling her back. "Give me your name and address. We want girls occasionally."

When she had gotten safely into the street, she could barely hold back the tears. It wasn't just the last comment that upset her. The entire day had been thoroughly humiliating. She gave up on the idea of asking other department stores for work. Instead, she just wandered on, feeling a certain safety and relief in mingling with the crowd.

As she continued aimlessly, Carrie suddenly noticed a piece of paper tacked onto a door. It read, "Girls wanted—wrappers and sewers." She hesitated a moment, then entered.

Speigelheim & Co., makers of boys' caps, was filled with dimly lit machines and workbenches. Sitting at these worked young women, dressed in thin, shabby, shapeless cotton dresses and worn-out shoes. It was so hot that they had to roll up their sleeves and open their dresses at the neck. Their faces were stained with oil and dust, and their skin was pale from being confined in this dreary factory. But they were not timid.

Carrie looked around her, disturbed by what she saw and sure that she did not want to work here. She felt uncomfortable because no one paid her any attention, except for a few glances just to look her over. Finally, a foreman, wearing an apron and shirt sleeves rolled up to his shoulders, approached.

"Do you want to see me?" he asked.

"Do you need any help?" said Carrie, already learning how to speak directly to men.

"Do you know how to stitch caps?" he replied.

"No, sir," she replied.

"Have you ever had any experience at this kind of work?" he asked.

She answered that she had not.

"Well," said the foreman, scratching his ear as he thought it over, "we do need a sewer. We like experienced help, though. We really don't have time to break people in." He paused and looked away. "We might, though, be able to put you at finishing."

"How much do you pay per week?" asked Carrie, encouraged by the man's gentle, simple way of talking to her.

"Three-and-a-half dollars," he answered.

"Oh," she was about to exclaim, but stopped herself from saying what she thought.

"We don't exactly need anybody," he went on vaguely, looking her over the way he might look over a package. "You can come in on Monday morning, though," he added, "and I'll put you to work."

"Thank you," said Carrie weakly.

"If you come, bring an apron," he added.

He walked away and left her standing by the elevator, never even asking her name.

She knew that she could never work in such a dirty, confining place. She was used to a better life—to the free, outdoor life of the country. Still, Chicago was not so bad, after all. Since she was able to get a job offer already on her first day, later on she might find an even better one.

But she was not reassured by her experiences later that day. Each time she applied for a job in a more pleasant or impressive place, she was turned down. Many businesses required experience. All sent her away abruptly, even rudely. The most painful experience was being rejected from a job working in a miserably lighted coat factory.

"No, no," said the foreman, a rough, heavily built individual, "we don't want anyone. Don't come here."

As the afternoon light faded, so did her hopes, her courage, and her strength. She had been astonishingly persistent. Such effort deserved to be rewarded. But the world of business seemed massive, hard, set in its uncaring attitude—and closed to her. Men and women hurried by in long, shifting lines. There was so much competition that she lost all hope of ever finding work. She felt helpless, but even then did not realize just how insignificant she really was in this sea of activity. In vain, she looked around for another place to apply, but she didn't have the courage to enter one more building. It would be the same thing all over—a humiliating plea, rewarded by an abrupt "no." Discouraged and exhausted, Carrie started back toward Minnie's apartment. She passed the door of a large wholesale shoe company. Looking through the plate glass window, she saw a middle-aged gentleman, sitting at a small desk. On impulse, she made one last attempt to overcome defeat. She walked deliberately through the door and up to the gentleman. Her weary face caught his interest.

"What is it?" he said.

"Can you give me something to do?" asked Carrie.

"Now, I really don't know," he said kindly. "What kind of work is it you want? You don't know how to use office machines, do you?"

"Oh, no," answered Carrie.

"Well, we only employ bookkeepers and typists here. You might go around to the side and ask upstairs. They did want some help a few days ago. Ask for Mr. Brown."

She hurried up to the fourth floor and waited to see Mr. Brown.

When he found out why she was there, Mr. Brown commented, "So you want something to do. Have you ever been employed in a shoe factory before?"

"No, sir," said Carrie.

"What is your name?" he asked. Then he continued, "Well, I don't know that I have anything for you. Would you work for four-and-a-half dollars a week?"

Carrie had expected that he would offer her at least six dollars a week. But she was so worn down by defeat that she accepted the offer.

"Well," he said, "you report here at eight o'clock Monday morning. I think I can find something for you to do."

She was sure that she had found something at last. Having at least some possibilities lifted her spirits. Suddenly, the mood on the street seemed light. She noticed that men and women were smiling. Scraps of conversation and notes of laughter floated to her. People were pouring out of the buildings, having finished work for the day. She hurried home, tired, but no longer weary. Already she was warming up to the possibility of spending the long winter here in Chicago—with its lights, its crowds, its entertainment. This was a great, pleasing city after all! She was working for a fine company. After all, it had huge plate glass windows. She could probably do well there. Then she thought about Drouet, and about the things he had told her. Now life seemed better, livelier, more exciting. She felt revived by a pleasant rush of warmth and energy. She would live in Chicago, her mind kept saying to itself. She would have a better time than she had ever had before. And she would be happy.

CHAPTER 4

Expectations and Realities

Carrie spent the next two days imagining how she would spend her salary. Before going to bed, she sat in her rocking chair and looked out upon the pleasantly lighted street. She daydreamed about how much joy and how much jewelry her small income of four dollars and fifty cents per week might buy for her.

"I will have a fine time," she thought.

Her sister, Minnie, did not know about Carrie's imaginary shopping sprees. She was too busy scrubbing the kitchen woodwork and calculating how to stretch eighty cents to pay for Sunday's dinner. When Carrie returned home, excited to tell her about how she got her first job, her sister merely smiled in approval. And then she asked whether Carrie would have to spend any of it for transportation. This was something that Carrie hadn't considered before.

When Hanson came home at seven o'clock, he was usually serious, silent, and a little edgy after his hard day's work. But when he heard Carrie's

25

announcement that night, he brightened up somewhat.

"You didn't lose any time, did you?" he remarked, smiling a little.

"No," replied Carrie, with a touch of pride.

He asked her one or two more questions and then turned to play with the baby.

Later, at the dinner table, Minnie remarked, "It seems to be such a large company."

"Great big plate glass windows and lots of clerks. The man I saw said they hired ever so many people."

"It's not very hard to get work now," put in Hanson, "if you look right."

Minnie felt cheered by Carrie's good spirits and her husband's taking part in the conversation. She began to tell Carrie about some of the well-known things to see—things that could be enjoyed for free.

"You'd like to see Michigan Avenue. There are such fine houses. It is such a fine street."

"Where is H.R. Jacob's?" interrupted Carrie, interested in one of the popular theaters that put on melodramas.

"Oh, it's not very far from here," answered Minnie. "It's in Halstead Street, right up here."

"How I'd like to go there. I crossed Halstead Street today, didn't I?"

Neither Minnie nor her husband answered right away. But after Hanson left the room, the two sisters were able to speak more freely as they washed the dishes.

"I'd like to walk up and see Halstead Street, if it isn't too far," said Carrie, after a time. "Why don't we go to the theater tonight?"

"Oh, I don't think Sven would want to go tonight," answered Minnie. "He has to get up so early."

"He wouldn't mind—he'd enjoy it," said Carrie.

"No, he doesn't go very often," replied Minnie.

"Well, I'd like to go," responded Carrie. "Let's you and me go."

Minnie thought for a while—but not about whether she could go or would go. She had already decided not to go. Instead, she tried to find a way to interest her sister in another topic.

"We'll go some other time," she said at last, finding no easy way to get out of going.

Carrie immediately sensed the reason that her sister was against the idea.

"I have some money," Carrie said. "You go with me."

Minnie shook her head.

"He could go along," said Carrie.

"No," replied Minnie softly. She rattled the dishes to drown out the conversation so that her husband wouldn't hear what she said. "He wouldn't."

Carrie had changed since the last time Minnie saw her. Her nature had always been timid, rather than pushy, especially since she didn't have any money or power. But the one thing she would speak up about was her strong craving for fun.

"Ask him," she pleaded softly.

Minnie thought about how Carrie's income would help pay the rent. It would also make it easier to talk with her husband about spending money. But Carrie needed to give up these ideas of running around and spending all her money. Otherwise, how was her coming to the city going to profit them?

At last she asked Hanson, but only because Carrie insisted, not because Minnie wanted to go.

"Carrie wants us to go to the theater," she said, looking in on her husband. Hanson looked up from his paper. They exchanged a look, which said, "This isn't what we expected."

"I don't want to go," he responded. "What does she want to see?"

"H.R. Jacob's," said Minnie.

He looked down at his paper and shook his head "no." He could not understand how a young woman like Carrie could even think about wasting her life this way, especially when she had so little money.

Carrie was disappointed, but didn't argue.

On Saturday, Carrie went out by herself. She was impressed by the fine houses, which suggested that wealthy people lived inside. She was glad to be out of the apartment. Already she felt that it was a narrow, boring place. Interest and joy lay elsewhere. Her mind wandered freely, and occasionally she thought about where Drouet might be. She wondered whether he might pay her a visit on Monday night, after all. The possibility was a little disturbing, but she also felt a slight wish that he would.

On Monday, Carrie got up early and prepared to go to work. She put on a worn cotton blouse with blue polka dots, a faded brown wool skirt, old worn-out shoes, and a small straw hat, which she had worn all summer at Columbia City. She looked like most other young women who worked in the factories. But her facial expression was slightly more sweet, reserved, and pleasing than most other "shop girls." It wasn't easy getting up early, after having gotten used to sleeping until seven or eight, as Carrie had done at home. Although most of her fantasies had faded away, she still had a little hope. She imagined that she would meet the great owners of the company, and that she would work where stylishly dressed men might see her.

"Well, good luck," said Minnie, when she was ready to go. They had agreed that Carrie would try walking to work, because sixty cents a week was a lot of money to pay for transportation.

"I'll tell you how it goes tonight," said Carrie.

Once in the sunlit street of her own neighborhood, Carrie felt slightly reassured. But after she crossed the river, the business district seemed to shut her out with its dark red brick walls and its big, shiny clean windows. Young women her own age seemed to look down at her timid manner. To be able to do anything at all in such a magnificent place required knowledge and experience. She dreaded that she would not know how, that she would not be quick enough. Had all the other places refused her because there was something or other that she didn't know? She would be yelled at, sharply criticized, shamefully fired.

With weak knees and shortened breath, Carrie walked up the stairs to the great shoe company and entered the elevator. When she stepped out on the fourth floor, there was no one around—only huge aisles of boxes piled to the ceiling. Very frightened, she stood waiting.

Soon Mr. Brown arrived. He did not seem to recognize her.

"What is it you want?" he asked.

Carrie's heart sank.

"You said I should come this morning to see about work . . ."

"Oh," he interrupted. "Um . . . yes. What is your name?"

"Carrie Meeber."

"Yes," said he. "You come with me."

He led the way through dark, box-lined aisles, which had the smell of new shoes. Then they entered the factory itself. They crossed a large room with a low ceiling. Here, men in white shirts and blue gingham aprons were working at clacking, rattling machines. Then they took an elevator to the sixth floor, where Mr. Brown called over to a foreman.

"This is the girl," he said. Then he told Carrie, "You go with him."

Carrie followed her new supervisor to a little desk in a corner, which served as a kind of office.

"You've never worked at anything like this before, have you?" he questioned, rather sternly.

"No, sir," she answered.

Annoyed that he would have to bother training her, he led her to a line of young women. They were all in a row, sitting on stools in front of clacking machines. He walked over to one of the women, who was using her machine to punch eyelet holes in a piece of leather. This would be used as the upper piece of a shoe, and the holes were to hold the laces. The foreman put his hand on the shoulder of the young woman.

"You," he said. "Show this girl how to do what you're doing. When you get through, come to me."

The girl got up promptly and gave Carrie her place.

"It isn't hard to do," she said, bending over. "You just take this piece like this, fasten it with this clamp, and start the machine."

After watching Carrie a few times, the young woman left Carrie to do this job by herself.

The pieces of leather came from the young woman at the machine to her right, and were passed on to the young woman at her left. Each person had to keep up the pace. Otherwise, the work would pile up, and the next person in line would fall behind. Carrie had no time to look around her. She bent nervously over her work. Realizing her difficulty, the other young women tried to help her by slowing their own work, as much as they dared. Carrie felt other people's eyes watching her. She worried that she was not working fast enough.

Once she misplaced the leather slightly and fumbled with a clamp. Suddenly, a large hand appeared before her eyes and fastened the clamp for her. It was the foreman. Her heart thumped so much that she could hardly see to go on.

"Start your machine," he said. "Start your machine. Don't keep the line waiting."

She responded, hardly breathing until the shadow of the foreman moved away from behind her. Then she let out a deep breath.

Carrie became aware that the room was so dark that she had to strain her eyes to see. By now, the floor was covered with litter, even though it was swept every evening. She noticed an unpleasant smell of machine oil and fresh leather. As the morning wore on, the room became hotter. Carrie felt she needed a breath of fresh air and a drink of water. But she didn't dare move. Her stool had no back or footrest. Now she began to feel uncomfortable. Her back was beginning to ache. She twisted and turned from one position to another, but it didn't help for long. She was beginning to tire.

"Stand up, why don't you?" suggested the

young woman at her right. "They won't care."

Carrie looked at her gratefully. "I guess I will," she said.

She stood up from her stool and worked that way for a while, but it was a more difficult position. Her neck and shoulders ached from bending over.

Carrie did not venture to look around, but above the clack of the machine she could hear an occasional remark.

"Did you see Harry last night?" said the girl at her left, addressing her neighbor.

"No."

"You ought to have seen what he was wearing. Gee, he looked great."

"Ssh," said the other young woman, bending over her work. Instantly, they both put on serious expressions. The foreman passed slowly, observing each worker carefully. The moment he was gone, they continued their conversation.

"So," began the young woman at her left, "what d'ya think he said?"

"I don't know."

"He said he saw us with Eddie Harris at Martin's last night."

"No!"

They both giggled.

A young man with shaggy hair shuffled between the machines, carrying a basket of leather scraps. As he passed by, he grabbed one of the young women under the arm.

"Aw, let me go," she exclaimed angrily. "Stupid!"

He just grinned.

"Loser!" he called back roughly.

Carrie's legs began to tire, and she wanted to get up and stretch. Wouldn't the lunch break ever come? It seemed as if she had worked an entire day. Her eyes were tired from straining to see the exact point where the machine punch came down. Carrie was concentrating too much. Her work did not really require so much mental and physical strain. But the pieces of leather kept coming. Her hands began to ache at the wrists and then in the fingers. Her body became one mass of dull, complaining muscles, fixed forever in one position and performing a single mechanical movement. The work became unpleasant, and then absolutely nauseating. Finally, a dull-sounding bell clanged somewhere down an elevator shaft, and the end came. In an instant there was a buzz of action and conversation. Then the noise of the machines died away in a low hum. It was suddenly so quiet that ordinary speaking voices sounded strange.

Carrie looked around for a place to sit and eat. The women stood around the windows or sat at any workbenches that the men had not already taken. Too shy to join a group of women, Carrie returned to her own machine, sat on her stool, put her lunch box on her lap, and listened to the chatter around her.

"Say, Kitty," one man called over to a girl who

was doing a waltz step in front of the windows, "are you going to the ball with me?"

"Look out, Kitty," called another. "You might mess up the back of your hairdo."

"Get lost, Loser," was her only comment.

Carrie was not used to this type of tough talk. She felt that it was beneath her. And compared with Drouet, these young men seemed ridiculous. She was glad when the short half-hour break was over, thinking that none of the men would notice her once everyone was back at work. She was wrong. Soon a young man passing by casually poked her in the ribs with his thumb. She turned around, indignant. But he had gone on, and turned around only once to grin at her. She could hardly keep from crying.

The young woman next to her noticed and said, "Don't you mind. He's too fresh."

Carrie said nothing, but bent over her work. She felt as though she could hardly endure such a life. Her idea of work had been so entirely different.

All during the long afternoon, she thought of the city outside and its impressive activity, crowds, and fine buildings. Then she began to think about Columbia City and the good things about the home life that she had left behind. By three o'clock she was sure that it must already be six. And by four it seemed as if they had forgotten what time it was and were making everyone work overtime. She started to imagine that the foreman was a real monster, prowling around constantly, keeping her tied down to her miserable task. She had no interest in making friends with these crude people. When six o'clock came, she hurried away eagerly, her arms aching and her legs stiff from sitting in one position.

A young man, attracted by her looks, tried to flirt with her.

"Hey, Honey," he called. "If you wait, I'll walk with you."

She didn't even turn around to look at him.

In the crowded elevator, another dusty, grimy young man tried to make an impression on her by leering at her.

On the sidewalk just outside, yet another young man grinned at her as she passed.

"Ain't going my way, are you?" he called cheerfully.

Carrie turned her face away from him, looking toward the setting sun. She was relieved to escape. Through a great shiny window, she again saw the small desk where she had applied for this job. She felt discouraged. The crowds hurried by with the same buzz and enthusiasm as before. Again, Carrie felt ashamed as she compared herself to the better-dressed young women who passed her by. She felt that she deserved more. And her heart protested.

CHAPTER 5

An Evening's Entertainment

Drouet did not call on Carrie that evening. After receiving her letter, he didn't think anymore about her for now. Instead, he went out to have what he thought of as a great time. On this particular evening, first he dined at Rector's, a restaurant of some local fame. In Drouet's mind, successful men—professionals, actors—went to such places. Drouet did not drink a lot, nor did he have much money. But he craved the best. He loved fine clothes and good eating. But above all, he liked to know and spend time with successful men.

Gentlemen who were not yet wealthy, but hoped to become so, would say eagerly, "That's So-and-so over there." For to them, dining lavishly in such a fancy restaurant represented the dazzling height of luxury.

"You don't say so," would be the reply.

"Why, yes, didn't you know that? Why, he's manager of the Grand Opera House."

Overhearing these conversations, Drouet looked forward to the day when he, too, would be able to flash a roll of dollar bills. Even now, he could at least eat where they did.

Afterward, Drouet stopped by the popular saloon, Fitzgerald and Moy's. Like Rector's, this plush saloon shone with glistening chandeliers, brightly colored tile floors, and rich, dark, polished wood paneling on the walls. The long bar was a blaze of lights, polished woodwork, colored and cut glassware, and many fancy bottles.

There Drouet leaned over the splendid bar and swallowed a glass of whiskey. He purchased a couple of cigars, one of which he lighted.

Some time ago, at Rector's, Drouet had met Mr. G. W. Hurstwood, manager of Fitzgerald and Moy's. He had been pointed out as a very successful and well-known man about town. Hurstwood fit this description. Almost forty, he was solidly built and energetic. He wore fine clothes and fancy jewelry. And he had a strong sense of his own importance. Drouet immediately saw him as someone worth knowing.

Hurstwood was an interesting person. He was shrewd and clever, and he could create a good impression. Because of his hard work and persistence, Hurstwood had worked his way up from bartender in an ordinary bar to this important position as manager of the magnificent Fitzgerald and Moy's. But even though he managed the floor of the saloon, he was not given any responsibility for or control over financial matters. Only the owners and a cashier had access to the money.

Hurstwood mostly just lounged around, dressed fashionably in finely tailored, imported suits, a solitaire ring, a fine blue diamond tie tack, a flashy vest, a watch chain of solid gold, and an engraved watch of the latest design. He knew hundreds of actors, businessmen, and politicians by name. In fact, he became successful in part by greeting them personally. If a regular customer earned only fifteen dollars a week as an office worker, Hurstwood might greet him with a friendly, "How do you do?" With rich or famous people who frequented the place, he would say even more warmly, "Why, old man, how are you?" But with people who were very rich, famous, or successful, he remained professionally tactful, dignified, and humbly respectful. With some men, who were not yet very rich or famous, Hurstwood simply enjoyed sharing friendship and a good conversation. He also loved to go out and have a good time once in a while. He went to the races, the theater, and the sporting events at some of the clubs. He had a racehorse, a wife and two children, and a nice house on the North Side near Lincoln Park. He was part of the American upper class—the first level below the luxuriously rich.

Hurstwood liked Drouet. He knew that Drouet was only a traveling salesman. But Bartlett, Caryoe & Company was a large and successful business, and Drouet was well regarded there. Drouet's easy manner, pleasant sense of humor, and ability to tell a good story helped in that business. He talked with Hurstwood about horseraces, women he met, cities he visited. Tonight he was in a particularly good mood because business was going well.

"Why, hello, Charlie, old man," said Hurstwood, as Drouet came in that evening about eight o'clock. "How goes it?"

Drouet shook hands good-naturedly, and they strolled toward the bar.

"Oh, all right."

"I haven't seen you in six weeks. When did you get in?"

"Friday," said Drouet. "Had a fine trip."

"Glad of it," said Hurstwood, with warmth that was genuine, for once. They drank some whiskey and sodas together, chatted about people they knew in common, and enjoyed each other's company.

After a while, Hurstwood asked Drouet if he had any other plans for the evening.

Drouet replied that he was planning to see a popular show.

"Well, you'd better be going. It's half past eight already," Hurstwood observed, pulling out his watch.

The crowd was already thinning out. Some men were going to the theater, and some to their clubs. And some men headed off for the pleasure that they found even more fascinating than the others—the ladies.

"Yes, I guess I will," said Drouet.

"Come around after the show. I have something I want to show you," said Hurstwood.

"Sure," said Drouet, delighted.

"You don't have anything planned for later tonight, do you?" added Hurstwood.

"Not a thing."

"Well, come 'round, then."

"By the way, I ran into quite a little peach as I was coming in on the train Friday," remarked Drouet, as he was leaving. "Oh, that's right. I must go and call on her before I leave town again on Wednesday."

"Oh, never mind her," Hurstwood remarked.

"You know, I must say that she was a real dandy," Drouet confided, trying to impress his friend.

"Twelve o'clock," said Hurstwood.

"OK," said Drouet, going out.

And so, Carrie's name was lightly tossed about in such an entertaining place. At the same time, Carrie was having serious regrets about her own bleak situation. And these two events were linked, even from the early stages of this, her unfolding fate.

CHAPTER 6

A Knight in Shining Armor

At the apartment that evening, Hanson asked Carrie, "Well, how did you make out?"

"Oh," said Carrie, "it's pretty hard. I don't like it."

Both Minnie and Hanson seemed surprised, and even a little annoyed, that Carrie seemed so disappointed and dissatisfied with her work. To Carrie, the one relief of the whole day would have been a cheerful home, a bright dinner table, and a sympathetic person saying, "Oh, well, try to put up with it a little while. You will get something better." But she saw that they thought she had no right to complain. Instead, she was supposed to keep working and say nothing. But unlike her sister, Carrie was still young, energetic, and idealistic. Her days of dating and falling in love still lay ahead. She could think of things she would like to do, of clothes she would like to wear, and of places she would like to visit. These were the things on her mind. And yet, there was no one here who could understand or share her feelings.

She had forgotten until now that Drouet might come. So after dinner she changed her clothes. When she was neatly dressed, she looked rather sweet, with her large eyes and sad mouth. Her face had an expression of expectation, dissatisfaction, and depression. After doing the dishes, she went downstairs to stand in the doorway to the building. If Drouet came, she could meet him there. Besides, Carrie never tired of observing the life of the streets. She imagined where people were going and what they were doing. She kept thinking about money, looks, clothes, and enjoyment.

After Carrie left the room, Hanson said to Minnie, "If I were you, I wouldn't let her stand in the door down there. It don't look good."

"I'll tell her," said Minnie.

A little later, Hanson decided to buy a loaf of bread at the bakery on the first floor of the building. That way, he could also see what Carrie was doing. She knew then that he didn't trust her, and it made her dislike him even more.

Finally, Carrie realized that Drouet was not coming. Somehow she felt a little resentful, as if she had been abandoned, as if she weren't good enough. Disappointed and weary, Carrie went upstairs. She said nothing except that she was going to bed.

"Yes, you'd better," replied Minnie. "You've got to get up early, you know."

The next day at the shoe factory, Carrie found the work a little less exhausting, but even more routine and dull.

At one point, the head foreman, making his rounds, stopped by her machine.

"Where did you come from?" he demanded.

"Mr. Brown hired me," she replied.

"Oh, he did, eh!" And then he added, "See that you keep things going."

Carrie became even less impressed with the shop girls who were working at the machines beside her. They seemed common and hardened. Carrie thought she had more imagination and better taste in clothes. They flirted freely with the men in the shop—both young and old. But Carrie was shocked by their rude comments. And she was worried that she might be treated the same way.

At noon that day, one of the men said to her, "Hello. You're a daisy."

He really expected Carrie to respond, "Aw! Go chase yourself!" Instead, Carrie silently moved away from him. There was nothing for him to do except retreat, in shame, grinning awkwardly.

That night, Carrie could hardly stand the loneliness and boredom inside the apartment. This time, after standing in the doorway awhile, looking out, she dared to walk away from the building. Her relaxed, slow way of walking caught the attention of a well-dressed thirty-year-old man. As he passed by her, he looked her over, slowed down, turned back toward her, and said, "Out for a little stroll, are you, this evening?"

Carrie looked at him in amazement, and finally replied, "Why, I don't know you." Offended, she started backing away from him.

"Oh, that don't matter," said the other pleasantly.

She exchanged no more words with him, but hurried away. By the time she reached her own door, she was completely out of breath. There was something in the man's look which frightened her.

The rest of the week was very much the same.

Then one morning it rained. Carrie realized that she had no umbrella. Minnie lent her one of hers, which was worn and faded. This bothered Carrie. So she went to one of the fine department stores and bought one for herself. She had to use a dollar and a quarter of her small savings to pay for it.

"What did you do that for, Carrie?" asked Minnie, when she saw it.

"Oh, I need one," said Carrie.

"You foolish girl."

Carrie resented this, though she said nothing. She was not going to be a common shop girl, she thought. And they shouldn't think so, either.

On the first Saturday night, Minnie accepted Carrie's payment of four dollars. She felt just a little guilty about taking the money. But her husband would not be able to understand if she took less than the entire four dollars. Hanson, on the other hand, was pleased that he could then spend less money on household expenses, and save more toward their payments on the new property. But Carrie was becoming frustrated because she couldn't figure out how to pay for clothes and entertainment on only fifty cents a week.

"I'm going up the street for a walk," she announced after dinner.

"Not alone, are you?" asked Hanson.

"Yes," answered Carrie.

"I wouldn't," warned Minnie.

"I want to see something," said Carrie. The way she said this made Minnie and Hanson realize, for the first time, that she was not pleased with them.

"What's the matter with her?" asked Hanson, when Carrie went into the front room to get her hat.

"I don't know," said Minnie.

"Well, she ought to know better than to want to go out alone."

Carrie did not go very far, after all. Soon she returned and just stood in the doorway.

The next day they went out to Garfield Park, but Carrie wasn't pleased. She felt that she did not look good enough.

The next Saturday Carrie paid another four dollars to Minnie, keeping only fifty cents for herself. But she had discovered that the other shop girls were able to keep more of their earnings for themselves. And their boyfriends took them out. But, after her experience with Drouet, Carrie thought that the young men who worked in the shop were too rough and immature for her tastes.

As the days grew colder, Carrie started to

worry that she didn't have any winter clothes. What was she to do? She had no winter jacket, no hat, no shoes. It was difficult to speak to Minnie about this, but at last she worked up enough courage to do so.

"I don't know what I'm going to do about clothes," she said one evening when they were together. "I need a hat."

Minnie looked serious.

"Why don't you keep part of your money and buy yourself one?" she suggested. But she was worried about explaining to her husband why she would have less money to give him at the end of the week.

"I'd like to for a week or so, if you don't mind," Carrie dared to suggest.

"Could you still pay two dollars?" asked Minnie.

Delighted to be able to keep a little more money, Carrie agreed. She immediately started figuring out what to buy. She needed a hat first of all. Although she never knew what Minnie told Hanson, the atmosphere in the apartment now became even more unpleasant.

And then one cold, rainy afternoon, Carrie left the warm shop at six. She still had no jacket, and she shivered as the wind hit her. In the morning she was sneezing. Going downtown made it worse. That day her bones ached, and she felt lightheaded. Toward evening she felt very ill. When she reached home, she was not hungry. She just stood by the stove, with her teeth chattering. Then she went to bed sick. The next morning she had a fever.

Minnie was worried about her. Hanson said that perhaps she had better go back home for a while.

When Carrie got up after three days, it was taken for granted that she had lost her job. It was almost winter, she had no clothes, and now she was out of work.

"I don't know," said Carrie. "I'll go down Monday and see if I can get something."

If anything, her job hunting was even less successful this time than the last. Her clothes were not suitable for the fall weather. She had spent her last money on a hat. For three days she wandered around, thoroughly discouraged. The atmosphere in the apartment was becoming unbearable. She hated to think of going back there each evening. Hanson was so cold. She knew it could not last much longer. Soon she would have to give up and go home.

On the fourth day, she spent all day downtown. Minnie had lent her ten cents to buy lunch. She had applied for jobs in the cheapest kinds of places—but still without success. She even answered a sign in the window of a small restaurant. They wanted a waitress, but only one with experience. Carrie moved through the thick crowd of strangers, feeling completely defeated. Suddenly a hand pulled her arm and turned her around.

"Well, well!" said a voice. It was Drouet—not just rosy-cheeked, but radiant. He was the essence of sunshine and cheer. "Why, how are you, Carrie?" he said. "You're a daisy. Where have you been?"

Carrie smiled, warmed by his irresistible friendliness.

"I've been at home," she said.

"Well," he said, "I saw you across the street. I thought it was you. I was just coming out to your place. How are you, anyhow?"

"I'm all right," said Carrie, smiling.

Drouet looked her over and saw something different.

"Well," he said, "I want to talk to you. You're not going anywhere in particular, are you?"

"Not just now," said Carrie.

"Then let's go up here and have something to eat. Gee! I'm glad to see you again."

In his radiant presence, Carrie felt relieved, looked after, and cared for. She gladly accepted his invitation, though she tried not to appear too eager.

"Well," he said, as he took her arm. And he said this word with such genuine friendliness that her heart glowed.

They went into the old Windsor dining room. It was a large, comfortable restaurant with excellent food and gracious service. Drouet selected a table near the window. He loved looking out at the busy, ever-changing street scenes. Indeed, he liked to see as well as be seen when he dined.

"Now," he said, getting Carrie and himself comfortably settled, "what will you have?"

Carrie looked over the large menu without really paying attention to it. She was very hungry, and everything on the menu tempted her. But she could not think about anything except the high prices. "Half broiled spring chicken—seventy-five cents. Sirloin steak with mushrooms—one dollar twenty-five cents." She had heard about such dishes, but she wasn't used to ordering them.

"I'll fix this," exclaimed Drouet. "Sst! Waiter."

The attentive waiter approached.

"Sirloin with mushrooms," said Drouet. "Stuffed tomatoes."

"Yes, sir," the server nodded in agreement.

"Hashed brown potatoes."

"Yes, sir."

"Asparagus."

"Yes, sir."

"And a pot of coffee."

Drouet turned to Carrie. "I haven't had a thing since breakfast. Just got in from Rock Island. I was on my way to lunch when I saw you."

Carrie smiled and smiled.

"What have you been doing?" he went on. "Tell me all about yourself. How is your sister?"

"She's well," replied Carrie.

He looked at her closely.

"Say," he said, "you haven't been sick, have you?"

Carrie nodded.

"Well, now, that's a darn shame, isn't it? You don't look very well. I thought you looked a little pale. What have you been doing?"

"Working," said Carrie.

"You don't say so! At what?"

She told him.

Drouet was indignant. "Rhodes, Morgenthau and Scott! Why, I know that company. They're really stingy. What made you go there?"

"I couldn't get anything else," said Carrie frankly.

"Well, that's an outrage," said Drouet. "You shouldn't be working for those people. The factory is right behind the store, isn't it?"

"Yes," said Carrie.

"That isn't a good company," said Drouet. "You don't want to work at anything like that, anyhow."

He chatted on rapidly, asking questions, explaining things about himself, telling her what a good restaurant it was. Then the waiter returned with a huge tray, filled with the delicious, hot dishes they had ordered. Drouet seemed to shine as he served the food. He looked handsome, sitting behind the white tablecloth and silver platters. As he cut the meat, Carrie noticed his strong arms and glittering rings. His new suit rustled as he stretched to reach the plates, break the bread, and pour the coffee. He gave Carrie a large serving. The abundant food and his warm manner renewed her body and her spirits. He was a splendid fellow. And he completely charmed Carrie.

Carrie easily accepted this lucky turn of events. She felt a little out of place. But the gracious room soothed her, and the view of the well-dressed crowds outside was splendid. Oh, to have money! How wonderful to be able to come in here and dine! Drouet must be fortunate. He rode on trains, dressed in such nice clothes, was so strong, and ate in these fine places. He seemed quite an impressive man. And she was amazed by his friendship and interest in her.

"So you lost your place because you got sick, eh?" he said. "What are you going to do now?"

"Look around," she said. Her desperate need for work had followed her even inside this fine restaurant, like a hungry dog, nipping at her heels.

"Oh, no," said Drouet, "that won't do. How long have you been looking?"

"Four days," she answered.

"Imagine that!" he exclaimed. "You shouldn't be doing anything like that. Those girls," and he gestured as though to include all shop and factory girls, "don't get anything. Why, you can't live on it, can you?"

He acted like a brother toward her. But at the same time, he noticed that Carrie was really very pretty. Even then, in her cheap clothing, he could see that she had a nice figure, and her eyes were large and gentle. Drouet gazed at her, and his thoughts reached their target. She felt his admiration. And behind it, she felt his easygoing good nature. She felt that she liked him—that she could continue to like him ever so much. And there was something else running through her mind, even deeper and richer, like a hidden undercurrent. Every now and then her eyes would meet his, and the feelings that flowed from each of them made a complete link.

"Why don't you stay downtown and go to the theater with me?" he said, pulling his chair closer. The table was not very wide.

"Oh, I can't," she said.

"What are you going to do tonight?"

"Nothing," she answered, a little drearily.

"You don't like being out there where you are, do you?"

"Oh, I don't know."

"What are you going to do if you don't get work?"

"Go back home, I guess."

Her voice started to tremble as she said this. Somehow, he was having a powerful influence on her. They had come to an understanding of each other without putting it into words. He understood her situation. She knew that he understood.

"No," he said, "you can't make it on your own!" For a moment, genuine sympathy filled his mind. "Let me help you. You take some of my money."

"Oh, no!" she said, pulling back from him.

"What are you going to do?" he said.

She sat and thought this over, shaking her head.

He looked at her in a way that—for his type—was quite tender. There were some loose bills in his vest pocket. They were soft and noiseless. He found them and crumpled them up in his hand so that Carrie didn't notice.

"Come on," he said, "I'll see you through this, all right. Get yourself some clothes."

It was the first time he had mentioned her clothing. Carrie now realized just how badly off she was. In his clumsy way, Drouet had gotten through to her deepest feelings. Her lips trembled a little.

They were quite alone in their corner of the restaurant. Carrie's hand was resting on the table in front of her. Now Drouet put his larger, warmer hand over it.

"Aw, come on, Carrie," he said. "What can you do alone? Let me help you."

He pressed her hand gently. She tried to pull it away. At this, he held it tight, and she no longer protested. Then he slipped the bills into her palm. When she began to protest, he whispered, "I'll loan it to you. That'll make it all right. I'll loan it to you."

He made her take it. Now she felt bound to him by a strange tie of affection. They went out onto the street, talking.

"You don't want to live with those people, do you?" he said at one point. Carrie heard his comment, but she did not pay much attention to it.

"Come down and meet me tomorrow," he said. "We'll go to a matinee. Will you?"

Carrie protested awhile, but finally agreed.

"You're not doing anything right now. Go get yourself a nice pair of shoes and a jacket."

When Carrie was with him, she shared Drouet's hopeful, carefree, easygoing mood. She didn't think about how she would feel after he was gone.

"Don't you bother about those people out there," he said as they parted. "I'll help you."

Carrie left him, feeling as though a great arm had appeared before her—a great arm that would carry away all her problems.

What she had accepted were two soft, green, handsome ten-dollar bills.

CHAPTER 7

The Lure of Luxuries

Carrie, like most people, saw money as "something everybody else has and I must get." Some of it she now held in her hand—two soft, green, ten-dollar bills. And she felt that she was immensely better off for having them. Money was power. Even if she were cast away on a desert island, she would be happy as long as she had a bundle of money. Only after starving for a while would she realize that, in some cases, money has no value.

The poor young woman was thrilled as she walked away from Drouet. She felt a little ashamed because she had been weak enough to take his money. But her need was so great that she was glad anyway. Now she would have a nice new jacket! Now she could buy a nice pair of pretty button shoes! She would get stockings, too, and a skirt, and, and . . . By now she had spent twice as much money in her imagination as she had in her hand.

But Carrie was right about the way she had sized up Drouet. To her, and indeed to all the world, he was a nice, good-hearted man. There was nothing evil in the fellow. He gave her the money because he had a good heart—because he realized how much she needed it. Now, he might not have given the same amount to a poor young man. But after all, it was natural that he would find a poor young man less appealing than a poor young woman. He was a carefree person, in fine health. He was drawn to women and money instinctively, without thinking. Femininity touched his feelings. When he pursued women, he had no intention of harming them. He simply loved to flirt with them, seduce them, and have them yield to his charms.

When Carrie had gone, he congratulated himself for having won her over. Gee, it sure was a shame that young girls had to be pushed around like that. Cold weather coming on and no clothes. Tough.

He would go around to Fitzgerald and Moy's and get a cigar. It made him feel lighthearted just to think about her.

Carrie reached home in high good spirits, which she could not hide.

"How did you make out?" asked Minnie.

Carrie couldn't lie, so she said, "I have the promise of something."

"Where?"

"At the Boston Store."

"Is it promised for sure?" questioned Minnie.

"Well, I'll find out tomorrow," replied Carrie.

"If you shouldn't get it . . ." Minnie paused,

not knowing how to say what she needed to tell Carrie.

"If I don't get something pretty soon, I think I'll go home."

Minnie saw her chance.

"Sven thinks it might be best for the winter, anyhow."

Suddenly, Carrie understood. They were unwilling to keep her any longer if she did not have a job. Now, as she sat there, taking in Minnie's remark, she was glad she had Drouet's money.

"Yes," Carrie said after a few moments, "I thought of doing that."

But what was there for her in Columbia City? Here was the great, mysterious city. What she had seen only suggested its possibilities. But what to do? She couldn't buy her new shoes and wear them here. And in the morning, Drouet would expect to see her in a new jacket. Yet how could she wear new clothes in the apartment, when Minnie knew that she had no money? The Hansons expected her to go home. But even though Carrie wanted to get away from the apartment, she did not want to go back home. And what would they think about her getting money without work? Carrie began to feel ashamed of the way she had taken the money. The whole situation was so depressing. Everything had been so clear when she was with Drouet. Now it was all so tangled, so hopeless. And it was so much worse than before because now she had a way out of her problems—but it was a way out that she could not take. Carrie finally decided that she would just give back the money. It had been wrong to take it. She would go downtown in the morning and hunt for work. At noon she would meet Drouet, as agreed, and tell him her decision. As she made up her mind, her heart sank. Just holding the money in her hand was such a relief. Ah, money, money, money! What a thing it was to have. And having plenty of it would certainly take away all her troubles.

In the morning she got up and started out a little early to hunt for work. But it was no use. Suddenly she found herself once again at The Fair. She decided to go in and look at the jackets—just to relieve her distress. But unlike before, now she was able to take her time, pausing at each display. How would she look in this? How charming that would make her look! She lingered in the jewelry department. She gazed at the earrings, the bracelets, the pins, the chains. She would have given anything to have them all! She would look fine, too, if only she had some of these things.

The jackets were the greatest attraction. When she entered the store, she already had her heart set upon a little tan jacket with large pearl buttons, which was all the rage that fall. After looking over all the racks, she decided that this was definitely the jacket to buy. But then she realized that it was time to leave the store. And she needed to give back the money.

Drouet was on the corner when she arrived.

"Hello," he said. "So where is the jacket and . . ." looking down, "the shoes?"

"I came to tell you that—that I can't take the money."

"Oh, that's it, is it?" he replied. "Well, you come along with me. Let's go over here to Partridge's."

Carrie walked with him. Suddenly, all the doubt and impossibility had slipped from her mind. She could not remember what had bothered her before, nor what she needed to explain to him.

"Have you had lunch yet? Of course you haven't. Let's go in here." And Drouet led her into a very nicely furnished restaurant.

"I mustn't take the money," said Carrie, after they were settled in a cozy corner and Drouet had ordered lunch. "I can't wear those things out there. They—they wouldn't know where I got them."

"What do you want to do?" he smiled. "Go without them?"

"I think I'll just go home," she said, wearily.

"Oh, come now," he said. "You've been thinking about it too much. I'll tell you what you should do. You say you can't wear them out there. So why don't you rent a furnished room and leave them there for a week?"

Carrie shook her head. As a woman, she felt that she needed to object first, and only later let herself be convinced by the man. It was up to him to brush away the doubts and clear the way, if he could.

"Then why are you going home?" he asked.

"Oh, I can't get a job here."

"They won't keep you?" he remarked, intuitively.

"They can't," said Carrie.

"I'll tell you what you do," he said. "You come with me. I'll take care of you."

Carrie listened, but did not answer. It seemed like a way out of her difficulty. Drouet seemed to share her way of looking at things. He was clean, handsome, well dressed, and sympathetic. His voice was the voice of a friend.

"What can you do back at Columbia City?" he went on. His words created a picture in Carrie's mind of the dull world that she had left behind. "There isn't anything down there. Chicago's the place to be. You can get a nice room here and some clothes. And then you can do something."

Carrie looked out through the window into the busy street. There it was, the admirable city, the great city—so fine as long as you were not poor.

"What will you have if you go back?" asked Drouet. He imagined that she would have none of the things that he thought worthwhile.

Carrie sat still, looking out. She was wondering what to do. They would be expecting her to go home this week.

Drouet turned to the subject of the clothes that she was going to buy.

"Why not get yourself a nice little jacket?

You've got to have it. I'll loan you the money. You needn't worry about taking it. You can get yourself a nice room by yourself. I won't hurt you."

Carrie understood what he meant, but she could not express her thoughts. She felt more helpless than ever.

"If only I could get a job," she said.

"Maybe you can," Drouet went on, "if you stay here. You can't if you go away. They won't let you stay out there. Now, why not let me get you a nice room? I won't bother you. You needn't be afraid. Then, when you get fixed up, maybe you could find some work."

He looked at her pretty face, and it excited his senses. She was a sweet little creature to him—there was no doubt about it. She seemed to have a certain power about her. She was not like the common run of shop girls. She wasn't silly.

In reality, Carrie had more imagination than he—and more taste. It was her sensitivity that also made her feel depressed and lonely.

"Do you really think I could get a job?" she asked.

"Sure," he said, reaching over and filling her cup with tea. "I'll help you."

She looked at him, and he laughed reassuringly.

"Now, I'll tell you what we'll do. We'll go over to Partridge's, and you pick out what you want. Then we'll look around for a room for you. You can leave the things there. Then we'll go to the show tonight."

Carrie shook her head.

"Well, then, you can go out to the apartment. That's all right with me. You don't need to stay in the room. Just take it and leave your things there."

Carrie still hadn't made up her mind by the end of the meal.

"Let's go over and look at the jackets," he said.

Once in the store, the shine and rustle of new things took hold of Carrie's heart. The good meal and Drouet's glowing presence made the plan seem possible. Carrie looked around and picked out a jacket just like the one she had admired at The Fair. When she got it in her hand, it seemed even nicer. The saleswoman helped her put it on, and it just happened to fit perfectly. Drouet's face lit up as he saw the improvement. She looked quite attractive in it.

"That's just the thing," he said.

Carrie looked at herself in the mirror. A warm glow crept into her cheeks.

"Now," said Drouet, "just pay for it."

"But it's nine dollars," protested Carrie.

"That's all right," said Drouet. "Take it."

She reached in her purse and took out one of the bills. The woman asked if she would like to wear the coat. In a few minutes the purchase was complete.

From Partridge's they went to a shoe store, where Carrie tried on shoes. When Drouet saw how nice they looked, he said, "Wear them."

Carrie shook her head "no." She was worried about returning to the apartment in them.

Drouet then bought her a purse to go with the shoes, and a pair of gloves to go with the jacket. Then he let her buy some stockings.

"Tomorrow," he said, "you come down here and buy yourself a skirt."

But the more Carrie sank into this relationship, the less sure she was about whether it was a good idea. She imagined that everything depended on her doing certain things that she had not yet done. Still, as long as she had not done these, there would be a way out of her involvement with Drouet.

Drouet took her to a place in Wabash Avenue where she could rent a room. Before they entered, he explained, "Now, we'll pretend you're my sister."

He carried off all the arrangements with ease.

"Her trunk will be here in a day or so," he told the landlady, who seemed very pleased.

So Carrie left her things there.

"Now," said Drouet, "why don't you move in tonight?"

"Oh, I can't," said Carrie.

"Why not?"

"I don't want to leave them this way."

He started dealing with that issue as they walked along the avenue.

"Just leave them," he said. "They won't care. I'll help you get along."

She listened until all her doubts vanished. He

would show her around a little and then help her get a job. He really imagined that he would. Then when he was traveling, she could work.

"Now, I'll tell you what you do," he said. "You go back to the apartment and get whatever you want. Then come away."

She thought a long time about this. Finally she agreed. He would come out as far as Peoria Street and wait for her. She was to meet him at eight-thirty.

At five-thirty, she reached home. By six she had made up her mind to leave that very night.

"So you didn't get the job?" said Minnie.

Carrie looked at her out of the corner of her eye. "No," she answered.

At dinner, Hanson said, "Didn't find anything, eh?"

"No," Carrie replied.

Hanson had already decided that she would just have to go home. And once she was gone, there would be no coming back in the spring.

Carrie was afraid of what she was about to do. But she was even more relieved that this situation would soon be over. They would not care. Hanson would actually be glad when she left. He would not care what became of her.

After dinner she wrote a little note. "Goodbye, Minnie," it read. "I'm not going home. I'm going to stay in Chicago a little while and look for work. Don't worry. I'll be all right."

After she finished doing the dishes, Carrie told

Minnie, "I guess I'll stand down at the door a little while." She could hardly keep her voice from trembling.

Minnie responded, "Sven doesn't think it looks good to stand down there."

"Doesn't he?" replied Carrie. "I won't do it anymore after this."

She put the note under Minnie's hairbrush, got her hat, and went slowly down the stairs.

Drouet was waiting at the corner, in good spirits.

"Hello, Carrie," he said, as she hurried eagerly toward him. "Got here safe, did you? Well, let's take a trolley."

CHAPTER 8

Doubts Disappear

The next day, Drouet paid a visit to Carrie. It was Drouet's very nature to chase women. And so, he had no choice but to pursue Carrie. He was drawn to her instinctively, with hardly a second thought.

Carrie, too, followed her natural feelings and instincts. She was drawn to Drouet, in spite of what she thought and almost against her will. She wondered whether she would find a job. She wondered what Drouet would do. But for the moment, she enjoyed this new feeling of freedom. For once in her life, she saw possibilities in her future.

Carrie visited with Drouet in her room. He seemed as jolly and lively as ever.

"Aw," he said, "what are you looking so blue about? Come on out to breakfast. You want to get your other clothes today."

Carrie looked at him with large, troubled eyes. "I wish I could find a job," she said.

"You'll get that all right," said Drouet. "What's the use of worrying about it right now? Get yourself fixed up. See the city. I won't hurt you."

"I know you won't," she remarked, half-truthfully.

"Got on the new shoes, don't you? Stick 'em out. Gee, they look fine. Put on your jacket."

Carrie obeyed.

"Say, that fits like a T, don't it?" he remarked. Stepping back a few feet, he eyed with real pleasure the way it hugged her waist. "What you need now is a new skirt. Let's go to breakfast."

Carrie put on her hat.

"Where are the gloves?" he asked.

"Here," she said, taking them out of the bureau drawer.

"Now, come on," he said.

And with that, her initial doubts were swept away.

It was like this every time they met. Drouet did not leave her alone very often. He filled her time with sightseeing. He bought her a nice skirt and blouse. With his money she purchased some makeup. She appeared to be a different person. When she looked in the mirror, she saw that she was pretty, yes, indeed! How nicely her hat framed her face! And weren't her eyes pretty? She caught her little red lip with her teeth and felt her first thrill of power. Drouet was so good.

One evening on the way to the theater, they passed crowds of workers going home. Little shop girls hurried by, chattering and laughing. Suddenly a pair of eyes met Carrie's. They were looking out from a group of poorly dressed girls. Their clothes were faded and hung loosely. Their jackets were old, their makeup shabby.

Carrie recognized the glance and the face. It was one of those young women who worked at the machines in the shoe factory. Carrie felt as if some great sea had rolled in between them. Carrie was so startled that she jumped.

"What's the matter?" asked Drouet.

"Oh, I don't know," she said, her lip trembling.

"You must be thinking too much," said Drouet, and he led her off to the theater.

The show delighted Carrie. Its color and grace caught her eye. She pictured far-off lands and magnificent people. She imagined having status and power. When the show was over, they watched the wealthy ladies and gentlemen step into their fancy coaches.

"Isn't it fine?" observed Carrie.

"Great," said Drouet. He enjoyed this show of fine clothing and swirling gaiety as much as she. He pressed her arm warmly. At one point she looked up, her perfect teeth glistening through her smiling lips, her eyes glowing. As they were moving out, he whispered down to her, "You look lovely!"

Then he added, laughing, "You stick with me, and someday we'll have a coach."

They stopped in at a restaurant for a little after-theater supper. Carrie had a fleeting thought about how late it was. But she no longer had anyone at home to set rules for her. And yet, she had not learned to follow those rules on her own. Otherwise, she might have been more worried about what she was doing. But Carrie was soothed by Drouet's romantic manner, by the warming food, and by the city's powerful influence.

"Well," said Drouet at last, "we had better be going."

Their eyes met, and he touched her hand.

At last, they got up from the table and went out into the street. Drouet had Carrie's arm in his, and he held it closely. When they arrived at Carrie's building, she stood on the first step, her head now even with his own. He took her hand and held it warmly. He looked steadily at her as she glanced around, caught up in her own thoughts.

A week or so later, Drouet strolled into Fitzgerald and Moy's saloon, looking and acting quite stylishly.

"Hello, Charlie," said Hurstwood, looking out from his office door.

Drouet strolled over to the manager.

"When do you go out on the road again?" asked Hurstwood.

"Pretty soon," said Drouet.

"Haven't seen much of you this trip," said Hurstwood.

"Well, I've been busy," said Drouet.

After they chatted for a few minutes, Drouet said, "Say, I want you to come out some evening."

"Out where?" asked Hurstwood.

"Out to my house, of course," said Drouet,

smiling.

Hurstwood looked up, a question on his face, a slight smile on his lips. He studied the face of Drouet in his wise way. Then, acting like a true gentleman, he answered, "Certainly. Glad to."

"We'll have a nice game of cards."

"May I bring a nice little bottle of Sec?" asked Hurstwood.

"Certainly," said Drouet. "I'll introduce you."

CHAPTER 9

A Fine House, A Flawed Home

Hurstwood lived with his wife, two children, and a maid in a house that was decorated in a way that seemed perfect. There were soft rugs, richly upholstered sofas, a grand piano, and a marble statue of Venus made by some unknown artist. But, despite the comfortable furniture, Hurstwood's house lacked the warm feeling of a true home.

At one time he had been very fond of his daughter, Jessica. But now that she was seventeen years old, she was becoming more independent. She liked nice clothes and asked for them constantly. At school she met girls whose parents were truly rich, and she wanted to share that lifestyle. Hurstwood's son, George, Jr., was twenty years old. He kept his money and his thoughts to himself, because he was not interested in sharing anything with his family. Mrs. Hurstwood longed to be accepted into high society, but she knew that it was not possible for her. She hoped for better things for her daughter. Through Jessica, she might rise a little. Or at least she might someday be able to point proudly to George, Jr.'s possible success. And if her husband's real estate investments paid off, she might even be able to improve her status.

Mrs. Hurstwood was ambitious, demanding, and difficult to please. Hurstwood was used to hearing her announce that she had fired yet another maid. When told, his only reply was, "All right." He had long ago grown weary of arguing. And he never talked openly with his wife. If he couldn't fix something, he just ignored it. He simply walked away from anything that seemed impossible to change.

A typical conversation would go something like this.

"I'm going up to Fox Lake tomorrow," announced George, Jr., at the dinner table one Friday evening.

"What's going on up there?" asked Mrs. Hurstwood.

"Eddie Fahrway's got a new speedboat, and he wants me to come up and see how it works."

"How much did it cost him?" asked his mother.

"Oh, over two thousand dollars. He says it's a dandy."

"Old Fahrway must be making money," put in Hurstwood.

"He is, I guess. Jack told me they were shipping their latest product, 'Vegacura,' to Australia now. He said they sent a whole box to Cape Town last week."

"Just think of that!" said Mrs. Hurstwood. "And only four years ago, they worked out of that basement in Madison Street."

"Jack told me they were going to put up a six-story building next spring in Robey Street."

"Just think of that!" said Jessica.

On this particular occasion, Hurstwood decided to leave the table early.

On another occasion, Jessica remarked to her mother, "What do you think? That Herbert Crane tried to make friends with me."

"Who is he, my dear?" asked Mrs. Hurstwood.

"Oh, no one," said Jessica, her pretty lips frowning. "He's just a fellow at school. He doesn't have any money."

But another day young Blyford walked Jessica home from school. He was the son of a wealthy soap manufacturer. Mrs. Hurstwood happened to notice them from her third-floor window. She approved of having this fine young man stroll with her daughter. Yes, it certainly was a most satisfactory sight, indeed.

But Hurstwood did not think too much about his home life. His real life was the life of the saloon that he managed. He spent most of his time there. When he went home in the evening, the house looked nice. He thought his children looked fine. And he was pleased that his wife dressed in a showy fashion. This was much better than looking plain. But there was no love between them. Neither was there any great feeling of dissatisfaction. They simply did not talk to each other enough to get into any arguments. Once in a while, Hurstwood met women who were young, cheerful, and good-natured. At those moments, he would feel slightly dissatisfied with his wife. But the feeling quickly passed. After all, to keep his job, he needed to lead a dignified, respectable life. So he was careful about everything he did. And on Sundays he made sure that he took his wife out in public.

When someone he knew was caught cheating on his wife, Hurstwood shook his head at the man's foolishness. "It was all right to do what he did," he observed. "All men do those things. But why wasn't he careful? A man can't be too careful."

As for his own situation, Hurstwood saw that his wife was friendly and vain. He realized that she might be easily seduced by another man's flattery. Yet as long as she loved him strongly, Hurstwood would continue to trust her. But if her feelings changed and the chain that tied him to her was broken . . . well, then something might happen.

During the last year or two, his family's expenses seemed to be increasing. Jessica wanted fine clothes. Mrs. Hurstwood, not to be outdone by her daughter, also bought fancy clothes for herself. In the past, Hurstwood had never said anything about this. But one day he murmured a comment, while admiring one of his own perfect vests in the mirror. "It seems to me that Jessica has recently been spending a good deal of money on dresses."

"Well, she's going out more," explained his wife. But she noticed a tone in his voice that she had not heard before.

Hurstwood did not travel much. But when he did, he usually took his wife along with him. One time recently, though, Hurstwood had been invited to join a business trip to Philadelphia.

"Nobody knows us down there," said one of his fellow businessmen. "We can have a good time." His left eye gave the slightest hint of a wink. "You ought to come along, George."

The next day Hurstwood announced his plans to his wife.

"I'm going away, Julia," he said, "for a few days. I'll have to leave you behind this time."

"All right," she replied finally. But, before he went away, she asked him some more questions. That irritated him. He began to feel that she was an annoying attachment.

He enjoyed himself thoroughly on this trip. When it was over, he was sorry to be back. They never talked about what had happened. But Mrs. Hurstwood found a way to make up for his leaving her behind. She simply went out more often, dressed better, and saw more shows.

Such an atmosphere could hardly be considered a true home life. The household kept going by force of habit and public opinion. But as time went on, it became drier and drier. And like wood that has become dry, it could easily be lighted and destroyed.

CHAPTER 10

A Friend Pays a Visit

Drouet had rented a three-room apartment. One room overlooked Union Park. Above its trees rose the steeple of the Union Park Congregational Church. The towers of several other churches could be seen in the distance.

Inside, the rooms were comfortably furnished. On the floor was a rich carpet patterned with impossibly gorgeous flowers. On the wall between the two windows was a tall, ornate mirror. A large, soft plush couch, several rocking chairs, a few pictures, some rugs, and various small knickknacks filled the room. The bedroom contained Carrie's belongings. Her closet held quite a collection of clothing—more than she had ever owned before. And they looked very attractive on her, as well. The third room served occasionally as a kitchen. Drouet would ask Carrie to prepare snacks of oysters and other delicacies that he enjoyed. Finally, there was a bath. Carrie's hard work helped make the whole apartment cozy, warm, cheerful, and extremely pleasant.

Many people would say that Carrie had found

herself a comfortable little place. People who were homeless and starving would say that she had found a safe and peaceful shelter from the wind and rain. But what had she lost? Carrie was no longer burdened by material concerns. But now she had to face a moral dilemma. She looked into her mirror and saw a prettier Carrie than she had ever seen before. Then she thought about how other people would see her. Did her behavior reflect her own views of right and wrong? She was torn between these images. Which one was right?

"My, but you're a little beauty," Drouet often exclaimed to her. But he thought to himself, "Oh, how delicious is my conquest."

Carrie would look at him with large, pleased eyes.

"You know it, don't you?" he would continue.

"Oh, I don't know," she would reply, delighted that someone should think so.

But in her conscience she heard a different voice.

"Oh, you're such a failure!"

"Why?" she asked this inner voice.

"Look around you at people who are good. How they would look down on you for what you have done! And look at the girls who are good. Think how they will back away from you when they find out that you have been so weak."

When Carrie was alone, looking out across the park, she would argue, plead, and make excuses to her conscience. But then another voice would remind her that it was cold and windy out there. She was alone, she was ambitious, and she was afraid of the dark, harsh winter. Like many people, Carrie needed material things, pleasurable activities, and artificial lights to feel happy and safe. And when she couldn't figure out a way to meet both her material and her moral needs, she simply turned her back on the dilemma.

At the same time, Drouet treated her well—at least, given his nature and her situation. He took her out often, spent money on her, and took her with him when he traveled. Occasionally she would be alone for two or three days, but generally, she saw him a great deal.

"Say, Carrie," he said one morning. "I've invited my friend Hurstwood to come out someday and spend the evening with us."

"Who is he?" asked Carrie, unsure about the idea.

"Oh, he's a nice man. He's the manager of Fitzgerald and Moy's."

"What's that?" asked Carrie.

"The finest club in town. It's a high society, swell kind of place."

Carrie was wondering how much Drouet had told him about her, and how she should act.

"It's all right," said Drouet, sensing her concerns. "He doesn't know anything. You're Mrs. Drouet now."

There was something about this which struck Carrie as slightly inconsiderate. She could see that

Drouet was not particularly sensitive.

"Why don't we get married?" she then asked, thinking of the generous promises he had made.

"Well, we will," he said, "just as soon as I get this little deal of mine closed up."

This little deal seemed to require quite a lot of attention, work, and so forth. As a result, somehow or other he was never free to do what he said he really wanted to do.

"Just as soon as I get back from my Denver trip in January, we'll do it."

This answer gave Carrie some hope, and a way to ease her conscience. Eventually things would be made right. Her actions would be justified. She really didn't love Drouet. She was more clever than he. And she was beginning to see what he lacked. In a way, it was better that she didn't think too highly of him, that she wasn't so sure what she wanted to do. Otherwise, she would have been dreadfully afraid that he might lose his interest in her. And if that happened, she would be afraid of being left adrift, with nowhere to go.

When Hurstwood came to visit, Carrie saw that he was more clever than Drouet in a hundred ways. His great charm was being attentive to women. He was mild-mannered, calm, assured. He gave the impression that he wished only to be of service, to do something that would please the ladies. And he was particularly interested in pleasing fine and pretty ladies.

Drouet used the same strategy, but with less

polish than Hurstwood. He was too lively, too jolly, too assured. He succeeded only with women who were inexperienced and coarse. Although Carrie was not coarse, she was still innocent enough to fall for Drouet's charms. A few years later, she would have gained too much experience and success. Had she met Drouet then, she would never have let him even get close to her.

"You ought to have a piano here, Drouet," said Hurstwood, smiling at Carrie, "so that your wife can play."

Drouet had not thought of that.

"So we ought," he quickly agreed.

"Oh, I don't play," admitted Carrie.

"It isn't very difficult," replied Hurstwood. "You could do very well in a few weeks."

Hurstwood was elegantly dressed that evening. His clothes looked particularly new and rich, but in an understated way. His rich plaid vest was set with a double row of mother-of-pearl buttons. He wore a shiny, but subtle silk tie. His shoes were of soft, black calf's leather, polished to a dull shine. Carrie noticed how much more elegant these were than Drouet's flashy, hard, patent leather shoes. And besides, she was used to Drouet's appearance.

"Why don't we have a little game of cards," suggested Hurstwood, after a light round of conversation. Hurstwood was respectful and pleasant toward Carrie, and avoided any hint that he knew anything about Carrie's past. As a result, he put

Carrie at ease and kept her amused. He pretended to be seriously interested in all she said.

"I don't know how to play," said Carrie.

"Charlie, you are neglecting a part of your duty," he teased Drouet. "Between us, though," he went on, "we can show you."

His attention to Carrie made Drouet appreciate Carrie even more. At the same time, it made him feel closer to Hurstwood.

"Now, let me see," said Hurstwood, looking over Carrie's shoulder very attentively. "What do you have?" He studied for a moment. "That's a rather good hand. You're lucky. Now, I'll show you how to beat your husband. You take my advice."

"Now look here," Drouet protested lightly. "If you two are going to scheme together, I won't stand a chance. Hurstwood's a regular card shark."

"No, it's your wife. She brings me luck. Why shouldn't she win?"

Carrie looked gratefully at Hurstwood, and smiled at Drouet. Hurstwood was just a friend, nothing more.

Instead of playing one of his own high cards, Hurstwood let Carrie win a hand. "I'd call that clever playing for a beginner."

Carrie laughed with delight. It was as if she were invincible when Hurstwood helped her.

When Hurstwood occasionally looked at Carrie, it was with a gentle, kind, friendly light in his eye. He replaced his usual clever, sharp gleam with an innocent look. Carrie couldn't know that he had anything more in mind than an evening of pleasant entertainment.

"It's unfair to let such playing go without earning something," he said after a time, slipping his finger into the little coin pocket of his coat. "Let's play for dimes."

"All right," said Drouet, fishing for some money.

Hurstwood was quicker. His fingers were full of new ten-cent pieces. "Here we are," he said, supplying each person with a little stack.

"Oh, this is gambling," smiled Carrie. "It's bad."

"No," said Drouet, "it's only for fun. If you never play for more than dimes, you can still go to Heaven."

"Don't you pass judgment," said Hurstwood to Carrie gently, "until you see what happens to the money."

Drouet smiled.

"If your husband gets the dimes, then he'll tell you how bad gambling is," Hurstwood teased playfully.

Drouet laughed loudly. Even Carrie thought this was funny.

"When do you leave?" Hurstwood then asked Drouet.

"On Wednesday," he replied.

"It must be hard to have your husband running around like that, isn't it?" Hurstwood asked Carrie.

"She's going along with me this time," said Drouet.

"You must both come with me to the theater before you leave."

"Certainly," said Drouet. "Eh, Carrie?"

"I'd like it ever so much," she replied.

Hurstwood did his best to see that Carrie won the money. He delighted in her success, kept counting her winnings, and finally gathered and put them in her extended hand. They had a bite to eat, and Hurstwood served the wine.

When he was ready to leave, he looked first at Carrie and then at Drouet. "So, be ready at seven-thirty. I'll come and get you." Then he added, speaking to Drouet with a friendly tone, "Next time you leave your wife alone, you must let me show her around a little. It will break up her loneliness."

"Sure," said Drouet, quite pleased at Hurstwood's attention.

"You're so kind," observed Carrie.

"Not at all," said Hurstwood. "I would want your husband to do the same for me."

He smiled and went lightly away. Carrie was thoroughly impressed. She had never come in contact with such grace. As for Drouet, he was equally pleased.

"There's a nice man," he remarked to Carrie, as they returned to their cozy room. "A good friend of mine, too."

"He seems to be," said Carrie.

CHAPTER 11

Changing Fashions, Changing Passions

Carrie quickly learned how to imitate the ways of the wealthy—at least, on the surface. Clothing was her special passion. Occasionally her conscience reminded her that it was wrong to accept Drouet's gifts. But as she walked through the fine clothing stores, each item seemed to beg her to take it home.

"My dear," a lace collar from Partridge's almost called out to her, "I fit you beautifully. Don't let me go."

"Ah, such little feet!" The leather of the soft new shoes seemed almost to speak to her. "How perfectly I could protect them. It would be such a shame not to allow me to come to their aid."

And once Carrie tried on a blouse or a shoe, she could never give it up.

Drouet encouraged her to dress and act stylishly. He loved to watch the fashionable ladies as they walked down the street. If he saw a woman swing her hips daintily, he pointed out to Carrie how gracefully she moved. But each remark made Carrie wonder whether she wasn't fine enough. So she, too, studied these women. Then she tried to imitate them. Surely she could do what they did.

Drouet tried to educate Carrie by comparing her to other women. But that was a tactical error. The more he held up other women as perfect examples, the more he wounded Carrie. And the less he complimented her, the less she cared about him. Drouet simply did not understand Carrie's feelings.

Carrie continued learning about wealthy people in her own apartment building. Mr. and Mrs. Frank A. Hale lived on the floor above Drouet and Carrie. They were a respectable couple, who spent every one of the forty-five dollars that Hale was paid each week as a theater manager. Mrs. Hale, an attractive thirty-five-year-old, was more interested in being entertained than in taking care of a house and raising a family. For a long time, she was Carrie's only companion. She loved money and gossip about popular actors and wealthy theatergoers. These interests formed Carrie's view of the world and pulled her constantly toward wanting a better life.

Across the hall were a young girl and her mother from Evansville, Indiana. They were the wife and daughter of a railroad treasurer. The daughter was in Chicago to study music, the mother to keep her company. Although not extremely wealthy, the young woman wore fancy clothing, and the jewels on her rings flashed as she played the piano. Sometimes the young woman's wistful music awoke in Carrie longings for those things that she did not have. It also caused her to cling more closely to the things she already possessed. One time at dusk, Carrie sat at her window, looking out and daydreaming. Drouet had been out since ten in the morning. She had amused herself by taking a walk, by reading a book that Drouet had left for her (but which she didn't like very much), and by changing her dress for the evening. Carrie gazed out across the park, wistful and depressed. For a moment, she felt guilty and sorry about what she had done with her life.

While she was in this mood, Drouet entered in an entirely different frame of mind. He noticed that her eyes were still wet with a few vague tears. But he didn't have the sensitivity to try to console her. Instead, he exclaimed, using one of his nicknames for her. "Hey, Cad. You've been crying. Pshaw, you don't want to do that."

Good-natured, but self-centered, Drouet assumed that Carrie was simply feeling lonely because he had been out of the house all day. So he took her hand and pulled her up to dance with him. "Come on, now," he said cheerfully. "Everything's fine. Let's just waltz a little to that music."

It was the last thing that Carrie wanted to do. Carrie saw his lack of sympathy as a defect in Drouet and a difference between them. It was his first big mistake.

By this time, Carrie's appearance had changed. She was a natural imitator. She looked in the mirror and pursed up her lips, adding a little toss of the head, just the way her neighbor did. She learned how to pick up her skirts with an easy swing. Soon she began to get the hang of those vain little things that graceful, pretty women did. She became a young woman of considerable taste.

Drouet noticed this.

And so did Hurstwood. When he first came to visit, Carrie seemed much more attractive than Drouet's first description of her. Hurstwood thought she was pretty, graceful, and richly appealing in her timid manner. There was something childlike in her large eyes, which captured the fancy of this stiff, old-fashioned, pretentious man. It was the ancient attraction of the fresh for the stale. He looked into her pretty face and sensed the youthfulness radiating out from her. He had become so cynical, while she remained so innocent. He would have found even her vanity to be charming. She seemed much more sensitive than Drouet. As he rode away from the apartment after his first visit, he wondered how Drouet had managed to win her.

"Why, next time I'll bring her some flowers," Hurstwood thought. He wasn't at all bothered by the fact that Drouet had won her first. He simply let his thoughts wander, hoping that something would come of them. He did not know, he could not guess, what the result would be.

A few weeks later, right after he returned to Chicago from a short trip, Drouet happened to run into one of his well-dressed lady acquaintances. He had intended to hurry home to surprise Carrie. But he was enjoying his conversation with the woman.

"Let's go to dinner," he said, thinking it unlikely that he would see anyone he knew.

"Certainly," said his companion.

They visited one of the better restaurants for a social chat. It was five in the afternoon when they met. It was seven-thirty before they had picked clean the last bone. Drouet was smiling as he finished telling a little story to his dinner date.

At that moment, he looked up and saw Hurstwood, who had just come into the restaurant. Their eyes met. Seeing Drouet with another woman, Hurstwood drew his own conclusion.

"Ah, the rascal," he thought. "He thinks I think he cares for Carrie. That's got to be pretty hard on the little girl," he thought sympathetically.

At first Drouet wasn't alarmed. But then he realized that Hurstwood was pretending not to notice. By golly, he'd better explain all this to Hurstwood. Otherwise, he might think that his dinner tonight was something more than just a little half-hour with an old friend.

The next time that Drouet drifted into Fitzgerald and Moy's, Hurstwood teased him. "I saw you," he joked, pointing his finger at him like a scolding parent.

"Just an old acquaintance that I ran into as I was coming up from the train station. Couldn't get away from her."

"So how long are you in town this time?" asked Hurstwood.

"Only a few days."

"You must bring your girlfriend down tonight and join me for dinner," he said. "I'm afraid you keep her cooped up out there. I'll get a box for us at the theater."

"Sure I'll come," answered the traveling salesman.

This pleased Hurstwood immensely. Even though he liked Drouet, he was also beginning to envy him. He saw him as a rival, and tried to find his weak points. He certainly had to be a failure as a lover. Hurstwood could trick him, all right. If he could just let Carrie see something like what he'd seen at the restaurant last Thursday, that would be the end of her involvement with Drouet. But Drouet had no idea that his friend was examining him with the eye of a hawk, about to attack its prey.

As the two men were planning how to entertain Carrie that evening, Carrie wasn't thinking about either of them. When Drouet returned home, he found her getting dressed in front of the mirror.

"Why, Cad," said he, catching her looking at herself. "I believe you're getting vain."

"Not at all," she replied, smiling.

"Well, you're mighty pretty," he went on, slipping his arm around her. "Put on that navy blue dress of yours, and I'll take you to the theater."

"Oh, I've promised to go with Mrs. Hale to the art show tonight," she said, apologetically.

"You did, eh?" he said. "I sure wouldn't want to go to that."

But Carrie didn't offer to break her promise to her neighbor just to go out with Drouet.

"Hurstwood has invited us to join him at the theater where Joe Jefferson is performing," explained Drouet. "So what do you say to that?"

Although Carrie was eager to accept the invitation, she did not show her true feelings. "You had better make the decision, Charlie," she answered.

"I guess we ought to go, if you can break your promise to Mrs. Hale," said Drouet.

"Oh, I can," said Carrie, having already forgotten about her commitment to her friend.

"Shall I wear my hair the way I did yesterday?" she asked, as she tried to decide which dress to wear.

"Sure," he replied, not realizing how excited she was.

She was relieved to see that Drouet did not suspect anything. Somehow, the combination of Hurstwood, Drouet, and herself seemed like the most pleasant way of all to spend the evening. Carrie took great care in the way she finished getting dressed.

"I say," said Hurstwood, as they entered the theater lobby. "We are exceedingly charming this evening."

Carrie fluttered under his approving glance.

"Now, then," he said, leading the way into the theater.

Hurstwood sent Drouet to go get some programs, while he and Carrie settled into their seats in the cozy box. He then tried to impress her with his knowledge about the performer.

Carrie was almost hypnotized by the dazzling environment, the elaborate box seats, her companion's elegance. Several times their eyes accidentally met. When that happened, she was flooded with feelings that she had never before experienced.

Drouet took part in the conversation. But in comparison to Hurstwood, he seemed so dull. Carrie knew instinctively that Hurstwood was the better man—stronger and higher. By the end of the third act, Carrie was sure. Drouet was kind, but he had little else to offer.

"I have had such a nice time," said Carrie, when it was all over and they were coming out.

"Yes, indeed," added Drouet, who had no idea that he was losing the battle for Carrie.

"Well, you have saved me a dreary evening," returned Hurstwood. "Goodnight."

He took Carrie's little hand, and a current of feeling swept from one to the other.

On the trolley ride home, Carrie said, "I'm so tired." She did not want Drouet to spoil the mood by talking to her.

"Well, you rest a little while I smoke," he said. But his next mistake was leaving her, alone with her daydreams, to go have a cigarette.

CHAPTER 12

Undercurrents of Feeling

Mrs. Hurstwood was not aware that her husband might be interested in another woman. But she was a cynical, cold, self-centered woman. She kept her thoughts to herself, so that Hurstwood had no idea what she might do if she found out. Mrs. Hurstwood simply watched and waited, calculating the best time and method to seek revenge. In the meantime, she found ways to hurt the other person. She just made sure that no one knew that she was the one who caused the pain.

Hurstwood, though, was not fully aware of his wife's shrewdness. And so he was not afraid of her. He thought that she would never risk losing her social status by ending their marriage. And yet, he knew that she held tremendous power over him. When he had cared more about her, he had signed over much of his property to his wife. Not knowing what she might do if she became dissatisfied, Hurstwood acted cautiously.

It just so happened that on the night when Hurstwood, Carrie, and Drouet were at McVickar's

Theater, George, Jr., was sitting in the sixth row with the daughter of a wealthy dry goods manufacturer.

The next morning at breakfast, Hurstwood's son announced, "I saw you last night."

"Were you at McVickar's?" responded Hurstwood casually.

"Yes," said young George.

Mrs. Hurstwood watched her husband's reaction closely. Then she asked, "How was the play?"

"Very good," returned Hurstwood. "Only it's the same old thing, 'Rip Van Winkle.'"

"Who did you go with?" asked his wife, pretending not to care.

"Charlie Drouet and his wife. They are friends of the boss."

Normally, Mrs. Hurstwood would not have been suspicious, since occasionally her husband had to entertain people as part of his job. But lately he had said that he could not go out with her because he needed to work late at the office. In fact, he had done so only yesterday.

"I thought you were going to be busy," she remarked, very carefully.

"So I was," he exclaimed. "I couldn't help the interruption. But I made up for it afterward by working until two."

That was the end of the discussion, at least for the time being.

Hurstwood had a new interest, which seemed like a bright light shining on the horizon. His wife now seemed old, dull, like the pale light at dusk.

He found it annoying to spend time with her. She, on the other hand, expected him to follow through on his duties as a husband, even if his heart was not in it.

Recently, when she asked him to go out with her, he had been saying that he was too busy.

"You find time to go out with other people, though," she would reply, irritated.

"Nothing of the kind," he would answer. "I can't avoid business relations, and that's all there is to it."

"Well, never mind," she would exclaim.

But her lips would tighten. His interest in Drouet's little shop girl would grow. And with each incident, the tension between them would increase.

When the winter season had passed and the first fine days of the early spring appeared, Mrs. Hale invited Carrie to go for a carriage ride along the fashionable North Shore Drive. Mrs. Hale pointed out subtle differences in degrees of wealth, and taught Carrie all about money and status. The glow of a more showy life awakened in Carrie a desire to have all the luxuries enjoyed by the very rich. And in the mellow radiance of the early evening, Carrie looked at these elegant mansions and remembered childhood tales of fairy palaces and king's castles. She looked through the richly carved wood-paneled doors with stained glass that sparkled like jewels from the glow of the crystal lamps inside. She was perfectly certain that beyond those entranceways there were no cares, no unsatisfied desires—only happiness. If only she could stroll up the broad walk, cross that rich entranceway, and sweep gracefully into the luxurious mansion, which she would possess and command. In that instant, all her sadness, all her heartache would disappear.

"If we could have a home like that," said Mrs. Hale sadly, "how delightful it would be."

"And yet, they do say," said Carrie, repeating moral views that she had been told many times, "that no one is ever happy."

Mrs. Hale responded, with wry humor, "Then I guess that rich people try pretty hard to make up for their great misery by living in fine mansions."

When Carrie returned home to her apartment, it seemed even smaller in comparison with the mansions she had just seen. She no longer thought about how much better her apartment was than any place she had ever lived before. Instead, she sat at her window, rocking back and forth, and gazed out across the lamp-lit park to the lamp-lit houses beyond. What, after all, was Drouet? What was she? Some old tunes came to her lips. As she sang them, her heart sank. She longed and longed and longed. First she longed for the old cottage room in Columbia City, then for the grand mansion on the North Shore Drive, then for the fine dress of some lady, then for the elegance of some scene in the theater. She was sad beyond measure, and yet uncertain, wishing, fancying. She felt lonely and abandoned, and couldn't keep from crying. She hummed and hummed as the moments went by, sitting in the shadow by the window. And though she didn't realize it, this was as happy as she would ever be.

While still in this frame of mind, Mr. Hurstwood arrived at the apartment building and asked to see Mr. and Mrs. Drouet.

"I guess he doesn't know that Charlie is out of town," thought Carrie.

After checking her appearance in the mirror, Carrie went downstairs to greet him.

No, Hurstwood hadn't heard that Drouet was out of town. But he didn't seem to mind. Instead, he spoke easily with Carrie about subjects that he thought would interest her. He pulled his chair up close to hers, and focused all his attention on her. He spoke in a soft, deep voice, as though what he said were very private and confidential, just between the two of them. Once when he touched her hand for emphasis, she smiled, warmed by his radiance. He was never dull. And he brought out the best in her. He made her feel brighter, more clever. She felt that she was more clever with him than with anyone else. At least, he seemed to find her brilliant. And, unlike Drouet, he did not seem to look down on her.

When Carrie first met Drouet, she was overwhelmed by distress. And so when he offered to help her, she simply gave in to him. That was all there was between them, nothing more. But with Hurstwood, a subtle, secret current of feelings flowed between them, under the surface. Carrie deeply, strongly sensed his growing desire for her, although she could not put her thoughts into words. But Hurstwood's glance, appearance, and voice touched her spirit. It was like music playing softly in the background. And her heart listened.

"Have you ever seen the houses along the Lake Shore on the North Side?" asked Hurstwood.

"Why, I was just over there this afternoon— Mrs. Hale and I. Aren't they beautiful?"

"They're very fine," he answered.

"Ah, yes," said Carrie, thoughtfully. "I wish I could live in such a place."

Slowly, after a slight pause, Hurstwood raised his eyes solemnly and looked into hers.

"You're not happy," he said, hoping to strike a deep chord, to touch her innermost feelings.

He leaned over quietly and held her in his steady gaze. She tried to move, but it was useless. He looked and looked. And the longer the situation lasted, the harder it was for Carrie to resist. The little shop girl was getting into deep water. She was letting her few supports float away from her.

"Oh," she said at last, "you mustn't look at me like that."

"I can't help it," he answered.

She relaxed a little. He took advantage of this to make his next move.

"You are not satisfied with life, are you?"

"No," she answered, weakly.

He saw that he was the master of the situation— he felt it. He reached over and touched her hand.

"You mustn't," she exclaimed, jumping up.

"I didn't mean to," he answered, easily.

She did not run away, as she might have done. She did not make him leave. Instead, she let him chat pleasantly for a little while longer. When he was ready to go, he stood up, and Carrie felt that he was in charge.

"You mustn't feel bad," he said, kindly. "Things will straighten out eventually."

She made no answer, because she could think of nothing to say.

"We are good friends, aren't we?" he said, extending his hand.

"Yes," she answered.

"Don't say a word, then, until I see you again."

He held onto her hand.

"I can't promise," she said, uncertain.

"You must be more generous with me than that." He said this in such a simple way that she was touched.

"Let's not talk about it anymore," she replied.

"All right," he said, brightening.

After he left, Carrie looked in the mirror. Ashamed of herself, she said, "I'm becoming a terrible person. I don't seem to do anything right. But what else can I do?"

Hurstwood returned to his office, merrily whistling a song that he had not thought about for fifteen years. "Well," he thought, "she likes me. That's for sure."

CHAPTER 13

A Knight and His Lady

Afterward, Carrie did not know what to think, and there was no one who could give her advice. She owed something to Drouet, she thought. After all, he had helped her when she was so worried and distressed. She had kind feelings toward him. She gave him credit for his good looks and his generous feelings. And when he was away, she forgot about how conceited he could be. But she didn't feel that she had to stay tied exclusively to him.

In fact, Drouet did not expect, or even seek, a long-term relationship. He just went merrily along, in his lighthearted carefree manner. He assumed that women would always find him charming. If one woman left him, he knew that another one would soon come along.

As for Hurstwood, he had not stopped thinking about Carrie since he saw her two days ago. Her giving in to him heated his passion. He felt he must succeed with her, and do so quickly.

His interest, his fascination with Carrie was deeper than just desire. Some time ago, his feelings had dried up and almost died, like a flower in barren soil. After he married his wife, he never had another love affair. But he knew that it had been a mistake to marry a woman like her. His experience with her, and with other women that he met, led him to think that all women were selfish, cold, ignorant, flashy. And so, he looked at most women with cynicism and suspicion. But Carrie was a young, unsophisticated, innocent soul—a better woman than had ever before appealed to him. Carrie was like a fly caught in a spider web. She had wandered innocently into the city, and now was caught in Drouet's net. Hurstwood thought that this was a mistake, so he sprang to her rescue. He wanted to win Carrie because he thought that she would have a better life with him than with Drouet. And he envied Drouet more than he had ever before envied another man. So Hurstwood wanted to grab Carrie, the way he would pick the fresh fruit of a tree. When he was with her, he felt fresh and alive. In his heart, he was young again— a knight with a duty to rescue a lady in distress.

It would be easy for Hurstwood to see her again. He was so responsible in his work that he was allowed to take time off during the day whenever he wanted. His employers asked only that he close up the saloon at the end of the evening. So Hurstwood faithfully returned every evening before midnight to take care of the last hour or two of business. He made sure that everything was safe and that all the employees had left the building. In fact, the owners trusted him so much that for years they had not even stopped by the saloon after five o'clock to check up on his work.

On this Friday afternoon, Hurstwood made up his mind to see Carrie. He could not stay away any longer. When he arrived, Carrie was a little flustered and excited, but mostly nervous. For just a moment, she felt that she had to be careful with Hurstwood. Hurstwood, too, felt nervous. But her simple, charming manner gave him courage. And her nervousness chased away his own fears.

"How are you?" he said, easily. "I could not resist the temptation to come out this fine afternoon. Would you care to take a walk?"

Afraid to be seen with Carrie in public, Hurstwood decided to rent a horse-drawn carriage and drive out of the city along a country road. That way, no one would see or hear them.

Once in the carriage, Hurstwood waited for a break in the conversation to make his move.

"Do you know," he said, "I have spent the happiest evenings in years since I have known you?"

"Have you?" she said, pretending to take his comment lightly, though she was excited by his persuasive tone of voice.

"I was going to tell you the other evening," he added. "But somehow the opportunity slipped away."

Carrie didn't know what to say. He seemed to win over all her doubts about whether she was doing the right thing.

"I came out here today," he went on, solemnly, "to tell you just how I feel—to see if you might listen to me."

In his own way, Hurstwood was capable of strong feelings—often poetic ones. And when he really wanted something, he could speak passionately and persuasively.

"You know . . ." he said, putting his hand on her arm. There was a solemn silence, while he put his thought into words. Then he continued, ". . . that I love you?"

Caught up in the silent mood that Hurstwood had created, Carrie did not reply.

Hurstwood waited for a few moments, and then repeated the words.

"You must not say that," Carrie said, weakly.

She spoke only because she thought that she needed to say something. But her words were not convincing at all. So he paid no attention to them.

"Carrie," he said, using her first name as though they had been friends for a long time, "I want you to love me. You don't know how much I need someone to waste a little affection on me. I am practically alone. There is nothing in my life that is pleasant or delightful. It's all work and worry, with people who mean nothing to me."

As he said this, Hurstwood really imagined that his life was pitiful. He managed to see what he wanted to see. Now, as he spoke, his voice trembled with intense feeling. And Carrie's heart heard that tone.

"Why, I would have thought," she said, turning toward him with large eyes, which were full of sympathy and feeling, "that you were very happy. You know so much of the world."

"That is it," he said, the tone of his voice dropping to a soft, sad, minor key. "I know too much of the world."

As Carrie listened, she felt all the mystery and strangeness of the city. And here was the greatest mystery of all. Sitting beside her was a powerful businessman, with status and money and rich clothing. And he was appealing to her for her help. She didn't know what to think or say, and she didn't bother trying to figure it out. She just warmed herself in the glow of his feeling. She felt grateful, the way that people who are cold are grateful when they can warm themselves by a blazing fire. Hurstwood burned with his own intensity, and the heat of his passion was already melting away her worry that she was doing something wrong.

"You think," he said, "that I am happy, that I shouldn't complain? But what if, all day long, you met with people who cared absolutely nothing about you? What if, day after day, you went to a job where everything was cold and fake? What if, among all those people you knew, there was not a single person who sympathized with you or brought you pleasure? Then perhaps you would be unhappy, too."

Now he struck a chord that Carrie could hear, a pain that she could feel. She knew what it was like to meet with people who were cold to her, to walk alone among so many people who cared absolutely nothing about her. Wasn't she at this very moment quite alone? Who among all those people that she knew could give her advice or sympathy? Not one. She was left to herself to worry and wonder.

"I could be content," Hurstwood went on, "if I had you to love me. If I had you to go to. If I had you for a companion. As it is, I simply move about from place to place without any satisfaction. Time hangs heavily on my hands. Before you came, I did nothing but hang around and drift from one thing to another. Since you came—well, I've had you to think about."

Carrie began to believe the old illusion that someone needed her help. She truly pitied this sad, lonely person. With all his fine things, he felt that he had nothing without her. And at the same time, she, too, was so lonely, drifting through life without an anchor.

"You probably think that I run around," he said apologetically, "and do all sorts of bad things. Yes, I have taken some bad risks. But I could change. I need you to pull me back from evil if my life is ever to amount to anything."

Carrie looked at him tenderly. She hoped that her goodness could make him a better person. But how bad could he be? His manner and his things were all so fine. He made himself seem so lonely that she was deeply moved.

He slipped his arm around her waist, and she

could not find the heart to pull away. With his free hand he seized her fingers.

"Tell me," he said, softly, "that you love me."

She looked down.

"Admit it, Dear," he said, passionately. "You do, don't you?"

She said nothing. But he felt his victory.

"Tell me," he said, richly, pulling her so close that their lips almost touched. He pressed her hand warmly, and then released it to touch her cheek.

"You do?" he said, pressing his lips to her own.

Still she said nothing. But her lips replied.

"Now," he said, joyously, his fine eyes ablaze, "you're mine, aren't you?"

In answer to his question, her head rested softly upon his shoulder.

CHAPTER 14

Seeing and Not Seeing

Mrs. Hale, from her upper window, saw Carrie come in that afternoon.

"Hmm," she thought to herself, "she goes riding with another man when her husband is out of the city. He had better keep an eye on her."

And Mrs. Hale was not the only one who noticed. The housekeeper greeted Hurstwood when he arrived. She thought Carrie was cold and unpleasant, and Hurstwood stiff and critical. She liked Drouet's easy, merry manner. Sometimes he even tossed a pleasant remark her way, as he did with all women. So she wondered why Hurstwood came so frequently, and why Mrs. Drouet went out with him that afternoon. She expressed her concerns to the cook. As a result, gossip began to hum, secretly, through the entire building.

Carrie began to look for a way out of her situation with Drouet. Their relationship seemed morally wrong. Carrie saw Hurstwood's dignity and grace as a way to lead a more honorable life.

Hurstwood, on the other hand, was thinking

only of having some pleasure, without any responsibility. He could enjoy spending some time with Carrie, while his life at home and at work would go on as they had, undisturbed.

As they dined together that Sunday evening, Carrie kept Hurstwood at a distance. She gave in to only casual displays of affection. Hurstwood soon realized that Carrie took their relationship more seriously than he had expected. He saw that he could not possess her just for the asking. He would have to continue pretending to believe that she was married to Drouet.

As they returned to her apartment, he asked, "When will I see you again?"

"I don't know," she answered, wondering herself.

"I'll tell you what I'll do," he suggested. "I'll write to you, in care of the West Side post office. Could you check there next Tuesday?"

Carrie agreed.

Unfortunately for the smooth progression of this affair, Drouet returned from his trip. Hurstwood was sitting in his little office the next afternoon when he saw Drouet enter.

"Why, hello, Charles," he called warmly. "Back again?"

"Yes," smiled Drouet.

"Been home yet?" Hurstwood asked, after they had chatted for a while.

"No, but I'm on my way there," said Drouet.

"I remembered your little girlfriend out

there," said Hurstwood. "So I called once. Thought you wouldn't want her left all alone."

"Right you are," agreed Drouet. "How is she?"

"Very well," said Hurstwood. "Rather anxious about you, though. You'd better go out now and cheer her up."

"I will," said Drouet, smiling.

"Like to have you both come down and go to the show with me Wednesday," offered Hurstwood as Drouet was leaving.

"Thanks, old man," said his friend. "I'll see what the girl says and let you know."

They separated in a very friendly manner.

"There's a nice fellow," Drouet thought to himself, as he started toward home.

"Drouet is a good fellow," Hurstwood thought to himself, as he went back into his office. "But he's not the man for Carrie."

When Drouet entered the apartment, he caught Carrie in his arms as usual. But she responded to his kiss with a slight tension, a hint of resistance.

"Well," he said, "I had a great trip. I surprised the people at the office. I've sold more goods this last quarter than any of the other traveling salesmen in our company. I'm going to ask for a raise in June. They can afford to pay it, as much business as I turn in. I'll get it, too, you'd better believe it."

"I hope you do," said Carrie.

"And then if that little real estate deal goes through, we'll get married." He put on a show of being serious and sincere, while he brushed his hair, looking at himself in the mirror.

"I don't believe you ever intend to marry me, Charlie," Carrie said sorrowfully. Hurstwood's recent declarations of love had given her courage to say this.

"Oh, yes, I do—course I do—what put that into your head?"

He stopped admiring himself in front of the mirror and moved over closer to Carrie. For the first time, Carrie felt as if she needed to move away from him.

"But you've been saying that for so long," she said, with her pretty face looking up at his.

"Well, yes, and I mean it, too. But it takes money to live as I want to. Now, when I get this increase, I can come pretty near fixing things, all right. And then I'll do it. Now, don't you worry, Girlie."

He patted her reassuringly upon the shoulder. But Carrie now realized how useless her hopes had been. She could clearly see that this easygoing man had no intention of marrying her. He was simply letting things drift because he preferred having his pleasure without being trapped by any legal ties to Carrie.

In contrast, Hurstwood appeared strong and sincere. He seemed more serious, less easygoing and carefree. He sympathized with her. And he showed Carrie her true value. He needed her, while Drouet did not care one way or the other.

"Oh, no," she said bitterly. "You never will."

"Well, you wait a little while and see," he insisted. "I'll marry you all right."

Carrie looked at him and felt justified. She had been looking for a way to calm her conscience, and here it was. He had faithfully promised to marry her, but he was not keeping his promise.

"Say," he said, after he thought he had pleasantly gotten rid of the marriage question. "I saw Hurstwood today. He wants us to go to the theater with him."

Carrie jumped at the name, but Drouet didn't notice.

"When?" she asked, pretending not to care.

"Wednesday. We'll go, won't we?"

"If you want to," she answered, restraining her excitement. Drouet noticed something, but he thought it was left over from their talk about marriage. "He said he came by to see you once."

"Yes," said Carrie, "he was out here Sunday evening."

"Was he?" said Drouet. "I thought from what he said that he had stopped by a week or so ago."

"So he did," answered Carrie, unaware of what her lovers might have said to each other. She was all at sea mentally, afraid that she might become tangled up in her answers.

"Oh, then he came over twice?" said Drouet, the first shade of misunderstanding showing in his face.

"Yes," said Carrie innocently, now realizing that

Hurstwood must have mentioned only one visit.

Drouet imagined that he must have misunderstood his friend. He did not think it was very important, though.

"What did he have to say?" he asked, with slightly more interest.

"He said he came because he thought I might be lonely. You hadn't stopped by the saloon for so long that he wondered what had happened to you."

"George is a fine fellow," said Drouet, feeling flattered by Hurstwood's interest in his life.

On Tuesday morning, Carrie stopped by the post office and read Hurstwood's letter to her. "I told him I called on you, Dearest, when he was away. I did not say how often, but he probably thought once. Let me know of anything you may have said. I want to speak with you before we meet at the theater."

Carrie wrote back immediately. "I said you called twice. He didn't seem to mind. I will try to meet you. But I know that it's wrong to act as I do."

When Hurstwood met her, as they had arranged, he reassured her that she was doing nothing wrong. "You mustn't worry, Sweetheart," he said. "Just as soon as he goes on the road again, we will arrange something. We'll fix it so that you won't have to deceive anyone."

Carrie imagined that this meant he would marry her right away, though he had not said so directly.

At the theater, Carrie watched Hurstwood with pleasure. She almost forgot about Drouet. Hurstwood did not give the slightest hint of any change in their relationship. If anything, he paid even more attention to his old friend than usual.

But Drouet, without knowing it, made himself look foolish.

There was one scene in the play where the husband was away, and the wife was seduced by her lover. After watching this, Drouet said, "Served him right. I find it hard to pity a man who would be such a fool."

"Well, you never can tell," responded Hurstwood gently. "He probably didn't think he was doing anything wrong."

"Well, a man ought to pay more attention to his wife than he did—especially if he wants to keep her."

After the show, they walked through the showy crowd and onto the street. Hurstwood heard a voice at his side. It begged him, "Please, Mister. Can you give me a little change?"

But Hurstwood was busy talking to Carrie, trying to impress her. So he just ignored the man.

"Honest to God, Mister. I don't have any place to sleep."

But Drouet noticed how thin, poor, and miserable this thirty-year-old man looked. He suddenly felt pity in his heart, and handed over a dime. Hurstwood hardly noticed the incident. Carrie quickly forgot.

CHAPTER 15

Old Ties and New

The more Hurstwood focused his feelings on Carrie, the less attention he paid to his own family. He began to see his son and daughter as shallow. It was as though a river ran between him and his wife, cutting off their feelings for each other. Her demanding voice began to irritate him, especially when it called him back from his daydreams about Carrie. His marriage seemed like a chain that bound his feet and kept him from moving forward.

As they sat in the living room before dinner, his family would demand things from him. His wife wanted him to use his business connections to get her special season tickets to the horseraces. As usual, they would argue. And then his seat at the dinner table would be empty.

His daughter complained that all her friends were going to Europe, but she never got to travel abroad. Except when she wanted something from her father, she felt that what she did was none of his business.

His son did whatever he pleased, and no one even bothered to tell Hurstwood. He acted as if he were already a grown man and demanded his privacy.

All Hurstwood seemed to do was pay the bills. It was not that he minded giving his family a fair share of all that he earned. But he did not like to be forced to do so against his will.

He comforted himself with the thought that, after all, his life was not completely without love. Whatever happened inside his house, he knew that Carrie would be waiting for him outside of it. Once again he felt the urge that quickens a lover's feet, a feeling that he had almost forgotten. Looking at his reflection in her young eyes, he felt young again.

In his mind, he looked into Carrie's apartment. He thought how charming it would be once they'd gotten rid of Drouet forever. Every evening she would be waiting for him in their cozy little home. He assumed that Drouet would have no reason to tell Carrie that Hurstwood was already married. Things were going so smoothly that he believed they would not change. Soon he would persuade Carrie to leave Drouet, and everything would be fine.

Carrie was, indeed, worth loving. She reminded Hurstwood of all the innocence, passion, and wonder of youth—feelings that his experiences had taken away long ago. Her soft eyes glowed with longing and expectation that had not yet been disappointed. But she was still timid enough that she did not make demands or try to dominate him. She wanted pleasure, she wanted status, and yet she was confused about what these things really were. Her interests kept changing. One moment, her attention was attracted by something shiny. This became the object of all her desires. But then the light would change. And some other object would become the beautiful, the perfect thing she craved.

Carrie's mouth also appealed to Hurstwood. Its shape gave the impression that she was on the verge of tears, though she had not yet experienced real grief. From the depths of her heart, she pitied the poorly dressed shop girls who hurried by her window each evening. They had so little, she thought. The way their faded clothes fit them so badly made her eyes hurt. "And they have to work so hard!" she would say. She sympathized with people who had to live in the world of hard labor. It was a world she had so recently escaped—a world that she knew better than the one she was in now.

Though Hurstwood did not know it, Carrie's feelings were just this tender and delicate. And though he did not know it, this was what attracted him to her. Being close to Carrie lightened his feelings. It made the morning worthwhile.

The day after their theater visit, Hurstwood began to write Carrie regularly. Every morning he sat at the desk in his office and wrote her a letter. He seemed to be working so seriously that everyone in the saloon respected him even more than before.

One morning, Hurstwood wrote to Carrie, asking her to meet him the next day in Jefferson Park. The following afternoon, while waiting for

Carrie to arrive, he dreamed he was a young man again, not yet tied to a wife and job. He remembered the light, carefree spirit of going out with young women—how he had danced with them, escorted them home, hung over their gates as they said goodnight. He almost wished he could go back in time, for then he felt totally free.

At two o'clock, Carrie appeared, almost skipping up to him. She was wearing a fashionable hat with a pretty blue and white polka dotted silk band. Her skirt was of a rich blue material. Her matching snow-white blouse was decorated with fine blue stripes. Her brown shoes peeked occasionally from beneath her skirt. She carried her gloves in her hand.

Hurstwood looked up at her with delight.

"You came, Dearest," he said eagerly, taking her hand.

"Of course," she said, smiling. "Did you think I wouldn't?"

"I didn't know," he replied.

They looked into each other's eyes—happy to be near each other. Finally, he asked, "When is Charlie going away again?"

"I don't know," she answered. "He says that right now he has some work to do around here."

Hurstwood grew serious, lost in quiet thought. He looked up after a time and said, "Come away and leave him."

Then he looked away, as though it were not an important request.

"Where would we go?" she asked in much the same manner, looking casually around her.

"Where do you want to go?" he asked.

"We can't stay in Chicago," she replied.

He had never thought that she might want to leave the city.

"Why not?" he asked softly.

"Oh, because," she said, "I wouldn't want to."

"But then I would have to give up my job," he said.

Carrie thought a little, at the same time enjoying the pretty scene.

"I wouldn't like to live in Chicago and have him here," she said, thinking of Drouet.

"It's a big town, Dearest," Hurstwood answered. "Moving to the South Side of Chicago would be almost the same as moving to another part of the country."

He had already been thinking about living in that neighborhood.

"Anyhow," said Carrie, "I shouldn't want to get married as long as he is here. And I wouldn't want to run away."

Carrie's suggestion of marriage came as a blow. How could he get around this problem of marrying Carrie while still married to his own wife? Carrie was the one part of his life that seemed to be going somewhere. When he looked at her now, he thought how beautiful she was. What a thing it was to have her love him, even if he became tangled up in a relationship. Here was something worth struggling for. He thought even more highly of her because she objected to living with him unless he married her. How different— how much better—she was from the women who yielded willingly! He swept the thought of bigamy from his mind.

"And you don't know when he'll go away?" asked Hurstwood, quietly.

She shook her head.

He sighed.

"You're a determined little miss, aren't you?" he said, after a few moments, looking up into her eyes.

She felt a wave of feeling sweep over her. She was proud that he seemed to admire her. And she liked this man, because he could see such fine qualities in her.

"No," she said coyly, "but what else can I do?"

Again he folded his hands and looked away.

"I wish," he said sorrowfully, "that you would come with me. I don't like to be away from you this way. What good is there in waiting? You're not happier without me, are you?"

"Happier!" she exclaimed softly. "You know better than that."

"Here we are then," he went on in the same tone. "We are wasting our days. If you are not happy, do you think I am? I sit and write to you all the time. I'll tell you what, Carrie," he exclaimed passionately, holding her with his eyes. "I can't live without you, and that's all there is to it! So now," he appealed, gesturing helplessly, "what shall I do?"

He seemed to be asking Carrie to tell him what to do. His appeal for help touched Carrie's heart.

"Can't you wait a little while longer?" she asked tenderly. "I'll try and find out when he's going away."

"What good will it do?" he asked.

"Well, perhaps we can arrange to go somewhere." She really didn't know what to do. She had no idea that Hurstwood had a wife and family. But out of sympathy, she was beginning to give in to him.

Hurstwood finally came up with a plan that would persuade her to leave Drouet.

"Carrie," he said. He gazed at her with a serious look that he did not feel. "Suppose I were to come to you next week, or this week for that matter—tonight, even—and tell you I had to go away. Suppose I told you that I couldn't stay another minute and wasn't coming back anymore. Then would you come with me?"

His sweetheart looked at him affectionately. She was ready to answer before the words were out of his mouth.

"Yes," she said.

"You wouldn't stop to argue or arrange?"

"Not if you couldn't wait."

He smiled because she seemed to think he was being serious. He thought about telling her that he was only joking. But her sweet seriousness was so delightful. And besides, another thought just came to him.

"Suppose we didn't have time to get married here?" he added.

"If we got married as soon as we got to the other end of the trip, it would be all right."

"I meant that," he said.

"Yes."

The morning seemed strangely bright to him now. Whatever could have put such a thought into his head? It was impossible, of course. But he had to smile at how clever he had been. There was no doubt in his mind. He would find a way to win her over.

"Well, then," he said, joking. "One of these evenings, I'll just come out and take you away with me."

Then he laughed.

Thinking it over, Carrie said seriously, "I wouldn't stay with you, though, if you didn't marry me."

"I don't want you to," he said tenderly, taking her hand.

She was extremely happy now that she seemed to understand everything. She loved him even more for wanting to rescue her. As for him, he didn't think much more about the marriage part of his proposal. He was thinking only that if she felt this way about him, nothing could get in the way of his eventual happiness.

CHAPTER 16

The Promise of the Theater

Drouet soon realized that, in order to get ahead, he needed to become more involved with the Elks, a men's association that he had joined. So he paid a visit to the local headquarters and chatted with Mr. Harry Quincel, one of its most powerful members.

Suddenly, Mr. Quincel exclaimed, "I say, Drouet. You're just the man that can help us out."

Mr. Quincel then explained that they were going to put on a melodrama, *Under the Gaslight*, which was popular among amateur theater groups. The Elks would use the show to raise money for their lodge. The members would play the male roles. But they needed a woman to take the part of Laura. Did Drouet know a young lady who could take the part?

Anxious to continue socializing with important people that he could meet through the Elks, Drouet agreed. But as soon as Mr. Quincel stopped talking, he forgot about his promise.

The next day, however, he received a letter from Mr. Quincel. Would he kindly forward the young lady's address to him right away, so that they could deliver her part to her?

"Now, who in the world do I know?" he wondered, going over in his mind all the women he knew. Finally, he decided to ask someone who lived near the lodge. He promised himself that he would go see her about it that very evening. But again he forgot.

The next day, he was reading the local newspaper when he saw a small announcement that the play would be performed on the 16th.

"By golly!" exclaimed Drouet. "I forgot all about that!"

"About what?" asked Carrie.

"Why, the play that my lodge is putting on. They wanted me to get them some young lady to take a part."

"What is it they're going to play?"

"*Under the Gaslight.*"

"Well, why don't you ask someone?" asked Carrie.

"I don't know anyone who could do it," he replied.

Suddenly he looked up.

"Say," he said, "how would you like to take the part?"

"Me?" said Carrie. "I can't act."

"How do you know?" asked Drouet.

"Because," answered Carrie, "I never did."

Even so, she was pleased to think that he would ask her. Her eyes brightened, for she loved the theater. True to his nature, Drouet held onto this idea, seeing it as an easy way out.

"That's not a problem. You'll be able to practice as much as you want."

"No, I can't," said Carrie, starting to give in. She was very much drawn toward the idea, and yet also fearful.

"Yes, you can. Now, why don't you do it? They need someone, and it will be lots of fun for you."

"Oh, no, it won't," said Carrie seriously.

"You'd like it. I know you would. I've seen you dancing around here and doing imitations of other people. That's why I asked you. You're clever enough, all right."

"No, I'm not," said Carrie shyly.

"Now, I'll tell you what to do," said Drouet, eager to settle the matter. "You go down and see about it. It'll be fun for you."

"I don't believe I could act, Charlie," Carrie insisted. "You don't think I could, do you?"

"Sure. Out o' sight. I bet you'll be a hit. Now you do want to go, I know you do. I knew it when I came home. That's why I asked you."

"What is the play, did you say?"

"*Under the Gaslight.*"

"What part would they want me to take?"

"Oh, one of the heroines—I don't know."

"What sort of a play is it?"

"Well," said Drouet, "it's about a girl who gets kidnapped by a couple of crooks. She had some money, and they wanted to get it. I don't remember exactly what happened."

"And what's my part like?"

"I think there's a girl in it that was stolen off the streets or something when she was an infant. She almost gets drowned—no, that's not it. But I'll get the script for you tonight."

"Well, I don't know," said Carrie. Her interest and desire to shine dramatically struggled with her fear that she might not be able to master the part. "I might try it if you thought I'd do all right."

"Of course, you'll do fine," said Drouet, trying to fire Carrie's enthusiasm. "Do you think I'd urge you to do something if I didn't think you could do it? You can act, all right. It'll be good for you."

"All right," said Carrie, finally giving in. "I'll do it. But if I'm a failure, it'll be your fault."

"You won't fail," assured Drouet. "Just act as you do around here. Be natural. You're all right. I've often thought you'd make a really fine actress."

"Did you really?" asked Carrie.

"That's right," said the traveling salesman.

As he left to pick up the script, Drouet had no idea that he had lighted such a secret flame in Carrie. Passive, sympathetic, impressionable, she was a natural mimic. Sometimes she stood in front of the mirror, practicing some graceful little expression of the mouth or eyes that she had observed in others. Drouet teased her about admiring herself. But she was really just trying to imitate a gesture that she had admired in someone else. And drama, after all, is simply such a re-creation of reality.

Drouet's praise made her body tingle with satisfaction. His words were like a flame melting together loose pieces of dreams into a solid mass. Drouet had pulled together floating feelings about her acting ability—ideas that she had felt, but never believed. By giving words to her feelings, he gave her a spark of hope. She had often wondered how she would look, and how delightful she would feel if only she had a chance to perform onstage. The glamour, the excitement, the fine clothes, the applause—these had lured her until she felt that she, too, could act. She, too, could make other people feel her power. It was a delightful sensation while it lasted.

When Drouet was gone, she sat down in her rocking chair by the window to think about it. As usual, her imagination exaggerated the possibilities. It was as if he had put fifty cents in her hand. But in her mind, she imagined spending a thousand dollars. She saw herself performing with a trembling voice and sorrowful manner. She imagined scenes of luxury and drama. She would be the guiding star—the center of everyone's attention and admiration. As she rocked back and forth, she imagined all kinds of emotions—the intense sadness of abandonment, the magnificent anger of betrayal, the quiet sorrow of defeat. She thought of all the charming women she had seen in plays. And every illusion she ever had about the stage flooded her with excitement and determination.

When Drouet stopped by the lodge, Quincel

asked, "Where is that young lady you were going to get for us?"

"I've got her," said Drouet.

"You do?" said Quincel, rather surprised by his promptness. "That's good. I'll send her a copy of the part. What's her address?"

Now Drouet was surprised. If Quincel saw Carrie's address, he might realize that they were living together.

"Well, I'd be happy to take it to her," offered the traveling salesman. "I'm going right by her house in the morning."

"What did you say her address was? We want it just in case we have any information to send her."

"Twenty-nine Ogden Place."

"And her name?"

"Carrie Madenda," said Drouet without thinking. He couldn't call her Mrs. Drouet because the lodge members knew that he wasn't married.

"That sounds like somebody that can act, doesn't it?" said Quincel.

"Yes, it does."

Drouet took the part home to Carrie. He handed it to her as though he were the one doing her a favor.

"He says that's the best part. Do you think you can do it?"

"I won't know until I look it over. You know I'm afraid, now that I've said I would."

"Oh, don't worry. What is there to be afraid of?"

"Well, I'll see," said Carrie, pleased to have the part, in spite of her doubts.

Drouet fidgeted a moment while he figured out how to approach the next problem. Finally he said, "They were getting ready to print the programs. So I gave them the name of Carrie Madenda. Was that all right?"

"Yes, I guess so," said his companion, looking up at him. She was thinking it was a little strange that he didn't say she was his wife.

"You know . . . just in case you weren't a hit," he tried to explain.

"Oh, yes," she answered, rather pleased now with his caution. It was pretty clever for Drouet.

"I didn't want to introduce you as my wife, because then you'd feel worse if you didn't pull it off. They all know me so well. But you'll be fine, all right. Anyhow, you'll probably never meet any of them again."

"Oh, I don't care," said Carrie desperately. She was determined now to give this fascinating game a try.

Drouet breathed a sigh of relief. He had been afraid that she would bring up the question of marriage again.

The part of Laura was full of suffering and tears, in the tradition of old-fashioned melodrama. Carrie was surprised at how small the part seemed. She didn't realize that she would have to remain onstage during the entire show.

"I think I can do that, though," she concluded,

after looking at the script.

When Drouet came home the next night, he asked how she was coming along with her part.

"All right," she laughed. "I think I have it almost memorized."

"That's good," he said. "Let's hear some of it."

"Oh, I don't know whether I can get up and say it here," she said shyly.

"Well, I don't know why you shouldn't. It'll be easier here than it will there."

"I don't know about that," she answered.

Eventually she tried performing the ballroom scene. She let her feelings take over. As she got deeper into the part, she forgot all about Drouet.

"Good," said Drouet. "Fine! Out o' sight! You're all right, Caddie, I tell you."

He was really moved by her portrayal of a poor little character that sways and finally faints. As she fell to the floor, he jumped up to catch her. Now he held her, laughing, in his arms.

"Aren't you afraid you'll hurt yourself?" he asked.

"Not a bit."

"Well, you're a wonder. Say, I never knew you could do anything like that."

"I never did, either," said Carrie merrily, her face glowing with delight.

"Well, you can bet that you're all right," said Drouet. "You can take my word for it. You won't fail."

CHAPTER 17

Stars in Her Eyes

To Carrie, this performance was so important that she immediately wrote to Hurstwood about it.

As he read her letter, he smiled indulgently. "I've got to see this."

He wrote back right away. "I have no doubt that you'll be a hit. You must come to the park tomorrow morning and tell me all about it."

When they met the next day, Carrie shared all the details about this exciting event. Afterward, Hurstwood commented, "Well, that's fine. I'm glad to hear it. Of course, you will do well, you're so clever."

He had never before seen her so lively. As she spoke, her eyes were bright, her cheeks radiant. For all her doubts—and she had many—she was still happy. She was delighted to be doing this little thing—something that most people would consider unimportant.

Hurstwood was charmed by the fact that Carrie had some ability. Her ambition to express this talent made her seem even brighter, more powerful, and more beautiful.

Carrie innocently imagined that this performance would help her discover some purpose in her life.

"I'd like you to be there," said Carrie, "if you want to come. But I don't see how you can unless he asks you."

"I'll be there," said Hurstwood affectionately. "You know, I'm a member of the same lodge. I can fix it so he won't know you told me. You leave it to me."

In fact, Hurstwood had a lot of status in the Elks' lodge. Already he was thinking about getting box seats, bringing some friends, and buying flowers for Carrie. He would make it a formal event, and give the little girl a chance.

The next afternoon, Drouet stopped by Fitzgerald and Moy's. He walked cheerfully over to Hurstwood. His new pair of tan shoes squeaked loudly, announcing his progress as he walked past a crowd of businessmen, actors, managers, politicians, and athletes.

"Well, sir," said Hurstwood, "I was wondering what had happened to you. I thought you had gone out of town again."

Drouet laughed.

As they strolled over to the bar, famous people stopped to shake Hurstwood's hand.

"I hear your lodge is going to give a performance," observed Hurstwood casually.

"Yes, who told you?"

"No one," said Hurstwood. "They just sent

me a couple of tickets. Is it going to be any good?"

"I don't know," replied Drouet.

Then, after thinking it over, Drouet decided to add, "I think the girl is going to be in it."

"You don't say so! How did that happen?"

"Well, they didn't have enough women for the parts. So they asked me to find them someone. I told Carrie, and she seems to want to try."

"Good for her," said the manager. "It'll be a real nice event. Do her good, too. Has she ever had any experience?"

"Not a bit."

"Oh, well, it isn't anything very serious."

"She's clever, though," said Drouet, defending Carrie's ability. "She learned her part quick enough."

"You don't say so!" said the manager.

"Yes, sir. By golly, she surprised me the other night. No kidding. She really did."

"We must give her a nice little send-off," said the manager. "I'll look after the flowers."

Drouet smiled at his friend's good nature.

Hurstwood continued, "After the show you must come with me, and we'll have a bite to eat."

"I think she'll do all right," said Drouet.

"She's got to do all right. We'll make her." At this, the manager gave one of his quick, steely half-smiles—a smile that was both good-natured and shrewd.

At the first rehearsal, the director was frustrated by the actors' lack of talent. He forgot that these were only volunteers and not paid performers. He bossed them around rudely and yelled at them as they read their lines flatly. The director was in despair. Then Carrie walked onto the stage. Suddenly, she forgot about everyone around her. She began to feel the part. Just as the script suggested, she put a cold smile on her lips, turned away from the other character, and walked toward the window. She did it with a grace which was fascinating to watch.

"Who is that woman?" asked the director, watching Carrie in her little scene.

"Miss Madenda," said Quincel.

"I know her name," said the director. "But what does she do?"

"I don't know," said Quincel. "She's a friend of one of our members."

"Well, she's got more energy than anyone I've seen here so far. She really seems to take an interest in what she's doing."

"Pretty, too, isn't she?" observed Quincel.

The director strolled away without answering.

In the second scene, Carrie did even better, winning the smile of the director. Fascinated by her, he decided to come over and speak with her.

"Have you ever been on the stage before?" he asked, trying to find out more about her.

"No," said Carrie.

"You do so well, I thought you might have had some experience."

Carrie only smiled.

Mrs. Morgan, who had a smaller part in the play, watched what was going on. She glared at Carrie with envy and anger. "I'll bet she's just some cheap professional," she thought. That would explain why the director smiled at her performance, but only yelled insults at Mrs. Morgan. It made her scorn and hate Carrie even more.

After the rehearsal, Carrie went home, feeling that she had done quite well. The words of the director were still ringing in her ears. She longed for a chance to tell Hurstwood. She wanted him to know just how well she was doing. In the meantime, she could hardly wait until Drouet asked her about the rehearsal. She wanted to tell him all about it. But she was too modest to bring up the subject herself. She wasn't good at introducing topics of conversation. So she usually waited to be asked a question.

But the traveling salesman had other things on his mind tonight. The little things that she did during the day did not strike Drouet as very important. He took it for granted that she was doing very well. So he didn't worry anymore about it.

Carrie felt sharply his lack of interest in her accomplishments. This irritated her, and made her long to see Hurstwood. It was as if he were now the only friend she had on earth.

The next morning, Drouet was interested again in her rehearsal. But it was too late. The damage had been done.

Carrie got a pretty letter from Hurstwood, saying that he would be waiting for her in the park. When she saw him, he seemed to shine upon her as brightly and warmly as the morning sun.

"Well, my dear," he asked, "how did you make out?"

"Well enough," she said, still somewhat discouraged by Drouet's lack of interest.

"Now, tell me just exactly what you did. Was it pleasant?"

Carrie told him all about the rehearsal, warming up as she went along.

"Well, that's delightful," said Hurstwood. "I'm so glad. I must get over there to see you. When is the next rehearsal?"

"Tuesday," said Carrie, "but they don't allow visitors."

"I imagine I could get in," said the manager.

His interest in her lifted her spirits and delighted her. But she made him promise not to stop by during rehearsals.

"Now, you must do your best to please me," he said encouragingly. "Just remember that I want you to succeed. We will make it a worthwhile performance. You do that, now."

"I'll try," said Carrie, full of affection and enthusiasm.

"That's the girl," said Hurstwood fondly. "Now, remember," shaking an affectionate finger at her, "do your best."

"I will," she answered, looking back.

For Carrie, the whole earth was overflowing

with sunshine that morning. She almost danced away. The clear sky seemed to pour liquid blue into her soul. Earnest and innocent, she took great pleasure in having a purpose in life and working hard to achieve it.

CHAPTER 18

Behind the Scenes

By the evening of the performance on the 16th, Hurstwood was able to bring to the theater a crowd of well-dressed, influential people, who would support and flatter the actors. He used his influence to make people think that they really ought to go to this event. He persuaded his friends to attend. And he arranged for announcements in all the newspapers. But he did all this so that no one knew he was the reason why the little event was so successful.

Carrie had mastered her part. But she still trembled as she thought about performing in front of the glaring lights. She was afraid that she would forget her lines or be overwhelmed by stage fright. At times she wished that she had never agreed to do the show. She worried that she would become paralyzed with fear. What if she froze—drew a blank, gasped for air, forgot what to say? Why, she could spoil the entire performance!

That evening, the lodge sent a carriage to bring her to the theater. Drouet left her at the door. He wanted to go pick up some good cigars to pass around to his friends in the lodge. The little actress marched nervously into her dressing room. She began putting on her makeup. This would change Carrie, a simple shop girl, to Laura, the beautiful and admired "Belle of Society."

Since her arrival in the city, many things had influenced her. But those forces had always been remote, separate from her own life. The great, brilliant mansions had waved her coldly away, permitting her only to wonder in awe from a distance. This new atmosphere of the theater was more friendly. It took her by the hand kindly, as someone who says, "Come in, my dear." This door opened for her, welcoming her as if she were one of its own. Before, she had only marveled at the greatness of the names on the billboards, the wonder of the long announcements in the newspapers, the beauty of the dresses on the stage. From a distance she had admired the atmosphere of carriages, flowers, elegance. But here was an open door to see all of that. She had come upon it as one who stumbles upon a secret passage. And, behold! Suddenly she was in a world of diamonds and delight! And it was really happening.

As she dressed with a flutter, she could not help thinking what a delight this would be if only it would last. How perfect life would be if only she could do well now. Then someday she could get a job as a real actress. The thought took hold of her. It kept humming in her ears, like the melody of an old song.

Outside of Carrie's dressing room, another scene was being acted out in the little lobby. There Hurstwood met Drouet, who had just returned from his trip to buy more cigars. Hurstwood had reserved a box of seats for his friends. Among these was Drouet.

Hurstwood, whose job gave him an air of power and authority, was looked upon as influential and prosperous. Tonight he was in his element, the center of attention in the lobby. He knew and greeted everyone who entered the theater.

At one point, a respectable-looking citizen in a starched white shirt asked him, "How goes it with you?"

"Excellent," replied Hurstwood.

"Wife here?"

"She couldn't come tonight. She's not well."

"Sorry to hear it. Nothing serious, I hope."

"No, just feeling a little ill."

Some of Hurstwood's wealthier friends now began to drive up in carriages. They came drifting in with a great show of finery, looking self-important and pleased with themselves.

"Here we are," said Hurstwood. He turned from the group with whom he was talking, to welcome the newcomers.

One of these gentlemen pulled Hurstwood aside and whispered, teasing, "And say, if this isn't a good show, I guess I'll have to punch you in the face."

"Heck with the show," Hurstwood replied.

"It's worth the price of the ticket just to see your old friends."

Then another friend asked, "Is it something really good?"

"I don't know. I doubt it. But it's for the lodge."

And so the little theater rang with the babble of successful voices, the rustle of fine clothes, the chatter of small talk. All this was commanded by one man's influence. Hurstwood was a powerful star among the people that greeted him. His position and his personality reflected their ambitions. They respected him, appreciated him, and flattered him. They tried to win his favor. In a way, they saw him as a celebrity. It was greatness in a way, small as it was.

:·: CHAPTER 19 :·:

Putting on an Act

At last the curtain was ready to go up. Hurstwood stopped talking and sat down with Drouet and his friends.

"Now, we'll see how the little girl does," he said to Drouet, so no one else could hear.

The first characters onstage were stiff with fright. They were so nervous that they merely spoke their lines, nothing more. It took all the hope and uncritical good nature of the audience not to show their pity.

Hurstwood didn't care. He took it for granted that the show would be worthless. He cared only that the audience could endure it enough to put on a display of congratulation afterward.

Then Carrie walked onto the stage. One glance at her, and both Hurstwood and Drouet saw plainly that she, too, was terrified. She came faintly across the stage, saying her lines in a thin, flat voice. The lack of feeling in her performance was ridiculous. Carrie seemed to be talking in her sleep. It looked as if she would be a wretched, hopeless failure. Drouet looked away from the stage at the audience. The audience kept hoping,

141

silently, that things would improve. Hurstwood fixed his eye on Carrie, as if to hypnotize her into doing better. He was trying to pour his own determination into her. But Carrie did not recover. She wandered through the whole scene, straining the patience of the audience. Finally, she left the stage, much to their relief.

"She's too nervous," said Drouet, understating the situation. For once, he actually recognized that he was lying.

"Better go back and say a word to her."

Drouet was glad to do anything for relief. Carrie was standing in the wings. She was waiting weakly for her next cue, all the spark and courage gone out of her.

"Say, Cad," he said, looking at her, "you mustn't be nervous. Wake up. Those guys out there don't amount to anything. What are you afraid of?"

"I don't know," said Carrie. "I just don't seem to be able to do it."

She was grateful for Drouet's presence, though. The other actors seemed so nervous that they took away her own strength and confidence.

"Come on," said Drouet. "Pull yourself together. What are you afraid of? Go on out there now and do the trick. What do you care?"

Drouet's excited, nervous energy revived her a little.

"Did I do so very bad?"

"Not a bit. All you need is a little more jazz.

Do it the way you showed me. Toss your head the way you did the other night."

Carrie remembered her triumph in the apartment. She tried to think that she really could do it.

"Well, now you do the next scene good and lively," said the salesman. "Put in a little spark, that's the thing. Act as if you didn't care."

"Your turn next, Miss Madenda," said the prompter.

"Oh, dear," said Carrie.

"Well, you're a fool for being afraid," said Drouet. "Come on now. Pull yourself together. I'll watch you from right here."

"Will you?" said Carrie.

"Yes, now go on. Don't be afraid."

She started out onstage, weak as ever. But suddenly she thought of Drouet looking on, and she felt a little stronger.

"She's more relaxed," thought Hurstwood to himself.

Carrie didn't perform as well as she had at rehearsal. But at least she did not irritate the audience.

Carrie left the stage, warm and nervous.

"Well," she asked, looking at Drouet, "was it any better?"

"I should say so. That's the way. Put life into it. You did that about a thousand percent better than you did the other scene. Now go on and fire up. You can do it. Knock 'em out."

"Was it really better?"

"Better, I should say so. And you can sure do the next scene all right."

"I don't know," answered Carrie.

"Why, woman," he exclaimed, "you did it for me! Now you go out there and do it. It'll be fun for you. Just do it the way you did at home. If you can pull it off that way, I'll bet you'll be a hit. Now, what'll you bet? You go do it."

The traveling salesman usually spoke with warm, good-natured enthusiasm. But this time he really did think that Carrie had acted this particular scene very well. And he wanted her to repeat it in public.

Drouet began to make Carrie feel as if she had done very well. He lifted her confidence and buoyed her up. That old, sad, deep feeling of desire came back to her.

"I think I can do this."

"Sure you can. Now you go ahead and see."

On the stage, the other characters were cruelly accusing her character, Laura, of being fake, pretentious, wicked—and beneath them. They were leaving the scene because they distrusted and disdained her.

Carrie listened, and started to catch a sense of something—she did not know what. She began to feel the bitterness of the situation. The feelings of being an outcast returned to her. Lost in her own thoughts, she heard hardly anything except the pounding of her own blood.

Carrie began to move forward with a steady

grace, born of inspiration. She appeared before the audience, glowing handsome and proud. Then, as the other characters moved away from her scornfully, she shifted into a cold, white, helpless object.

Hurstwood blinked his eyes and caught the feeling. The magic of passion spread across the theater, like waves breaking against the farthest walls. The attention of the audience, which had been wandering before, now focused on Carrie. They moved as she moved. Their eyes were fixed on Carrie's eyes.

At this moment, the character's lover was trying to choose between his fiancée, who came from a wealthy family, and Laura, who had risen from the slums. As the fiancée turned to leave, Carrie's voice rang out.

"No!" she commanded, with a force that was new to her. "Stay with him!"

As the curtain fell, Carrie returned to her dressing room. Drouet had been fascinated by Carrie's personality onstage, and his affection for her was rapidly reviving.

"Well, well," said Drouet, "you were out of sight. That was simply great. I knew you could do it. Oh, but you're a little daisy!"

Carrie's eyes flamed with the light of achievement.

"Did I do all right?"

"Did you? Well, I should say so. Didn't you hear the applause?"

There was still the sound of some faint clapping.

"I thought I got it . . . I got something like . . .

I felt it."

In his box seat, Hurstwood, too, realized that he was seeing something extraordinarily good. The audience's applause made it even better. He thought now that Carrie was beautiful. She had done something which was on a level above his own. He felt intense delight in realizing that she was his. His feelings overflowed with enthusiasm and joy. He was almost swept away by the strength and feeling she had shown. His only desire was to pour forth his praise to her. As her lover, his feelings knew no boundaries. Seized by a sudden impulse, he went around to the stage door.

But when Hurstwood entered her dressing room, there was Drouet. Instinctively Hurstwood felt the change in the other man. He saw that the traveling salesman was getting close to Carrie. Jealousy burned inside him. In a flash of thought, he blamed himself for having sent Drouet backstage to encourage Carrie. He hated the man because he seemed like an intruder. He could hardly calm himself down enough to congratulate Carrie in the way that a friend would, not as her lover. But finally Hurstwood pulled himself together. He acted the part, and it was a triumph.

Looking at Carrie, he said, "I thought I would come around and tell you how well you did, Mrs. Drouet. It was delightful."

Carrie took the cue, and replied, "Oh, thank you."

"I was just telling her," put in Drouet, "that I

thought she did fine." Now he, too, was delighted that Carrie was his possession.

"Indeed you did," said Hurstwood. Turning toward Carrie, his eyes said more than his words.

Carrie gave a rich laugh.

"If you do as well in the rest of the play, you will make us all think you are a born actress," said Hurstwood smoothly.

Carrie smiled again. She understood Hurstwood's feelings, and she wished deeply that she could be alone with him. But she did not understand the change in Drouet.

Too envious and grudging of Drouet to speak anymore, Hurstwood bowed out of the room. Once outside, he muttered between clenched teeth, "Damn it! Is he always going to be in the way?"

During the next act, Drouet joined Hurstwood again in their box seats. Drouet was feeling so excited that he wanted to whisper to his friend. But Hurstwood was thinking his own thoughts, and the thoughts were wretched.

Carrie, from now on, was easily the center of interest. After their first gloomy impression, the audience now went to the other extreme and thought she was better than she really was. She performed well, but with nothing like the intensity that had aroused the audience's feeling at the end of the first act.

In front of the stage lights, Carrie seemed even more charming. Drouet thought that her talent for acting made her seem more appealing than before. He longed to be at home with her until he could tell her what she meant to him. He waited impatiently for the end of the play, when they would go home alone.

Hurstwood, on the other hand, could have cursed the man beside him. Carrie's new attractiveness made his own situation seem even more miserable.

At one point during the last act, Carrie came onstage alone. The strength she had shown at the end of the first act was returning. She seemed to be gaining feeling, now that the play was drawing to a close and the opportunity for great action was passing.

"Poor Pearl," she said, speaking of her lover's fiancée. "It is a sad thing not to have happiness. But it is a terrible thing to see another person groping blindly for it, when it is almost within their grasp."

Carrie now gazed sadly out upon a backdrop of the open sea.

Hurstwood began to feel deep pity for her and for himself. He felt that she was almost talking directly to him. The illusion on the stage made these lines seem as if they were directed only to him, like a sad melody that becomes forever a personal and intimate thing.

"And yet, Pearl could be very happy with him," the little actress continued. "Her sunny temper, her joyous face would brighten any home."

She turned slowly toward the audience, looking out without seeing them.

"I shall set aside my longings for what I may not have," Carrie spoke with a sigh. "Only two people will have known me in all the wide world. And I shall find joy only through the joy of that innocent girl who will soon be his wife."

Hurstwood was charmed by Carrie's pale face and by her graceful figure, which was draped in pearl gray, with a coiled string of pearls at the throat. She had the air of one who was weary and in need of protection. And under the spell of this make-believe, his feelings were so aroused that he was ready in spirit to go to her. He would ease her out of her misery, at the same time adding to his own delight.

Carrie continued, "I must return to the city, no matter what dangers may lurk there. I must go—secretly if I can, openly if I must."

Laura's lover returned to the scene, explaining why he had left Pearl.

"But she is your fiancée," Carrie said, softening her voice until it was low and musical. "The way you act now will affect your entire married life together. Ray, my friend, do not let your life be an unhappy one."

"When I lost you," he replied, seizing her little hand, "I was at the mercy of any flirt who happened to look twice at me. It was your fault. You know it was. Why did you leave me?"

Carrie turned slowly away. She seemed to be struggling to master some impulse. Then she turned back.

"Ray," she said, "the greatest happiness I have ever felt has been knowing that you would give all your love forevermore to a good woman—a woman from a fine family, a woman with wealth and accomplishments. What a time to reveal your feelings for me! Why do you keep denying yourself a chance to be happy?"

She asked this question so simply that the audience and the lover heard it as a personal thing, meant only for their ears.

The lover at last exclaimed, "But why can't you be with me the way you used to be?"

Carrie answered, with touching sweetness, "I can no longer be with you that way, for the Laura you used to love is forever dead to you. But this is what she would say."

Hurstwood leaned forward. The whole audience was silent and intent.

"It doesn't matter whether the woman you desire is wise or foolish, beautiful or plain, rich or poor. A woman has only one thing that she can really give or refuse—her heart."

Drouet was so moved that he felt his throat tighten.

"Her beauty, her wit, her accomplishments—these she may sell to you. But her love is a treasure that has no price and which cannot be bought."

Hurstwood felt that this was a personal appeal. It came to him as if he and Carrie were alone. He felt such sorrow for the hopeless, pitiful, and yet dainty and appealing woman whom he loved. He could hardly hold back his tears. Drouet, too, was beside himself. At that moment, he made up his mind. He would be for Carrie the kind of man he had never been before. By golly, he would even marry her! She was worth it.

Carrie put the tone of her voice in harmony with the sad melody that the orchestra was playing. "She asks only one thing in return. When you look upon her, let your eyes speak of your devotion. When you speak to hear, let your voice be gentle, loving, and kind. Don't look down on her if she doesn't understand right away all your thoughts and ambitions. For when misfortune and evil have destroyed your goals and defeated you, her love remains to comfort you. You look up at the trees and admire their strength and greatness. Do not look down at the flowers because all they have to give is their fragrance. Remember," she concluded tenderly, "love is all a woman has to give. But it is the only thing that we can carry with us after we die."

The two men watching Carrie from their box seats were in agony. They scarcely heard the rest of the scene. They saw only their idol, moving about with appealing grace, continuing to reveal an unexpected power.

Hurstwood made up his mind about a thousand things. And so did Drouet. They joined equally in the burst of applause which pulled Carrie out for another curtain call. Drouet pounded his hands until they ached. Then he jumped up and ran to meet Carrie backstage. As he left, Carrie saw a huge basket of flowers being rushed down the aisle toward her. They were Hurstwood's. She looked toward his box for a moment, caught his eye, and smiled. He could have leaped out of the box to fold her in his arms. For a moment, he forgot that he was married to another woman, and that he needed to be cautious about showing his feelings for Carrie in public. No matter what, he would have that lovely girl, even if it took everything he had. He would act at once. One thing was certain. This would be the end of Drouet. He would not allow that traveling salesman to have her.

Hurstwood was so excited that he could not stay in the box. He went into the lobby, and then into the street, thinking. The last act was over, and he wanted to have Carrie alone. His desire was driving him crazy. He cursed the bad luck that made him have to smile, and bow, and put on an act with his friends after the show. All he wanted was to whisper to her alone, to tell her that he loved her. He groaned as he saw that his hopes were impossible. He would have to take Drouet and Carrie to dinner, still faking his feelings. He finally went backstage and tried to make small talk with her.

"We are going to supper, of course," he said, with a voice that was a mockery of his heart.

"Oh, yes," said Carrie, smiling.

The little actress was feeling wonderful. She was realizing for the first time what it was like to be admired, pursued, and flattered. Success gave her the first faint feeling of independence. Suddenly, she was looking down, rather than up, at her lover.

When she was ready, they climbed into the waiting carriage to drive downtown. Carrie was going to sit between the two men. But before Drouet had settled in beside her, she squeezed Hurstwood's hand in a gentle, impulsive manner. The manager was overwhelmed with emotion. He would have sold his soul to be with her alone.

"Oh," he thought, "the agony of it."

But Drouet was so self-centered that he didn't stop chattering about how wonderful he thought she was. The dinner was spoiled by his enthusiasm.

Hurstwood felt that he would die if he couldn't express his feelings for Carrie. So just before he went home, he whispered passionately to her, "Tomorrow." She understood. He then walked away from the traveling salesman and Carrie, his prize. At that moment, he felt that he could murder Drouet without any regret. Carrie also felt the misery of it all.

"Goodnight," he said, pretending a casual friendliness.

"Goodnight," said the little actress, tenderly.

"The fool!" he said to himself. He hated Drouet now. "The idiot! I'll get him yet. And I'll do it quickly! We'll see about it tomorrow."

Drouet, meanwhile, turned to Carrie and squeezed her arm.

"Well, if you aren't a wonder," he observed, feeling quite pleased with himself that things had turned out so well. "You are the dandiest little girl on earth."

CHAPTER 20

Acting and Reacting

Hurstwood was, by nature, a man of action. And so, he needed to pursue his passion by doing something right away. He couldn't sleep; he couldn't eat; he couldn't read the newspaper. He was harassed by thoughts of his love being held by the jolly, red-faced traveling salesman. He would have given anything to have Carrie agree to some kind of arrangement with him—one that would get rid of Drouet completely and forever.

What to do?

Hurstwood moved about in the same room with his wife, unaware of her presence. At breakfast, she broke the silence, interrupting his thoughts in an irritating way. "Have you made up your mind, George, when you will take your vacation?"

She was frowning. Most summers they had already started making their plans by now.

"Not yet," he said. "I'm very busy just now."

"Well, you'll want to make up your mind pretty soon, won't you, if we're going?" she replied.

"I guess we have a few days yet," he said.

"Hmff," she responded, aggravated. "Don't wait until the summer's over."

"There you go again," he observed. "One would think I never did anything, the way you talk."

"Well, I just want to know when we're going," she said.

"You've still got a few days," he insisted.

He was irritated that she was asking him to think about this now, when he wished to have his thoughts for other purposes.

"Well, we may want to leave soon."

"Then why did you make me get you season tickets to the horseraces?"

"Oh, hmff!" she exclaimed in disgust. "I won't argue with you."

With that, she got up from the table.

"Say," he demanded, as she was about to leave, "what's the matter with you lately? Can't I talk with you anymore?"

"Certainly, you can *talk* with me," she replied.

"Well, you wouldn't think so by the way you act. Now, you want to know when I'll be ready to go away. Well, here's your answer. Not for another month. Maybe not even then."

"Then we'll go without you."

"You will, eh?" he sneered.

"Yes, we will."

He was astonished at the woman's determination. And that made him even more irritated.

"Well, we'll see about that," he responded. "It seems to me that you've been trying to take over everything lately. You talk as though you were in charge of my life. Well, you're not. You don't control anything that's connected with me. If you want to go, then go. But you won't get me to make up my mind any faster by talking that way."

His dark eyes snapped, and he crunched his newspaper as he laid it down. Mrs. Hurstwood said nothing more. She turned on her heel and went upstairs.

Mrs. Hurstwood had not really expected to get into an argument with her husband. Still, she had come down to the breakfast table feeling a little tense. She had been working on a plan to help her daughter get ahead socially. She was hoping to arrange something for their summer vacation—something that her beautiful daughter would not find boring. But when she came down to the breakfast table, she sensed that something was wrong. She wasn't sure what it was, or just how the trouble had begun. But she was sure, now, that her husband was a bully. And under no circumstances would she let this go by unsettled. She would be treated more like a lady or she would know why.

For his part, Hurstwood was weighed down by this latest argument with his wife. As he left to meet Carrie, he started worrying about other concerns—love, desire, and the forces that stood in the way. He could hardly wait to see Carrie face to face. What was the night, after all, without her? What was the day? She must and should be his.

For her part, Carrie had been living in a world of fantasy and feeling since the night before. She had heard Drouet's enthusiastic chatter, although she did not pay much attention to what he said. He was only trying to make himself look good. But she listened carefully to what he said about her. She kept as much distance from him as she could, because she wanted to think about her own triumph. She felt that Hurstwood's passion was a delightful background to her own achievement. And she wondered what he would have to say. She also felt sorry for him. His misery contrasted with her own happiness. It was a special and new kind of sorrow for Carrie, as she felt the contrast between his misery and her success. For now she was moving from someone who needs help to someone who gives help. All in all, she was extremely happy.

The day after the show, Drouet instinctively felt that he needed to change the way she looked at him.

"I think that I'll straighten out that little deal of mine this month. Then we'll get married. I was talking with Mosher about that yesterday."

"No, you won't," teased Carrie. She was starting to feel a certain faint power that let her play around with his feelings.

"Yes, I will," he exclaimed, more passionately than usual. Then he added, with the tone of one who pleads, "Don't you believe what I've told you?"

Carrie laughed a little. But she answered, "Of course I do."

Drouet was feeling less sure of himself. Carrie was still with him, but she was no longer helpless and pleading. Her voice had a new lightness. Her eyes no longer expressed dependence. The traveling salesman felt the shadow of something dangerous which was coming. He hoped that he could keep it away by paying more attention to Carrie and by saying a few little words about marriage.

As soon as he left for work, Carrie hurried down the stairs to meet Hurstwood. At the corner she passed Drouet, but they did not see each other.

A little while later, Drouet realized that he had forgotten some papers that he needed for work. So he went back home, raced up the stairs, and burst into the apartment. There he found only the housekeeper, who was cleaning up.

"Hello," he exclaimed, surprised. "Has Carrie gone?"

"Your wife? Yes, she went out just a few minutes ago."

"That's strange," thought Drouet. "She didn't say a word to me. I wonder where she went."

Once he found the papers, he turned his attention to the housekeeper. She was good-looking and always seemed pleased to see him.

"Well, let me show you something," he said,

pleasantly. He came over to her, and handed her a clever little card he'd been given by a wholesale tobacco company.

"That's cute," she said.

"You can have it if you want it," he responded.

He took this opportunity to look at her hand, which now held the card. "That's a pretty ring you have," he said. He touched the cheap piece of jewelry on her finger.

"Do you think so?"

"I sure do," he answered. Pretending to look more closely at the ring, he held her finger in his hand. "That's a fine ring."

Now that the ice was broken, he continued talking about the ring, pretending to forget that he was still holding her fingers. But soon she slipped them out of his hand. She backed away from him, and leaned against the windowsill.

"I haven't seen you for a long time," she said, teasing, as she brushed off one of his attempts to make a pass at her.

"I've been away," said Drouet.

"Do you travel far?"

"Pretty far—yes."

"I wish I could travel," said the girl, gazing out of the window.

"Oh, you get tired of it after a while."

Then she asked, "What has become of your friend, Mr. Hurstwood?"

"He's here in town. What makes you ask about him?"

"Oh, nothing. Only he hasn't been here since you got back."

"How do you know him?"

"Why, I must have seen him stop by a dozen times in the last month."

"Get out," said Drouet, lightly. "He hasn't visited more than half a dozen times since we've been here."

"He hasn't, eh?" said the girl, smiling. "That's what you think."

Drouet wasn't sure whether she was joking or not.

"Tease!" he accused her. "What makes you smile that way?"

"Oh, nothing."

"Have you seen him recently?"

"Not since you came back," she laughed.

"Before?"

"Certainly."

"How often?"

"Why, almost every day."

She loved to gossip and spread rumors. And she was wondering how much trouble her words would cause.

"Who did he come to see?" asked the traveling salesman, still not believing her.

"Mrs. Drouet."

Afraid to look like a fool, he pretended not to be upset by this news.

"So," he said, "what of it?"

"Nothing," replied the girl, flirting with him,

her head tilted to one side.

"He's an old friend," he went on, digging himself in deeper.

Normally, he would have enjoyed flirting a little longer with her. But at the moment, it had lost its appeal.

"I've got to go," she said, lightly, as she moved away from him.

"Then I'll see you later," he said.

After she left, he sat down in a rocking chair to think it all over. No, Carrie hadn't been acting any differently. It couldn't be true that she was cheating on him. She hadn't acted that way. Why, even last night she had been as friendly toward him as could be—and Hurstwood, too. Look at how they acted! He could hardly believe they would try to deceive him. But then, again, she did act sort of funny at times. Why, this morning she went out and never even said a word.

He scratched his head and prepared to go downtown. He was still frowning as he left the apartment. But when he ran into the housekeeper in the hallway, she looked delightful in her white apron. When she smiled at him, he almost forgot about his worries. He put his hand on her shoulder, as though only in a friendly greeting.

"Got over being mad?" she said, still trying to stir up trouble.

"I'm not mad," he answered.

"I thought you were," she said, smiling.

"Quit fooling around," he said, casually.

"Were you serious?"

"Certainly," she answered. Then, she added, as though she never meant to create trouble, "He came lots of times. I thought you knew."

The game was over. Drouet could no longer pretend that he wasn't upset.

"Did he spend the evenings here?" he asked.

"Sometimes. Sometimes they went out."

"In the evening?"

"Yes. You shouldn't look so mad, though."

"I'm not," he said. "Did anyone else see him?"

"Of course," she replied, as if it really didn't matter.

"How long ago was this?"

"Just before you came back."

The traveling salesman chewed his lip nervously.

"Don't say anything, all right?" he asked, giving her arm a gentle squeeze.

"Certainly not," she returned. "I wouldn't worry about it if I were you."

"All right," he said, as he left her. But for once, he was seriously concerned. At the same time, he was also aware that he was making a most excellent impression on the housekeeper.

"I'm going to talk to her about that," he said to himself, passionately. He felt that he had been unfairly wronged. "By golly, I'll find out whether she'll act that way or not."

CHAPTER 21

A Flood of Feeling

When Carrie arrived, Hurstwood had already been waiting awhile. He was anxious to see the woman who had stirred his emotions so deeply the night before.

They walked on together, as if they were going to a specific place. Hurstwood could barely contain his joy, and he walked with a spring in his step. He drank in the radiance of her presence. The rustling sound of her pretty skirt was like music to him.

"Are you satisfied?" he asked, thinking about how well she had done the night before.

"Are you?" she replied.

"It was wonderful."

Carrie laughed with pure delight.

"That was one of the best things I've seen in a long time," he added.

Hurstwood remembered how attractive she had been the evening before. It added to the excitement he felt at being with her now.

Carrie felt the excitement and warm glow which this man created for her. She listened to the sound of his voice, and sensed that he was being drawn to her.

"Those were such nice flowers you sent me," she said, after a moment or two.

"Glad you liked them," he answered, simply.

But all the time he was thinking about how to change the subject so that he could talk about his own feelings. He wanted to plunge in and speak of his desire. Yet he found himself fishing for words.

"You got home all right," he said gloomily, remembering that Drouet had taken her home.

"Yes," replied Carrie, easily.

He looked at her steadily for a moment, slowing his pace. He fixed her with his eye.

She felt the flood of his feelings.

"How about me?" he asked.

This confused Carrie. She realized that the floodgates were open, and his feelings were starting to rush out. She didn't know exactly what to answer.

"I don't know," was the only thing she could think to say.

He bit his lower lip, then stopped and kicked the grass with his toe. He searched her face with a tender, appealing glance.

"Won't you come away from him?" he asked, intensely.

"I don't know," replied Carrie. She felt herself drifting. She found nothing to catch that would guide her. There was no logical way out of the problem. She saw before her a man she genuinely liked. He was gracious and sympathetic. She was delighted when he leaned toward her. She was also the victim of his keen eyes, his suave manners, his fine clothes. She could not resist the glow of his personality, the light of his eye. She almost convinced herself that she felt as much passion for him as he felt for her. And yet, there were thoughts and questions that disturbed her. In his eyes, was she Drouet's wife, or what? Would he marry her? Even while he talked, and she softened, and her eyes were lighted with a tender glow, she was asking herself these questions. Had Drouet told him that they were not married?

And yet, she was not worried about Hurstwood's love. Whatever he knew, he was evidently sincere. His passion was real and warm. There was power in what he said. What should she do? Her thoughts kept drifting, as though she were on a limitless sea of uncertainty.

"Why don't you come away?" he said, tenderly. "I will arrange for you to have whatever—"

"Oh, don't," said Carrie.

"Don't what?" he asked. "What do you mean?"

There was a look of confusion and pain in her face. Why did he have to bring up that miserable idea about being his mistress? She did not want to hear how he would arrange to provide for her without also marrying her.

He realized that it had been a mistake to mention such an arrangement. Still aroused by her presence and absorbed by his plan, he began again. This time he changed to a more respectful, almost reverent tone.

"Won't you come? You know I can't live without you—you know it—it can't go on this way—can it?"

"I know," said Carrie.

"I wouldn't ask if I—I wouldn't argue with you if I could help it. Look at me, Carrie. Put yourself in my place. You don't want to stay away from me, do you?"

She shook her head as if in deep thought.

"Then why not settle the whole thing, once and for all?"

"I don't know," said Carrie.

"Don't know! Ah, Carrie, what makes you say that? Don't torment me. Be serious."

"I am," said Carrie, softly.

"You can't be, Dearest, and say that. Not when you know how I love you. Look at last night."

His manner as he said this was incredibly quiet. Only his eyes moved, and they flashed with an intense, dissolving fire.

Carrie made no answer.

"How can you act this way, Dearest?" he inquired, after a time. "You love me, don't you?"

Then he turned to her with such a storm of feeling that she was overwhelmed. For the moment, all her doubts were cleared away.

"Yes," she answered, frankly and tenderly.

"Well, then, you'll come, won't you—come tonight?"

Carrie shook her head.

"I can't wait any longer," urged Hurstwood.

"If that is too soon, come Saturday."

"When will we be married?" she asked, timidly. She was so upset that she forgot that she was supposed to be already married to Drouet.

The manager jumped in alarm. Getting married would be even more difficult for him than for her.

"Anytime you say," he said lightly, covering his distress. He refused to let this miserable problem interfere with his present delight.

"Saturday?" asked Carrie.

He nodded his head.

"Well, if you will marry me then," she said, "I'll go."

The manager looked at his lovely prize—so beautiful, so charming, so innocent, so difficult to be won. His passion had reached the stage where it no longer responded to reason. In the face of such loveliness, he wasn't going to bother about little obstacles like his being married to another woman. He would promise her anything, everything. He would make a try for paradise, whatever the result might be. He would be happy—even if it cost him his honesty, even if he had to abandon the truth.

Carrie looked at him tenderly. It all seemed so delightful.

"Well," she said, "I'll try and get ready then."

Hurstwood looked into her face. He thought he had never seen anything more lovely than her expression. Her pretty face was crossed with little shadows of wonder and doubt.

"I'll see you again tomorrow," he said, joyously,

"and we'll talk over the plans."

"Yes," said Carrie, with pride and delight.

She felt so much enthusiasm that she believed she must be deeply in love. She sighed as she thought of her handsome adorer. Yes, she would get ready by Saturday. She would go, and they would be happy.

CHAPTER 22

Thunderclouds Gather

Jealousy caused the misfortune in the Hurstwood household. Mrs. Hurstwood's jealousy was born of her love for her husband. But it did not die when her love for him died. As he paid less attention to her, she became more suspicious of him. And Hurstwood made things worse because, as always, he avoided things that were no longer amusing or satisfying. Mrs. Hurstwood observed that he seemed more energetic, and even more careful about his looks than before. She seemed to sense the change, the way an animal sniffs out danger from far away. And her feelings of jealousy could easily be turned into resentment and hate. The atmosphere was charged with conflict. Like a sky full of blackening thunderclouds, a single gust of cold wind could turn the lowering clouds of suspicion into a pouring rain of rage and revenge.

There were frequent arguments because of each person's growing independence and selfishness. Mrs. Hurstwood, still angry at her husband's lack of interest in her plans, left the table and scolded her daughter for being late to breakfast. When Jessica responded coolly that it didn't matter, her mother continued, "Well, it matters to me. And, anyhow, I don't like it when you talk to me that way. You're too young to put on such an attitude with your mother."

"Oh, Mamma, don't pick at me," Jessica responded sharply and defensively. "I said I wasn't hungry. I don't want any breakfast."

"Mind how you address me, Missy. I'll not have it. Listen to me. I'll not have it!"

Jessica heard this as she walked out of the room, tossing her head and flicking her pretty skirts. She felt independent and not at all interested in being scolded by her mother.

George, Jr., was even touchier about his individual rights. He tried to make everyone feel that he was a man with a man's privileges—even though he was only nineteen.

But Hurstwood was a man of authority. It irritated him that he was surrounded more and more by a world that he understood less and less. It was a world that he was unable to manage or control. He was no longer leading. Instead, he was being made to follow. When his family addressed him with sharpness, anger, a sneer, or a cynical laugh, he was unable to keep his temper. He flew into a rage, and wished he could be free of the whole household. It seemed to be holding him back from all his opportunities and desires.

For all this, he still kept up the appearance of

leadership and control. But his wife was also straining to be independent and in control. All she needed was proof of one specific, improper action. Such knowledge would give her the power and justification she needed.

Her first hint came from their neighbor, Dr. Beale. On the day that Hurstwood had taken Carrie on a drive along Washington Boulevard, Dr. Beale happened to pass them, going in the other direction. He recognized Hurstwood, but only after they had passed each other. He was not so sure of Carrie. That is, he did not know whether she was Hurstwood's wife or daughter.

The next time he saw Mrs. Hurstwood, he teased her. "So, when you're out driving and run into your friends, you don't bother to speak to them, do you?"

"If I see them, I do. Where was I?"

"On Washington Boulevard," he answered, expecting her to remember right away.

She shook her head.

"Yes, out near Hoyne Avenue. You were with your husband."

"I guess you're mistaken," she answered.

"I know I saw your husband," he went on. "I wasn't so sure about you. Perhaps it was your daughter."

"Perhaps it was," said Mrs. Hurstwood. But she knew that it wasn't Jessica, either. She began to be suspicious, and wanted more details.

"Was it in the afternoon?" she asked, cleverly,

pretending that she knew something about the situation.

"Yes, about two or three."

"It must have been Jessica, then," said Mrs. Hurstwood, as though the incident were unimportant.

The physician had a thought or two of his own. But he did not say anything more about the matter.

Mrs. Hurstwood assumed that her husband had been riding with some other woman. And he did this after announcing to her that he was *busy*. Now she remembered other times that he had refused to go to places with her or to take part in the social activities that made her life pleasant.

He had already been seen at the theater with people whom he called Moy's friends. Now he had been seen driving. Most likely, he would have an excuse for that, too. Perhaps there were other situations that she had not yet heard about. Why else would he be so busy, so uninterested in her lately? In the last six weeks, he had become unusually irritable. Recently he seemed willing to get up and go out, whether things were right or wrong in the house. Why?

She recalled that he looked at her now with less satisfaction and approval than before. Maybe he was starting to see her as old and uninteresting. She was fading, and perhaps he saw her wrinkles. He was trying to hold onto his youthful vitality and elegance, while she . . . She found the whole situation bitter, and thoroughly hated him for it.

The day after Carrie's appearance on the Avery stage, Mrs. Hurstwood visited the races with Jessica and a young man she knew. They just happened to run into several of Hurstwood's friends. Two of them had attended the performance the evening before.

One of them tried to make casual conversation with her. "I see that you did not get over to our little entertainment last evening. I did see your husband, though."

"Yes," she said, cautiously, trying to find out more about what her husband had been doing behind her back. "Was it pleasant? He did not tell me much about it."

"Very. Really, it was one of the best amateur shows I ever attended. There was one actress who surprised us all."

"Indeed," said Mrs. Hurstwood.

"It's too bad you couldn't have been there, really. I was sorry to hear you weren't feeling well."

Not feeling well! For the moment, Mrs. Hurstwood felt wholly at sea. She was anxious to find out why her husband would have told his friends that she was ill when she was not. Here was another case of his not wanting to spend time with her, of making excuses. She made up her mind to find out more.

"Were you at the performance last evening?" she asked another one of Hurstwood's friends.

"Yes. You didn't make it."

"No," she answered. "I was not feeling very well."

"So your husband told me," he answered. "Well, it was really very enjoyable. Turned out much better than I expected."

"Were there many people there?"

"The theater was full. I saw quite a number of your friends—Mrs. Harrison, Mrs. Barnes, Mrs. Collins."

"Quite a social gathering."

"Indeed it was. My wife enjoyed it very much."

Mrs. Hurstwood bit her lip.

"So," she thought, "that's the way he acts. Tells my friends I am sick and cannot come." She wondered why he would want to go alone. There was something going on.

By the time Hurstwood came home that evening, distrust, anger, and evil curiosity had darkened her eyes. A savage desire for explanation and revenge set the hard lines of her mouth.

Hurstwood, on the other hand, came home in high spirits. He was proud of himself, proud of his success, proud of Carrie. He intended to be pleasant to everyone and to forget that his wife even existed. He found his wife brushing her hair, thinking her own thoughts. He planned to smooth over any hard feelings she might still have by a kind word or ready promise. But Mrs. Hurstwood ignored him and said nothing. So he sat down and read the evening paper.

At one point, he tried to get her attention by chuckling at something he read in the paper. But Mrs. Hurstwood kept on arranging her hair, not even giving him a glance.

He tried again to engage her in conversation by asking her if she had read the article in the paper about a lawsuit against one of the local railroad companies.

She finally managed to force herself to answer. "No," she replied sharply.

Hurstwood heard the edge in her voice. But he was so preoccupied with thoughts of Carrie and her promise to him that he underestimated her anger. He thought he could patch things up just by continuing to be agreeable. It was a mistake.

"Why do you feel so bad about our disagreement this morning?" he said, at last. "You know you can take a vacation in Waukesha if you want to."

"So you can stay here and fool around with someone else?" she exclaimed, turning to him with a sharp and angry sneer.

He stopped as if slapped in the face.

"What do you mean?" he said at last. He stared at the cold, determined figure of his wife. She paid no attention to him, but went on fixing her hair in front of the mirror.

"You know what I mean," she said, finally. She pretended that she already knew everything and did not need to tell him what she meant.

"Well, I don't," he said, stubbornly. But he was nervous and on guard for what would come next. He no longer felt in control of this battle.

She made no answer.

"Humph!" he murmured, turning his head to one side. It was the weakest thing he had ever done. It totally lacked confidence.

Mrs. Hurstwood saw his weak point. Like an animal, she turned on him, ready to strike a second blow.

"I want the money to go to Waukesha, and I want it tomorrow morning," she said.

He looked at her in amazement. Never before had he seen such a cold, steely determination in her eye—such a cruel lack of concern. She seemed to have completely mastered her emotions. And she seemed completely confident and determined to take away all his control. He felt unable to defend himself. And so he decided that he must attack.

"What do you mean?" he said, jumping up. "*You* want! I'd like to know what's got into you tonight."

"Nothing's *got* into me," she said, flaming. "I want that money. You can do your bragging afterward."

"Bragging, eh! What! You'll get nothing from me. What do you mean by your insinuations, anyhow?"

"Where were you last night?" she answered, furiously. "Who were you driving with on Washington Boulevard? Who were you with at the theater when George saw you? Do you think I'm a fool to be deceived by you? Do you think I'll sit at home and believe your lies about 'too busy' and 'can't come'? And let you parade around and tell everyone that I'm unable to come to a show? I want you to know that your days of pretending to be in charge have come to an end as far as I'm concerned. You can no longer tell me or my children what to do. I'm through with you entirely."

"It's a lie," he said, driven to a corner and knowing no other excuse.

"Lie, eh!" she said, fiercely, but regaining her control. "You may call it a lie if you want to, but I know the truth."

"It's a lie, I tell you," he said, in a low, sharp voice. "You've been searching around for some cheap accusation for months, and now you think you have it. You think you'll figure out something and then get the upper hand. Well, I tell you, you can't. As long as I'm in this house, I'm master of it. And neither you nor anyone else can tell me what to do. Do you hear?"

Something in the woman's cool, cynical, controlling manner—as if she were already the master—made him feel as if he could strangle her.

She stared at him—vicious as a python.

"I'm not telling you what to do," she replied. "I'm telling you what I want."

Her answer was so cool, so full of bravado, that he gave up. She seemed to have all the evidence. She seemed to know that the law was on her side, and all of his property was in her name. He was like a ship without a sail—powerful and dangerous, but rolling, unable to control its movement, and beginning to sink.

"And I'm telling you," he said in the end, slightly recovering himself, "what you'll not get."

"We'll see about that," she said. "I'll find out what my rights are. Perhaps you'll talk to a lawyer, even if you won't talk to me."

It was a magnificent play, and it had its effect. Hurstwood felt beaten. He knew now that she was not bluffing. He didn't know what to say. All the day's joy had gone away. He was upset, miserable, resentful. What should he do?

"Do as you please," he said, at last. "I'll have nothing more to do with you." And out he walked.

CHAPTER 23

Betrayal and Blame

When Carrie returned to her apartment, she was full of doubts and worries. She had given her word to Hurstwood, but should she keep her promise? She discovered little objections that had not occurred to her in the heat of the moment. First of all, she had agreed to marry him, even though supposedly she was already married. She remembered a few things that Drouet had done, and it seemed wrong to walk away from him without a word. She had a comfortable living situation with him. And that is important for a person who is somewhat afraid of the world.

Carrie thought, "There are terrible things outside. People end up begging. Women lead lives of misery. You never can tell what will happen. Remember the time you were hungry. Stick to what you have."

Right now, she was leaning toward Hurstwood. But he was not passionate enough to overwhelm her powers of reasoning. She imagined that she was in love only because she so much wanted to be loved. She longed to be protected, improved, and understood. That is why she found it difficult to refuse him.

Carrie was sitting by the window, rocking and looking out, when Drouet came home. He was determined to know all about her relationship with Hurstwood. But he didn't expect any serious consequences, and hoped to get the whole thing over with quickly. He hesitated, uncertain how to begin.

"When did you get home?" he asked, foolishly.

"Oh, an hour or so ago. What makes you ask that?"

"You weren't here," he said, "when I came back this morning. I thought you might have gone out."

"So I did," said Carrie simply. "I went for a walk."

Drouet hesitated to believe that the pretty woman before him was involved in anything so distasteful to him. He wanted to believe that everything was all right, after all. Yet he was still bothered by what the housekeeper had told him.

"Where did you go this morning?" he finally asked, weakly.

"Why, I went for a walk," said Carrie.

"You're sure you did?" he asked.

"Yes, what makes you ask?"

She was beginning to see now that he knew something.

"I thought maybe you didn't," he said, beating around the bush in the most useless manner.

Carrie saw that he was hesitating, so she boldly

continued to act as if she were innocent.

"What makes you talk like that?" she asked, wrinkling her pretty forehead.

They looked at one another for a moment, and then Drouet plunged desperately into his subject.

"What's this about you and Hurstwood?" he asked.

"Me and Hurstwood? What do you mean?"

"Didn't he come here a dozen times while I was away?"

"A dozen times," repeated Carrie, guiltily. "No, but what do you mean?"

"Somebody said that you went out riding with him and that he came here every night."

"I never did such a thing," answered Carrie. "It isn't true. Who told you that?"

Blood rushed to her face, as Carrie defended herself with denials.

"Well, someone," he said. "You're sure you didn't?"

"Certainly," said Carrie. "You know how often he came."

"I know what you told me," he said finally.

"Well, I know that I didn't tell you any such thing as that," said Carrie, recovering her confidence.

Ignoring this remark, Drouet went on, "If I were you, I wouldn't have anything to do with him. He's a married man, you know."

"Who—who is—?" asked Carrie, stumbling at the word.

"Why, Hurstwood," replied Drouet.

"Hurstwood!" exclaimed Carrie. She was so shocked that she forgot to cover up how upset she was at this news. "Who told you this?" she demanded, further revealing her guilt.

"Why, I know it. I've always known it," said Drouet. "I thought I told you."

"No, you didn't," she argued. "You didn't do anything of the kind."

"You shouldn't have had anything to do with him," said Drouet in an injured tone, "after all I've done for you."

"You?" said Carrie, "You! What have you done for me?"

Her mind had been overflowing with mixed feelings. She felt shame that her behavior had been exposed, shame that Hurstwood had betrayed her trust, and anger that Drouet had deceived her and made her look like a fool. Finally, one clear idea came into her head. Drouet was at fault. There was no doubt about it. Why had he brought Hurstwood over to visit them—Hurstwood, a married man—and never said a word to her? Never mind now about Hurstwood's betrayal. Why had Drouet done this to her? Why hadn't he warned her? There stood Drouet, guilty of betraying her. And he dared to talk about what he had done for her!

"Well, that's a fine thing to say!" exclaimed Drouet, not realizing how angry she was. "I think I've done a good deal."

"You have, eh?" she answered. "You've deceived me—that's what you've done. You've brought your old friends out here under false pretenses. You've made me out to be a—" With this, her voice broke, and she wrung her hands tragically.

"I don't see what that's got to do with it," said Drouet innocently.

"No," she answered, clenching her teeth. "No, of course you don't see. You never see anything. You couldn't have told me in the first place, could you? No, you had to wait until it was too late for me. Now you come sneaking around with your information and expect me to thank you for what you've done for me."

Drouet had never suspected this side of Carrie's nature—so full of anger and resentment.

"Who's the one that's been sneaking?" he asked. He was certain that he had been wronged. So he did not realize that this was the wrong approach to use with Carrie.

"You are," stamped Carrie. "You're a horrid, conceited coward, that's what you are. If you were a man, you wouldn't have thought of doing any such thing."

Drouet stared. "I'm not a coward," he said. "What do you mean by going out with other men, anyway?"

"Other men!" exclaimed Carrie. "Other men! You know better than that. I did go out with Mr. Hurstwood, but whose fault was that? Didn't you bring him here? You told him yourself that he should come over here and take me out. Now that it's happened, you come and tell me that I shouldn't go with him and that he's a married man."

She paused after the last two words and wrung her hands. Hurstwood's betrayal wounded her like a knife. "Oh," she sobbed. But she controlled herself wonderfully and kept her eyes dry. "Oh, oh!"

"Well, I didn't think you'd be running around with him when I was away," insisted Drouet.

"Didn't think!" said Carrie, now angered to the core by Drouet's attitude. "Of course you didn't. You thought only about what you wanted. You thought you'd make a toy of me—a plaything. Well, I'll show you that you won't. I'll have nothing more to do with you at all. You can take your old things and keep them!"

She took off a little pin he had given her and flung it onto the floor. Then she began to move around as if to gather up her belongings.

Drouet stared at her in amazement. Finally he said, "I don't see where you've got the right to be angry. You shouldn't have done anything wrong to me after all I did for you."

"What have you done for me?" asked Carrie, blazing.

"I think I've done a good deal," said the traveling salesman, looking around. "I've given you all the clothes you wanted, haven't I? I've taken you everywhere you wanted to go. You've had as much as I've had, and more, too."

Carrie was not ungrateful, but she was still

angry. She felt that Drouet had hurt her beyond repair.

Not knowing how to answer Drouet's argument, she replied, "Did I ask you to do that?"

"Well, I did it," said Drouet, "and you took it."

"You talk as though I had persuaded you," answered Carrie. "You stand there and throw in my face all that you've done. Well, I don't want your old things. You take them tonight and do what you want with them. I won't stay here another minute."

He started thinking about what he was about to lose. Hurt and angry, Drouet answered, "That's nice! Use everything and take advantage of me. Then just walk off. That's just like a woman. I take you when you have nothing. And then, when someone else comes along, I'm not good enough. I always thought it would come to this."

"That's not true," said Carrie. "And I'm not going with anybody else. You've been miserable and inconsiderate. I hate you, I tell you. And I wouldn't live with you another minute. You're a big, insulting . . ." Carrie hesitated, unable to find the right word. Then she finished, "Or you wouldn't talk to me that way."

By now she had slipped her jacket over her little evening dress and put on her hat. She was angry, humiliated, grief-stricken. But still her eyelids were dry. She didn't know what to do or think, and so she acted aimlessly. She didn't have the slightest idea how the whole thing would end.

"So, just pack up and pull out, eh?" said Drouet. "You must have been fooling around with Hurstwood, or you wouldn't act like that. Well, I don't want this old apartment. You don't need to move out for my sake. You can have this place for all I care. But by golly, you still haven't done me right."

"I don't want to live with you," responded Carrie. "You've done nothing but brag ever since you've been here."

"Aw, I have not," he answered.

Carrie walked over to the door.

"Where are you going?" he said, stepping between her and the door.

"Let me out," she said.

"Where are you going?" he repeated. In spite of his anger, he was worried about what would happen to Carrie if she wandered out alone.

Carrie merely pulled at the door, and then finally burst into tears.

"Now, be reasonable, Cad," said Drouet gently. "Why rush out like this? You don't have any-place to go. Why not stay here now and calm down? I won't bother you. I don't want to stay here any longer."

Still sobbing, Carrie went from the door to the window. She was so overcome that she could not speak.

"Be reasonable now," he said. "I don't want to hold you back. You can go if you want to. But why don't you think it over? Goodness knows I don't want to stop you."

Carrie didn't answer, but was beginning to calm down.

"You stay here now, and I'll go," he added at last.

Carrie was listening with mixed feelings—indignation, anger, and appreciation for both Hurstwood's and Drouet's good qualities. She thought about how threatening the outside world could be. She had failed there once before. Then she thought about how impossible the inside situation was right now. She had no right to stay here any longer. She felt like a small boat, beaten by the storms, without an anchor, able to do nothing except drift.

"Say," said Drouet, as he thought of another idea. He came over and put his hand on her.

"Don't!" said Carrie, pulling away from him.

Drouet continued, "Don't worry about this argument right now. Let it go. You stay here at least until the end of the month. Then you'll have a better idea of what you want to do. OK?"

Carrie did not answer.

"You'd better do that," he said. "There's no use in packing up your things now. You can't go anywhere."

Still he did not get a response.

"If you'll do that, we'll call things off for now, and I'll get out."

Carrie just looked out of the window.

"Will you do that?" he asked.

Still no answer.

"Will you?" he repeated.

She only looked vaguely onto the street.

"Aw! Comeon," he said. "Tell me. Will you?"

"I don't know," said Carrie softly, forced to answer.

"Promise me you'll do that," he said, "and we'll quit talking about it. It'll be the best thing for you."

Carrie heard him, but she could not bring herself to answer reasonably. She felt a pang of regret that this man was so gentle and still interested in her.

Drouet, too, had mixed feelings. He was jealous of Hurstwood, angry at being deceived, sad about losing Carrie, miserable about being defeated. He also felt justified in holding onto Carrie. And he had a right to make her feel that she had been wrong.

"Will you?" he urged.

"Well, I'll see," said Carrie.

This left things as open as before, but at least it was something. Drouet hoped that the fight might blow over if only they could find a way to talk to one another. Carrie was ashamed, and Drouet was offended. He pretended to start packing a suitcase.

Now, as Carrie watched him, she started thinking more logically. He made a mistake, true. But what had she done? Even though he was conceited, he was also kind and good-natured. On the other hand, there was Hurstwood—an even bigger deceiver. He had pretended all this affection, all this passion. But all the while he was lying to her.

And she had loved him. No, she would never again see Hurstwood. She would write to him and tell him what she thought. And then what would she do? Here was the apartment. Here was Drouet, begging her to stay. It would be better than the street, without a place to sleep.

But Drouet kept trying to find a way to make Carrie admit that he was right and she was wrong. He thought that then they could make up and shut out Hurstwood forever.

"Do you think," he said, after a few moments' silence, "that you'll try and get on the stage?"

"I don't know what I'll do yet," said Carrie.

"If you do, maybe I can help you. I've got a lot of friends in that field."

She didn't answer, but just kept rocking in her chair.

"Don't go and try to get along now without any money. Let me help you," he said. "It's not easy to go it alone around here."

Carrie only rocked back and forth in her chair.

"Why don't you just tell me what happened with Hurstwood, and then we can let it go. You don't really like him, do you?"

"Why do you want to start that all over again?" said Carrie. "You were to blame."

"No, I wasn't," he answered.

"Yes, you were, too," said Carrie. "You shouldn't have told me a story like that."

"But you didn't have much to do with him, did you?" Drouet went on. For his own peace of mind, he was anxious for her to deny any involvement.

"I won't talk about it," said Carrie, pained at how the peace between them had broken down.

"What's the use of acting like that now, Cad?" insisted the traveling salesman. "You could at least let me know where I stand."

"I won't," said Carrie. She felt that anger was her only defense. "Whatever has happened is your own fault."

"Then you do like him?" said Drouet, experiencing a rush of feeling.

"Oh, stop!" said Carrie.

"Well, I'm not going to be made a fool of," exclaimed Drouet. "You can play around with him if you want to, but you can't make me go along with it. You can tell me or not, whatever you want. But I won't play the fool any longer!"

He shoved a few remaining things into his suitcase and snapped it closed with a vengeance. Then he grabbed his coat, picked up his gloves, and started out.

"You can go to the devil as far as I am concerned," he said, as he reached the door. "I'm no sucker."

With that, he opened it with a jerk and then slammed it shut.

Carrie listened from her rocking chair by the window. She was surprised at how emotional this easygoing, good-natured man had become. But jealousy can fan the flame of love and make it blaze with heat.

CHAPTER 24

Thunderclouds Break

That night, Hurstwood stayed in a downtown hotel, trying to figure out how to respond to his wife's threats. He cursed himself for putting all his property in her name. Then he thought about his position as manager of Fitzgerald and Moy's. "If my name gets in the papers, they'll fire me." Even his friends would stay away from him. He kept trying to put together all the pieces of the puzzle, but he couldn't find a solution. At least tomorrow he would be able to meet with Carrie as usual. As for Saturday's plans to get married, he was sure that Carrie would be glad to wait if necessary. In his mind, he saw only her pretty face and lovely figure. He wondered why life wasn't arranged to allow the kind of constant joy that he felt with her. He would see what happened tomorrow, and then talk with Carrie. If only he could have enough time to think, perhaps something would turn up. Surely, surely, he would find a way out before this thing drifted along into a disaster.

Mrs. Hurstwood, in the meantime, took action

right away to force him to meet her demands. He would have to pay her money regularly, or there would be trouble. She really did not care whether he came home anymore or not. The household would be pleasanter without him. And she could do what she wanted without checking with him first. She planned to consult a lawyer and hire a detective.

The next morning, he opened his mail, expecting an angry letter from his wife. But there was nothing unusual. Then he went to the park, and waited and waited for an hour or more. But Carrie did not come. Could something have happened out there to keep her away? Could his wife have gotten in touch with her? Surely not. He thought so little of Drouet that it never occurred to him to worry that he might find out. Finally, Hurstwood decided that Carrie must not have been able to get away this morning. She would surely send him a letter instead. It would probably be on his desk when he got back.

The bright blue sky became overcast with clouds, which shut out the sun. His mood also darkened. By the time he reached his office, it was threatening to rain all afternoon. He went in and looked at his mail, but there was nothing from Carrie. Fortunately, there was nothing from his wife, either.

At one-thirty, he went to lunch. When he returned, a messenger was waiting for him.

"I'm supposed to bring back an answer," said

the young man.

Hurstwood recognized his wife's handwriting. He tore open the letter, which was worded in a sharp, cold, formal manner.

"I want you to send me the money at once. I need it to carry out my plans. You can stay away if you want to. It doesn't matter in the least. But I must have some money. So don't delay, but send it with the messenger."

Her boldness took his breath away. He was so angry that his first impulse was to write a four-word reply: "Go to the devil!" But instead, he simply told the messenger that there would be no reply. What would she do about it? The witch! Was she going to try to bulldoze him into obeying her? He would go up to the house and have it out with her. That's what he would do. She was carrying things too far.

But then he thought better of it. Something had to be done. He knew that once she decided on a plan, she would go through with it. She might go to a lawyer right away.

"Damn her!" he said softly, with his teeth firmly set. "I'll make things difficult for her if she causes me any trouble. I'll make her change her tone, even if I have to use force to do it!"

He went over to the window and looked out into the street. It had begun to rain. With all the umbrellas, the street looked like a sea of round, black cloth roofs, twisting, bobbing, moving. Everywhere people were shielding themselves as best they could. In his mind, he kept confronting his wife. He demanded that she change her attitude toward him. If not, he threatened to hurt her.

At four o'clock another note came. It simply said that if he didn't send her the money that evening, she would tell the whole story to his employers, Fitzgerald and Moy. Other steps would be taken to get the money.

Yes, Hurstwood would send her the money. In fact, he'd take it to her himself. He'd go there right away and have a talk with her.

His temper cooled as he thought more about the situation. What did she know? What had she done? Perhaps she really did have some evidence. Why else would she push him this way? She was shrewd. Maybe she was preparing a kind of secret ambush.

He began to wish that he had compromised—that he had sent her the money the first time she had asked. Perhaps he could work things out with her. He would go and see her, anyhow. He wouldn't argue with her. He took a cab out to his house. When he arrived, he went up the steps to the front door. He tried to put his key in the lock, but it was blocked from the inside. He shook the knob, but the door was locked. Then he rang the bell. No answer. He rang again—this time longer. Still no answer. He tried a few more times, but it was no use. He pushed it fiercely several times in a row, but still without success. The door to the kitchen was also bolted, and the windows were all shut. What could it mean? He rang the bell and then waited. Finally, seeing that no one was coming, he turned and went back to his cab.

"I guess they've gone out," he explained to the cab driver.

"I saw a young girl up in that window," the driver replied.

Hurstwood looked, but there was no face there now. He climbed back into the cab, upset, but also relieved.

So this was the game she was playing. Shut him out and make him pay. Well, by golly, that was a heck of a thing to do!

CHAPTER 25

Adrift in the Storm

When Hurstwood got back to his office again, he was more uncertain than ever. "Lord, Lord," he thought. What had he gotten himself into? How could things have taken such a violent turn, and so quickly? This impossible situation had suddenly fallen on him. He had done nothing to make it happen. Nor could he have done anything to prevent it.

And what was going on with Carrie? She had agreed to meet him that morning. Yet here it was, late in the evening, and no letter had come, no word of any kind. Tomorrow they were supposed to have met and gone off—but where? In the excitement of recent events, he had not worked out that plan. Suppose she had found out something? Suppose she also wrote him that she knew everything—that she, too, would have nothing more to do with him? Meanwhile, he still had not sent the money to his wife.

He was so shaken up that he paced and thought and drank more brandy and soda than usual. What

to do? For two or three hours, he debated the problem with himself. At last, he got out an envelope,
placed in it the amount of money requested, slowly
sealed it up, and sent it to his wife.

Now he felt beaten. Oh, the misery of being
forced like this! In his mind, he watched her take
the envelope. She would know that she had tri-
umphed. If only he had that letter back, he
wouldn't send it. Alone in his hotel room, he did
not sleep soundly that night.

The next day he returned to his office and
opened his mail, both suspicious and hopeful
about what he might find. No word from Carrie.
Nothing from his wife. Maybe by sending the
money he had bought himself some time to think.

It was Saturday, the day they were to have run
off together. The hours slipped by, and with them
the possibility of being with Carrie. Three o'clock
came. Then four, five, six—and still no letter.

The next day, Sunday, the saloon was closed.
He moped about, alone in his hotel room—shut
out from his home, the excitement of his work, his
union with Carrie. And there was not a single
thing he could do to change his situation. It was
the worst Sunday he had spent in his entire life.

In Monday afternoon's mail was a very legal-
looking letter from the law offices of McGregor,
James, and Hay. It was full of very formal phrases
like "Dear Sir," and "We beg to state." It informed
him that Mrs. Julia Hurstwood had hired them to
work out certain matters about her support and

property rights. Would he kindly see them about these matters immediately?

Hurstwood read it through carefully several times. Then he simply shook his head. It seemed as if his troubles were just beginning.

"Well!" he said finally. "I don't know."

Then he folded up the letter and put it in his pocket.

To add to his misery, there was no word from Carrie. She must have found out that he was married. She would be angry that he had deceived her. His loss seemed all the more bitter now that he needed her most. The possibility of losing her made her seem even more attractive. Come what may, he would work things out, and soon. He would go to her and explain everything. He would tell her how much he needed her. Surely she couldn't go back on him now? It wasn't possible. He would plead with her until her anger melted— until she forgave him.

Suddenly he thought, "Suppose she isn't out there? Suppose she has gone away?"

He even went to visit his son at work several times. But George, Jr., would not see him. Neither of his children seemed even to notice that he was gone.

Tuesday was the same. He finally managed to go out to see Carrie. But when he got near her apartment, he thought he saw a man watching him, so he went back to the office. He stayed at his desk until long after everyone else had gone home.

On Wednesday, he received another polite note from McGregor, James, and Hay. It read:

Dear Sir:
We beg to inform you that we shall wait until tomorrow (Thursday) at one o'clock. Then, on behalf of Mrs. Julia Hurstwood, we shall file a suit against you for divorce and alimony. If we do not hear from you, we shall consider that you do not wish to compromise in any way. And then we shall act accordingly.

Very truly yours,

"Compromise!" exclaimed Hurstwood bitterly. "Compromise!"

Again he shook his head.

So here it was, spread out before him. If he didn't go and see them, they would sue him. If he did, he would have to agree to terms that would make his blood boil.

He folded the letter and put it with the other one. Then he put on his hat and went for a walk around the block.

CHAPTER 26

Shut In and Shut Out

Carrie, left alone by Drouet, listened to his steps as he stormed out. She hardly realized what had happened. It took a few moments before she started to wonder whether he would return—not just now, but ever. The evening light was dying. She looked around at the apartment and wondered why she did not feel the same way about it anymore. She went over to light one of the lamps. And then she went back to the rocking chair to think.

Finally she collected her thoughts enough to see the truth. She was all alone. Suppose Drouet did not come back? Suppose she never heard anything more from him? She would have to leave the apartment before long.

To her credit, she never once counted on Hurstwood. She was shocked and frightened that he would have tricked her into a situation that was morally worse than the one she was already in. And yet, she could not keep him out of her mind. She kept picturing how he looked and acted. Only this one act of deception seemed strange and miserable.

It contrasted sharply with all she felt and knew about the man.

But now she was alone. Now what? Would she look around again for work in the business district? The stage! Oh, yes. Drouet had spoken about that. Was there any hope there? She rocked back and forth in her chair, deep in her thoughts.

Then she began to wonder how much money she had. There were only seven dollars in her purse. That was so little to live on. Still, at least the rent was paid until the end of the month. But what if she had stormed out into the street when she had first threatened to do so? What would she have done then? At least she had a little time. Perhaps everything would turn out all right, after all.

Drouet had gone, but what of it? He only acted as if he were angry. He would come back— of course he would. But suppose he did come back. Then what? She would have to talk with him and explain everything. He would want her to admit that he was right. And then it would be impossible for her to live with him.

On Friday, Carrie remembered her date with Hurstwood. She felt that she needed to act—to do something—if only to calm herself down. So she put on a brown street dress and went out to the business district once again. She must look for work. Soon the rain dampened her mood, just as it had dampened Hurstwood's. So she went home and spent the rest of the day indoors.

She could not help feeling that life must be a

joyous thing for people who did not need to worry about money. She did not want Drouet or his money. She did not want anything more to do with Hurstwood. But she longed for the peace of mind that she experienced when she was with these men. Even if she hadn't been happy, at least she had been happier then. For now she had to make her way alone.

The next morning, Saturday, she returned to the business district. She remembered what had happened the last time she went there to look for work. Her old fears and worries came back. But at least now her appearance and manner were much better than before. Men—some of them well dressed, like the ones who had coldly ignored her before—now looked her over with a soft light in their eyes. In a way, this made her feel satisfied and powerful. But it did not completely reassure her. She did not want any special favors because of her looks. No man should buy her with false promises or flattery. She wanted to earn her living honestly. By 12:15, she decided that it would be no use to try anymore that day. So she got on a trolley and went to Lincoln Park. There was always something to see there—the flowers, the animals, the lake. She imagined that she would get up early and look for work again on Monday. Besides, many things might happen between now and then.

Sunday passed with more doubts, worries, assurances, and changes in mood. Sometimes, with the sharpness of a lashing whip, she felt the need to take immediate action. At other times, she looked around at her apartment and assured herself that things were not so bad, after all. Certainly she would come out safe and sound. At those times, she thought of Drouet's advice about becoming an actress. She saw that as a good possibility. So she decided to look the next day for work in the theater.

And so, she got up early Monday morning and dressed herself carefully. She had no idea about how to find an acting job. She assumed that she should just go to a theater and ask for a position. She did not realize that jobs were sometimes given in return for sexual favors.

First she bravely entered the polished, golden lobby of the Chicago Opera House. But then she saw the pictures of the current star of the stage. She couldn't imagine ever reaching those heights of success and fame. She had enough courage only to look at the impressive pictures and then walk out. She began to feel that she had no right to be so ambitious.

That night, she sat down to think. Drouet had not put in an appearance. She had not heard from anyone else. She had spent one of her few and precious dollars for food and carfare. It was clear that she could not survive this way for long. She had no resources. For the first time since she had left to be on her own, she thought of her home in Columbia City, and then of her sister in Van Buren Street. But she felt that she could never go back. She kept thinking about Hurstwood. But that only brought her sorrow. How could he have deceived her so cruelly?

On Tuesday, she returned to the Chicago Opera House, ashamed that she had been so weak the day before. She forced herself to speak with the well-dressed man at the box office. He was impressed by Carrie's good looks.

"You'd better see the manager of the company," he explained. "He'll be in this afternoon."

He thought about how good-looking she was, and what she might be willing to do for a job.

Next Carrie went to the Grand Opera House. She asked to speak with the manager of the company. Carrie did not realize that he did not have the authority to hire actors. And even if there had been a part available, they would have hired an actor from New York, not from Chicago.

Carrie stood waiting, timidly. She was sure that she would be rejected, since she had no experience. So she pretended that she was asking only for advice.

"Can you tell me how to go about getting on the stage?" she finally asked.

Her trim appearance and innocent manner appealed to the manager. He looked her over boldly, wondering how to get her to go out with him.

"Well, you can't expect to get started out here in Chicago. You ought to be in New York. There's more chance there."

Carrie smiled warmly, grateful for his advice.

He noticed the smile, and interpreted it as an

invitation to flirt.

"Sit down," he said, pulling a chair closer to his desk and lowering his voice. "Have you ever tried to get a job as a chorus girl?" he asked, leaning toward her.

Carrie began to feel that there was something strangely intimate about his manner.

"No," she said.

"That's the way most girls begin. It's a good way to get experience on the stage."

He flashed her a friendly, persuasive smile.

"I didn't know that," said Carrie innocently.

"It's difficult," he went on, "but there's always a chance, you know."

Then, as if he suddenly remembered something, he looked at his watch. "I've an appointment at two," he said, "and I've got to go to lunch now. Would you care to come and dine with me? We can talk it over there."

"Oh, no," said Carrie. Suddenly the man's ulterior motive flashed on her. "I have an appointment, myself."

"That's too bad," he said, realizing that he had moved in on her too fast. "Come in later. I may know of something."

"Thank you," she answered nervously, and went out.

Angry that he had lost the game, the manager decided that Carrie wasn't so good-looking, after all. "She'd never make an actress," he thought. "Just another chorus girl—that's all."

Carrie then returned to the Chicago Opera House and spoke with the manager there. He said that there were absolutely no openings and thought she was foolish to look for one. "Chicago is no place to get a start," he said. "You ought to be in New York."

Discouraged, she decided to check at the post office to see if she had received any mail. There was a letter that Hurstwood had written on Saturday. He was so passionate and upset about not seeing or hearing from her that she pitied the man. Clearly he loved her. But it was wrong to dare to love her when he was already married to another woman. She would write and tell him that she knew he was married. She would say that she had a right to be furious at him for deceiving her. She would tell him that it was all over between them.

Back at her apartment, she wrote the letter, with difficulty.

I don't have to explain why I did not meet you. How could you deceive me so? You cannot expect me to have anything more to do with you. I wouldn't under any circumstances. Oh, how could you act so? You have caused me more misery than you can imagine. I hope you will get over your foolish love for me. We must not meet anymore. Goodbye.

The next morning, reluctantly, she dropped the letter into the mailbox. She was still uncertain whether she should do so or not.

Then she went downtown to look for a job in

a department store. Because of her neat and attractive appearance, she was treated more respectfully than most applicants. But she was still asked the same old questions. And she could not answer them any better than before.

"What can you do? Have you ever worked in a retail store before? Are you experienced?"

Besides, it was the slow season. No one was hiring.

When she returned home, weary and discouraged, she discovered that Drouet had been in the apartment. He had taken some of his things, but not all of them. So, he really was leaving for good. What was she to do now? Soon she, too, would have to leave. Her clothes would get poor. She wrung her hands. Large tears gathered in her eyes and broke hot across her cheeks. She was alone, very much alone.

Drouet really had stopped by, but for a very different reason from what Carrie thought. He had expected to find her at home. He planned to pretend that he had come just to get a few things. Then he would patch things up with her. But when he arrived, he was disappointed that Carrie wasn't there. He waited for a while, but Carrie did not return. After a while, he sat down in the rocking chair and looked out the window. Still no Carrie. Then he looked out of the window and saw storm clouds gathering. He had an appointment at three. So he picked up a few of his things, hoping it would scare her. Tomorrow he would come back and find out how things stood.

As he started to go, he felt truly sorry that he had missed her. He noticed a picture of her wearing the little jacket that he had first bought her. He was touched by her expression. It was more wistful than it had been recently. He looked into the eyes with an emotion that he didn't feel very often.

"You didn't do me right, Cad," he said, as if he were talking to her in person.

Then he went to the door, took a good look around, and walked out.

CHAPTER 27

One Door Opens, and Another One Closes

When Hurstwood returned to his office, he was thrilled to find a letter from Carrie. After reading it, he felt a little depressed. But then he desperately tried to convince himself, "She wouldn't have written at all if she didn't care about me." For the moment he forgot the letter from McGregor, James, and Hay. If only he could have Carrie, perhaps he could get out of this whole mess. Then, perhaps, nothing else would matter. He wouldn't care what his wife did if only he didn't lose Carrie. He kept dreaming his delightful dream of a life shared with this pretty woman that he loved.

But soon he remembered that he only had until one o'clock tomorrow to prevent a lawsuit. He had done nothing, and here the afternoon was slipping away. It was now almost four o'clock. At five, the attorneys would leave the office. But he still had tomorrow morning. Even as he thought, the last fifteen minutes passed, and now it was five o'clock. He gave up the idea of seeing them that day. Instead, he focused all his thoughts on finding a way to persuade Carrie. Nothing was wrong in that. He loved her dearly. Their mutual happiness depended upon it. If only Drouet were gone!

He left to buy a few things and then stopped by his hotel to drop them off. As he entered, he thought he saw Drouet going upstairs with a key. Surely not Drouet! Then he thought, perhaps they had moved temporarily. He went straight up to the desk.

"Is Mr. Drouet staying here?" he asked of the clerk.

"Yes, he is."

"Is that so?" exclaimed Hurstwood, trying to hide his surprise. "Alone?" he added.

"Yes," said the clerk.

Hurstwood thought, his spirits rising, "They must have had a fight."

Later that evening, he went out to Carrie's apartment and asked the housekeeper, "Is Mr. Drouet in?"

"He is out of the city," she answered, repeating what she had heard Carrie say.

"Is Mrs. Drouet in?"

"No, she has gone to the theater."

Hurstwood decided to return to the saloon, since he assumed that she must have gone with someone else.

At about ten o'clock, several important and famous men entered the bar and invited him to join them. Feeling upset and discouraged, Hurstwood drank more than usual. After a few drinks, he started to feel that his troubles were not so serious, after all.

At twelve o'clock, he said goodbye to his drinking companions, and watched the bartenders and cashier leave.

One of his duties, as manager, was to see that everything was locked up after everyone else had left the bar. Usually, the only cash kept at the saloon was the money taken in after the banks had closed. That money was always locked in the safe by the cashier. And only the cashier and the owners knew the secret combination to the safe. But it was Hurstwood's responsibility to make sure that everything was tightly closed. So every night he pulled on each of the cash drawers and the door to the safe. Then he locked up his office and left. This was his routine, even though he always found everything locked up tightly.

But this time, when he tried the safe, the door opened. Surprised, his first thought was, of course, to check the drawers and shut the door. When he looked in the first drawer, he noticed a stack of bills, bundled in a packet of a thousand, the way banks do. Then he pulled out the second drawer and found all the cash left from that evening.

"I didn't know Fitzgerald and Moy ever left so much money lying around like this," his mind said to itself. "They must have forgotten it."

He looked at the first drawer and paused again.

"Count them," said a voice in his ear.

There were fifty-dollar bills and one-hundred-dollar bills, bundled in packages of a thousand dollars. He thought he counted ten of them.

"What's keeping me from just shutting the safe?" his mind asked itself.

Then it answered with these strange words, "Did you ever have ten thousand dollars in cash?"

No, he hadn't. He had earned his property only a little at a time. Now he was worth more than forty thousand dollars. But his wife would get everything.

As he puzzled over this, he pushed in the drawers and closed the door. Then he paused, with his hand still on the knob. He could so easily lock it up beyond temptation.

Still he paused, thinking strange thoughts.

"The safe is open," said a voice in his mind. "There is just the least little crack in it. The lock has not been sprung."

The manager sank into a jumble of thoughts. His life was a tangle of problems. And here was a solution. Money would take care of everything. If only he had money—that and Carrie.

The manager was no fool. But he had been drinking. Alcohol made him think that ten thousand dollars would give him great opportunities. And that he could get Carrie. Oh, yes, he could! He could get rid of his wife, too. He wouldn't need to answer that letter tomorrow, after all.

He went back to the safe and put his hand on the knob. Then he pulled the door open again and took out the drawer with the ten thousand dollars in it.

Now that the money was right there in front of him, it would be foolish to think about leaving it there. Certainly it would. Why, with all this, he could live quietly with Carrie for years.

Lord! What was that? He looked around, fearfully. Nothing. Just a person passing by outside. He took the box and the money and put everything back in the safe. Then he partly closed the door again.

Hurstwood was caught between duty and desire, between instinct and reason. It was as if he were listening to a clock ticking in his mind: "Thou shalt." "Thou shalt not." "Thou shalt." "Thou shalt not."

After he had put the money back, he felt more relaxed. The drinks had not yet worn off. He went back and forth, from the safe to his desk, from his desk to the safe. Then he put his hand on the knob and opened it. There was the money! Surely no harm could come from just looking at it.

He took out the drawer again and picked up the bills. They were so smooth, so compact, so portable. It seemed like so little, after all. He decided he would take them. Yes, he would. He would put them in his pockets. No one would think anything of it, either. He would take it all. He put the empty drawers back. Then he pushed the iron door almost closed. He stood beside it, thinking.

Hurstwood could not bring himself to make a decisive move. He wanted to think it over—to decide whether it was the best thing to do. He didn't know what evil might result from it. But he was drawn by his desire for Carrie, and driven by his dismay at his own affairs. He never once thought about what was morally right and wrong. But now that he had the money, he felt disgusted. He would not do it—no! Think of what a scandal it would make. The police! They would be after him. He would have to run away. And where would he go? Oh, the terror of being a criminal, fleeing from justice!

He took out the two boxes and put all the money back inside. But in his excitement he forgot what he was doing, and switched the money between the two boxes. As he pushed the door closed, he realized his mistake and opened the door again. There were the two boxes, with the money mixed up.

He removed the boxes, and sorted out the money. But now the terror had gone. Why be afraid?

While the money was in his hand, the lock clicked. It had sprung! Did he do it? He grabbed at the knob and pulled it hard. It had closed. Heavens! Now he was in trouble, no doubt about it.

When he realized that the safe was locked for sure, he broke out into a sweat and started trembling. "Even if I do leave all the money on top of the safe, they'll know who took it out. I'm the last person to close up. And that will only be the start of my problems."

He looked around and decided instantly. There was no delaying now.

"I must get out of this," he thought. At once he became a man of action.

He put on his coat and hat, and opened the door to his office. Then he started having second thoughts. "I wish I hadn't done that," he said. "That was a mistake."

He walked steadily down the street, greeting the night watchman as he passed by him. He must get out of the city—and quickly. He looked at his watch. It was nearly one-thirty.

He called the Michigan Central Station to find out when the next train was leaving for Detroit.

"There is a mail train out of here at three o'clock," explained the ticket agent.

"All right," said Hurstwood. "What time does it get to Detroit?"

He was thinking that if only he could get there, then he could cross the river into Canada. Once he left the country, he would be safe. Then he could take his time getting to Montreal. He was relieved to learn that the train would reach Detroit by noon.

"They won't open the safe until nine," he thought. "So they won't be able to start tracking me down before noon."

Then he thought of Carrie. He needed to get her quickly if he were going to get her at all. She would have to come along with him.

He took a cab to her apartment, ran up the

stairs, and woke the housekeeper.

"Is Mrs. Drouet in?" he asked.

"Yes," she answered, astonished to see him at that hour.

"Tell her to dress and come to the door at once. Her husband is in the hospital, injured. He wants to see her."

The housekeeper rushed upstairs to tell Carrie. "Mr. Drouet is hurt and in the hospital. He wants to see you. The cab's downstairs."

Carrie dressed very rapidly, thinking only of what was necessary.

Once she was downstairs, Hurstwood told her, "Drouet is hurt. He wants to see you. Come quickly."

Carrie was so shocked and confused that she believed the whole story.

"Get in," said Hurstwood. He helped her into the cab and then jumped in after her.

He leaned forward and spoke quietly to the cab driver, so that Carrie could not hear. "Michigan Central Station—as fast as you can go."

CHAPTER 28

Escape or Capture?

By the end of the first block, Carrie was wide-awake. "What's the matter with Charlie?" she asked. "Is he hurt badly?"

"It isn't anything very serious," Hurstwood answered briefly. But he was too worried about his own situation to pay attention to Carrie. He wanted only to get safely out of reach of the law.

Carrie had not forgotten that there was something to be settled between her and Hurstwood. But she was so upset that she set aside that concern. The important thing was to finish this strange journey.

"Where is he?"

"Way out on the South Side," said Hurstwood. "We'll have to take the train. It's the quickest way."

Carrie became silent, wondering. The strange atmosphere of the city at night held her attention. She looked at the long receding rows of lamps and studied the dark, silent houses.

Hurstwood looked at his watch and urged the driver to hurry.

When they reached the station, he led Carrie into the waiting room and said, "You wait here while I get the tickets."

He bought the tickets, making sure that no one was observing him. The train was scheduled to depart in only four minutes.

"Is it far?" Carrie asked, as he hurried back.

"Not very," he said. "We must get right in."

At the gate, Hurstwood stood between Carrie and the ticket collector so that she could not see where they were going.

As soon as they sat down, the train started. Carrie was upset, but said nothing.

Hurstwood was thinking about his own danger, not about Carrie. He couldn't think about the future until he reached the Canadian border, beyond the reach of United States laws. His criminal deed and his running away from the law were like large shadows that weighed on his mind. Now that he was sober, he could hardly believe that the thing had been done, that he was a fugitive from justice. He kept going back and forth, reviewing the past. "What a fool I was to do that," he said over and over to himself. "What a mistake!" But then he thought, "What else could I have done?"

The train began to gain speed. Carrie saw the dark, silent streets flashing by, one after the other.

"Is it very far?" asked Carrie.

"Not so very," said Hurstwood. He found her innocence charming. He wanted to explain everything to her and calm her. But he also wanted to be far away from Chicago.

After another half-hour, Carrie thought that he must be taking her quite some distance, anyhow.

"Is it in Chicago?" she asked nervously. They were now far beyond the city limits. The train was rapidly crossing the state border.

"No," he said, "not where we are going."

There was something in the way he said this that made her suspicious. A frown wrinkled her pretty forehead.

"We are going to see Charlie, aren't we?" she asked.

He felt that it was time. An explanation might as well come now as later. So, very gently, he shook his head "no."

"What?" said Carrie.

He just looked at her in a kind, soothing way.

"Well, where are you taking me, then?" she asked. Her voice sounded frightened.

"I'll tell you, Carrie, if you'll be quiet. I want you to come along with me to another city."

"Oh!" Carrie's voice became a weak cry. "Let me off. I don't want to go with you."

She was shocked at the man's boldness. This was something that had never for a moment occurred to her. Her one thought now was to get off the train and away from this man. If only the speeding train could be stopped! Then this terrible trick would be undone.

She got up and tried to push past Hurstwood. She knew she had to do something. Hurstwood laid a gentle hand on her.

"Sit still, Carrie," he said. "Sit still. It won't do you any good to get up here. Listen to me, and I'll tell you what I'll do. Just wait a moment."

She was pushing at his knees, trying to get by. But he kept pulling her back. No one saw this little struggle, though, for the few other people in the train were asleep.

"I won't," said Carrie. She began to give in to him, though, even against her will. "Let me go. How dare you!" Large tears began to gather in her eyes.

Now Hurstwood was forced to stop thinking about his own situation. He must do something with this girl, or she would cause him trouble.

"Look here now, Carrie," he said. "You mustn't act this way. I didn't mean to hurt your feelings. I don't want to do anything to make you feel bad."

"Oh," sobbed Carrie. "Oh, oh—oo—oh!"

"There, there," he said. "You mustn't cry. Won't you listen to me? Listen to me a minute, and I'll tell you why I did this. I couldn't help it. Really, I couldn't. Won't you listen?"

"No, I won't," said Carrie, her anger flashing. "I want you to take me out of this, or I'll tell the conductor. I won't go with you. It's wrong." Again, sobs of fright cut off her words.

Hurstwood felt that Carrie had the right to feel the way she did. And yet he wished that he could straighten this thing out quickly. Soon the conductor would come through the car to check the tickets. He wanted no noise, no trouble of any kind. Above all else, he must make her quiet down.

"You can't get out until the train stops again," said Hurstwood. "It won't be very long until we reach another station. You can get out then if you want to. I won't stop you. All I want you to do is to listen a moment. You'll let me explain, won't you?"

Carrie seemed not to listen. She turned her head toward the window. Outside all was black and lonely. The train whistles sounded like sad music.

The conductor took the tickets from Hurstwood. Carrie was ready to spring to action. But she did not make a move.

After the conductor left, Hurstwood felt relieved.

"You're angry at me because I deceived you," he said. "I didn't mean to, Carrie. I swear I didn't. I couldn't help it. I couldn't stay away from you after the first time I saw you."

He wanted to convince her that his marriage was no longer an issue. He tried to shut out of his mind the stolen money and his tricking her into getting on the train.

"Don't talk to me," said Carrie. "I hate you. I want you to get away from me. I am going to get out at the very next station."

"All right," he said. "But you'll hear me out, won't you? After everything you said about loving me, at least you could listen to me. I don't want to hurt you. I'll give you money to take with you when you go back. I just want to explain, Carrie.

You can think what you want. But you can't stop me from loving you."

He looked at her tenderly, but she didn't reply. "You think I deceived you badly, but I didn't. I didn't do it willingly. I'm through with my wife. She has no hold on me. I'll never see her anymore. That's why I'm here tonight. That's why I came and got you."

"You said Charlie was hurt," said Carrie, savagely. "You deceived me. You've been deceiving me all this time. And now you want to force me to run away with you."

She got up and tried to get by him again. This time he let her. She sat down in another seat. Then he followed.

"Don't run away from me, Carrie," he said gently. "Let me explain. If you will just hear me out, you will see where I stand. I tell you, my wife means nothing to me. She hasn't meant anything to me for years. If she did, I wouldn't have ever come near you. I'm going to get a divorce just as soon as I can. I'll never see her again. I'm done with all that. You're the only person I want. If I can have you, I won't ever think of another woman again."

Carrie heard all this, and felt very upset and confused. It sounded sincere, despite what he had done. Still, he was married, and he had deceived her twice. She did not want anything more to do with him. And yet, something about his daring and power appealed to her. Even more, she thought he was like this because he loved her so much.

The train's speeding wheels put Chicago farther and farther behind them. Carrie could feel that she was being carried a long distance away. At times, she thought about crying out and making so much fuss that someone would come to her aid. At other times, she thought it would be useless, no matter what she did.

Hurstwood kept trying to appeal to her sympathy. "I was put in a situation where I simply didn't know what else to do."

Carrie pretended not to hear.

"You said you wouldn't come unless I married you. So I decided to put everything else behind me and get you to come away with me. I'm going off now to another city. I want to go to Montreal for a while. Then we can go anywhere you want. We'll go and live in New York, if you say so."

"I don't want to have anything to do with you," said Carrie. "I want to get off this train. Where are we going?"

"To Detroit," said Hurstwood. "Won't you come along with me? You won't need to do anything except travel with me. I won't bother you in any way. You can see Montreal and New York. Then, if you don't want to stay, you can go back. It would be better than trying to go back tonight."

Carrie saw a first gleam of fairness in this offer. It did seem reasonable, although she was still afraid that Hurstwood might try to keep her from going back to Chicago. Montreal and New York! Even as they talked, they were already speeding toward those great, strange lands. She could see them if she liked. She thought it over, but did not respond.

"Think about what I've given up," Hurstwood continued. "I can't go back to Chicago anymore. I've got to stay away. And I'll have to live alone now, if you don't come with me. You won't leave me now, will you, Carrie?"

"I don't want you to talk to me," she answered, resisting his pleas.

Hurstwood kept silent for a while.

Carrie felt the train slow down. She needed to act now, if ever.

"Don't think of going, Carrie," he said. "If you ever cared for me at all, come along with me. Let's start out right. I'll do whatever you say. I'll marry you, or I'll let you go back. Give yourself time to think it over. I wouldn't have wanted you to come if I didn't love you. I tell you, Carrie, before God, I can't live without you. I won't!"

He couldn't think of giving her up in his hour of distress. He clutched her hand and pressed it in passionate desperation.

The train stopped. Everything outside was dark and dreary. A few sprinkles on the window showed that it was raining. Carrie hung between decisiveness and helplessness. She wavered, totally unable to make a move. Minute after minute slipped by. Still she hesitated. Still he pleaded.

"Will you let me go back if I want to?"

"Of course," he answered. "You know I will."

Carrie began to feel as if she were in control.

She could give Hurstwood a temporary pardon.

The train again picked up speed. Hurstwood changed the subject. "I believe we're in for a heavy rain," he said.

"So it looks," said Carrie. Her nerves were quieting under the sound of the raindrops and the gusty wind. Frantically, the train swept on through the shadow to a newer world.

"See if you can rest a little," he said tenderly, arranging his coat so that she could rest her head on it.

In spite of her distress and anger, Carrie once again was touched by his thoughtfulness.

Hurstwood sat down beside her and went back to thinking about what he had done. He was in a terrible mess. He did not want to be a thief. He didn't even want the miserable amount of money that he had stolen. No amount of money could make up for what he had done to himself. It could not give him back his friends, his reputation, his house, his family. It couldn't even give him Carrie, the way he had wanted to have her. He was shut out from Chicago—from his easy, comfortable life there. He had robbed himself of his dignity, his merry get-togethers, his pleasant evenings. And for what? The more he thought about it, the more unbearable it became. Maybe he would try and go back to the way things were. He would return the stolen money and explain. Perhaps Moy would understand. Perhaps they would forgive him and let him come back.

By noon, the train rolled into Detroit. Hurstwood was extremely nervous and afraid. The police must be on his track by now. They had probably notified the police in all the big cities, and detectives would be watching for him.

"I think we had better go right on through to Montreal," he said to Carrie. "I'll see what the connections are when we get off."

The train stopped. They stepped onto the platform. Hurstwood carefully looked all around him. No one seemed to be watching him. He went to the ticket office, bought two tickets for Montreal, and led Carrie onto the train.

"I wish I was out of all this," Carrie exclaimed gloomily, feeling tired and weary.

"You'll feel better when we reach Montreal," he said.

"I don't have an earthly thing with me," said Carrie, "not even a handkerchief."

"You can buy anything you want as soon as we get there, Dearest," he explained.

Hurstwood breathed a sigh of relief as the train started. They just had to cross the river, and then they would be out of the country. At last, they reached the other side and entered Canada. Then he settled back with a sigh.

"It won't be so very long now," he said, remembering her in his relief. "We get there first thing in the morning."

Carrie hardly bothered to reply.

Then he added, "I'll see if there is a dining car. I'm hungry."

CHAPTER 29

Drifting Toward
the Open Sea

Travel to an unfamiliar place can be fascinating and comforting. The flood of new sights and sounds takes one's mind off other issues. Carrie looked out at the scenery that flew by the train window. She almost forgot that she had been tricked into this long journey against her will. She forgot that she had nothing with her. She forgot that Hurstwood was sitting beside her. She simply wondered at the homey farmhouses and cozy cottages in the villages that they passed. It was an interesting world to her. Her life had just begun. She did not feel herself defeated at all. The great city ahead of her offered so much. Maybe she would leave all the ties that bound her and finally become free. Who knows? Perhaps she would be happy. Even if she were wrong, at least she was hopeful.

The next morning, the train pulled safely into Montreal. Hurstwood was glad to be out of danger. Carrie wondered at this unfamiliar northern city.

They went directly to a hotel. Hurstwood registered under the false name of "G.W. Murdock and wife."

Once in their room, Carrie went over to the window and looked out. Hurstwood looked at himself in the mirror. He felt dusty and unclean. He suggested that Carrie bathe and get ready for breakfast, while he went out to a barbershop.

"All right," said Carrie. She sat down in one of the rocking chairs.

"You're not mad at me, are you?" he asked softly.

"Oh, no," she answered, not caring one way or the other.

"Don't you like me at all?"

Not answering, she looked steadily toward the window.

"Don't you think you could love me at least a little?" he pleaded. He took one of her hands, which she tried to pull away. "You once said you did."

"What made you deceive me so?" asked Carrie.

"I couldn't help it," he said. "I wanted you too much."

"You didn't have any right to want me," she answered.

He knew she was right. "Well, Carrie," he answered, "it's too late now. Here I am. Won't you try and like me a little?"

She shook her head "no."

"Let me start all over again. Be my wife from today on," he pleaded, still holding her hand.

Carrie stood up and tried to step away. He put

his arm around her and held her quite close. She struggled to get away, but it was no use.

Suddenly, desire flamed up in his body.

"Let me go," said Carrie, who was folded close to him.

"Won't you love me?" he said. "Won't you be mine from now on?"

Carrie had never disliked the man. In fact, she had just been starting to give in to him, as she remembered her old affection for him. He was so handsome, so daring!

But now this feeling changed to opposition. For a moment she protested.

But then she began to feel something else. This man, who held her so close to his body, was strong. He was passionate, he loved her, and she was alone. If she did not turn to him—accept his love—where else could she go? Her resistance half dissolved in the flood of his strong feeling.

He lifted her head and looked into her eyes. She was drawn to him, as to a magnet. For the moment, she forgot all about his many sins. He pressed her closer and kissed her. She felt that it was useless to try to resist.

"Will you marry me?" she asked, forgetting that he was already married to another woman.

"This very day," he said, with complete delight.

Finally, he released his hold upon her. "You'll get ready right now?" he asked.

"Yes," she answered, eager and excited.

"I'll be back in less than an hour."

For Hurstwood, life suddenly seemed worth fighting for. His recent victory over Carrie seemed to make up for what he had endured during the last few days. Maybe running away from everything that was familiar would bring him happiness. He imagined a rainbow at the end of the storm.

As he crossed the hotel lobby, a familiar voice greeted him. Instantly his heart sank. "Why, hello, George, old man!" said the voice. "What are you doing down here?"

Hurstwood recognized Kenny, a friend from Chicago.

"Just taking care of a little private matter," he answered, hastily. This man evidently did not know about the theft. Maybe he had not read the newspapers.

He invited Hurstwood to join him for breakfast. But Hurstwood kept giving him excuses and tried to get away.

"So," said Mr. Kenny, changing the subject, "how are things out in Chicago?"

"About the same as usual," said Hurstwood, smiling pleasantly.

"Wife with you?"

"No."

"Well, we must get together later today."

"Of course," said Hurstwood, moving away. The whole conversation felt like a trial to him. Every word complicated things. He forgot his triumph with Carrie. He realized that soon the papers would report what he had done. When the other man read them, he would see Hurstwood for what he really was—a criminal. He decided that he'd better leave this hotel.

But across the lobby, another man was observing him. He had been talking with the desk clerk, but now he was watching Hurstwood closely. He was probably a private detective. What would happen now? What could a detective do? He began to worry about whether he could be forced to leave Canada. Would he have to return to face trial in the United States? Would he be arrested? Oh, what if Carrie found out! Things were getting too hot, too risky in Montreal. He began to long to be out of this city.

When Hurstwood returned to their room, Carrie looked more delightful than ever. But her coldness toward him had returned. Love was no longer blazing in her heart. He felt it, and he worried even more. He could not take her in his arms. He did not even try. Something about her would not allow it. Or at least, what had happened in the lobby made him feel that way.

"If you're ready," he said kindly, "let's go out for breakfast."

As they left the hotel, Hurstwood noticed the detective standing at the corner, observing him.

Carrie found Montreal very different from Chicago. "What is there here, anyway?" she asked, wondering why Hurstwood would want to visit this town.

"Nothing much," he replied. He was glad that she was dissatisfied, because he wanted to leave as soon as possible. "We won't stay here long. You pick out your clothes as soon as breakfast is over. We'll go to New York soon. You'll like that. It's a lot more like a city than any place outside Chicago."

He planned to slip away to New York, where it was easy to hide. He realized that Fitzgerald and Moy would probably hire detectives to watch him. They might arrest him as soon as he tried to leave Canada. What if he had to stay here for months!

Back at the hotel, he wanted to look at the morning newspapers, yet was afraid. He saw that there was only a brief article about his crime. Again he wished that he could undo it all. He had made a huge mistake. There might have been an easier way out—if only he had known.

Carrie was busy looking out the window. He came over to speak with her. But before he could, there was a knock at the door. He went to answer it.

"You're Mr. Hurstwood, are you?" said the man who had been observing them earlier.

"Yes," said Hurstwood calmly. He stepped out into the hallway and closed the door.

"Well, you know what I am here for, don't you?" said the man quietly.

"I can guess," replied Hurstwood softly.

"Well, do you intend to try and keep the money?"

"That's my business," said Hurstwood grimly.

"You can't do it, you know," said the detective,

eyeing him coolly.

"Look here, my man," said Hurstwood firmly. "You don't understand anything about this case, and I can't explain to you. Whatever I do, I'll do it without any advice from you. You'll have to excuse me," he said, trying to move down the hall, where Carrie couldn't hear them.

"Well, now, we can make a lot of trouble for you if we want to. You've registered under a false name. You're not here with your wife. And soon the newspapers will figure out where you are. You might as well be reasonable."

"What do you want to know?" asked Hurstwood.

"Whether you're going to send back that money or not."

Hurstwood paused, and then said, "I'm no fool, you know. I know just what you can and cannot do. Now, listen to me. I've made up my mind what to do. I've already written Fitzgerald and Moy, so there's nothing more to say to you. You can wait until you hear more from them."

"Well, you can't get out of Canada with the money," said the detective.

"I don't want to get out," said the ex-manager. "When I get ready to leave Canada, there'll be no reason to stop me."

At this point, Hurstwood didn't even want the money anymore. He wasn't a thief. If only he could explain to Fitzgerald and Moy, maybe things would be all right again.

When he went back to the room, Carrie asked, "Who was that?"

"A friend of mine from Chicago."

Hurstwood felt depressed and disgusted. What hurt him the most was being chased like a thief. It was unfair that all the newspapers were looking at only one side. The only thing they reported was that he had taken the money. No one cared about how and why this tragedy came about. No one knew all the complicated things that had led up to it. He was accused without being understood.

He decided to send back the money. He made good his lie to the detective and wrote to Fitzgerald and Moy. He couldn't explain everything. So he wrote them simply that he had been entertaining friends, and that his mind was clouded from alcohol. He had found the safe open and taken the money out. But then he accidentally closed the door. He very much regretted what he had done. He was sorry that he had caused them so much trouble. He would undo what he could by sending back most of the money. The rest he would pay back as soon as possible. Maybe they would forgive him. Perhaps they would even ask him back. He forgot for a moment that he had already cut himself off from his past, the way a knife rips something apart. Even if he did manage in some way to go back, the jagged line where things had been separated and rejoined would always show.

By noon, the sun had come out. Its golden

light flooded through their open windows.

Hurstwood could not keep his eyes off Carrie. She seemed the one ray of sunshine in all his troubled world. Oh, if only she would love him wholly—how happy he would be! Her love would repay him for all his sacrifices. It would show him that he had not lost everything.

"Carrie," he said, coming over to her, "will you stay with me from now on?"

She was uncertain. But she melted with sympathy as she saw the love in his eyes—love now strengthened by difficulty and worry. She could not help smiling.

"Let me be everything to you from now on," he said. "Don't make me worry anymore. I'll be true to you. We'll go to New York and get a nice apartment. I'll go into business again, and we'll be happy. Won't you be mine?"

She felt neither love nor passion. But when he was close to her, she felt some affection for him. She used to admire him greatly. But now, she just felt rather sorry for him.

"You'll stay with me, won't you?" he asked.

"Yes," she said, nodding her head.

He drew her close, placing kisses on her lips and cheeks.

"You must marry me, though," she said.

"I'll get a license today," he answered.

"How?" she asked.

"Under a new name," he answered. "I'll take a new name and live a new life. From now on I'm

'Murdock.'"

"Oh, don't take that name," said Carrie.

"Why not?" he said.

"I don't like it."

"Well, what name shall I take?" he asked.

"Oh, anything. Only don't take that."

He thought a while, still holding her in his arms. Then he said, "How would 'Wheeler' be?"

"That's all right," said Carrie.

"Well, then, 'Wheeler,'" he said. "I'll get the license this afternoon."

They were married by a Baptist minister, the first member of the clergy that they could find.

At last a response arrived from Mr. Moy. He was shocked and very sorry that Hurstwood had done this. If he returned the money, they would not press charges. But there was no hope that he could get back his old job.

Hurstwood decided to send back $9,500 and keep $1,300 for his own use. He was still afraid that he might be arrested and taken back. But no one seemed to be observing him. They left on a train that night.

Carrie still did not know about his theft or his fears. So she enjoyed entering New York the next morning. She looked out the train window and filled her mind with the wonder of the great city. The East River delighted her. It was the first she'd seen of the great Atlantic Ocean.

When they got off the train, Hurstwood hailed a cab. But a disagreeable thought flashed through his mind. For the first time in years, he needed to be careful about little expenses. He decided it would be less expensive to rent an apartment than to stay in a hotel.

"Where are the residential neighborhoods?" asked Carrie. She did not realize that families lived in the five-story buildings around her.

"Everywhere," explained Hurstwood. "There are no lawns in New York. All these buildings are houses."

"Well, then, I don't like it," said Carrie. She was beginning to have a few opinions of her own.

CHAPTER 30

Desire and Disillusion

In Chicago, there were few millionaires and well-known celebrities. The sea of people was small enough that ordinary people could still feel satisfied with what they had and could still be noticed. But in New York, there were so many extremely rich and famous people that they overshadowed people of average income and status. Here, Hurstwood was hardly noticed. He was like a common fish in a great ocean. In other words, Hurstwood was nothing.

Like other ordinary people, he walked past the magnificent houses, splendid carriages, golden shops, fine restaurants. He noticed the laughter and the disdaining looks of people who lived in luxury. He felt the atmosphere of the high and mighty all around him. And he craved it like a drug. He saw it as the one dream that he desired, and that he must achieve, no matter what. Hurstwood no longer had the illusions and burning desires of younger people. But because he no longer had youthful hope, he became even more

distressed and bitter. New York had everything
that he most respected on this earth—wealth, status, fame. To be part of that world, he would need
huge amounts of money. And here he was, cut off
from his friends, robbed of his property and even
his name, and forced to begin all over again the
battle for status and comfort.

He soon found that it wasn't enough just to
escape being arrested. To survive, he needed to act
quickly to make money. He had kept thirteen hundred dollars of the money he had taken from
Fitzgerald and Moy. But he usually spent that
much money in only two months.

First he rented an apartment on the third floor
of a five-story building. Carrie noticed that the
rooms here were smaller than the ones in Chicago.
But she liked the fact that the apartment was new.
She was pleased that she could look out the windows and see the tops of the trees in Central Park
and the broad waters of the Hudson River.

Next, Hurstwood looked into some business
opportunities that were advertised in the local
newspapers. He hoped to buy part of a successful
downtown bar. But then he found out that the
most profitable places often made illegal deals with
police officers and political bosses.

At last he found an opportunity to buy a one-
third share of a saloon on Warren Street. The
owner claimed that business was excellent.
Hurstwood thought that he might be able to
increase profits by making a few improvements

and by managing the business more carefully.

"We deal with a very good class of people," the owner told Hurstwood. "Merchants, salesmen, and professionals. It's a well-dressed class. No bums. We don't allow 'em in the place."

Hurstwood listened to the cash register ring, and he watched the customers for a while.

"It's profitable enough for two, is it?" he asked.

"You can see for yourself if you're any judge of the liquor trade," said the owner. "I have another bar down on Nassau Street. I can't tend to both of them alone. So I wouldn't mind letting someone else manage this one."

Hurstwood wondered whether he could make enough money to meet his ordinary family expenses and be comfortable. But he hadn't been able to find the kind of bar that he really wanted. Now was not the time to hesitate. So he agreed to become a partner. He then paid one thousand dollars for his share of the business, and prepared to start managing it the next day.

At first, he was delighted, and he told Carrie that he thought he had made an excellent arrangement. In time, though, he thought differently. His partner was very unpleasant, especially after he had been drinking. Hurstwood also found that it would take a long time to make friends. The customers hurried in and out, not interested in developing friendships. Celebrities did not visit this bar. And the business did not pay as well as he had thought. He would have to watch his household expenses, which he found humiliating.

In the very beginning, he liked to join Carrie for a quick dinner before going back to the bar. It was a delight to find her, late at night, after work. But then the novelty wore off.

At the end of the first month, Carrie mentioned casually, "I think I'll go buy a dress."

Hurstwood, worried about his finances, asked, "Would you mind putting it off a few days?"

"No," replied Carrie. "Why?"

She did not catch the drift of his remarks. She had never before thought of him as having any money troubles.

"Well, I'll tell you," said Hurstwood. "This investment of mine is taking a lot of money just now. I expect to get it all back soon. But right now I'm a little short of cash."

"Oh!" answered Carrie. "Why, certainly, Dear. Why didn't you tell me before?"

"It wasn't necessary," said Hurstwood.

Something about the way he said this made Carrie just a little suspicious. It reminded her of the way Drouet always talked about being on the verge of making money on his little deal. It made her think about Hurstwood in a different way. She noticed that he dressed as nicely as usual. But he was still wearing the same clothes that he had brought to Canada. He did not suggest that they go out to dinner or the theater. He seemed concerned about his business. This was not the easygoing Hurstwood of Chicago—not the generous, luxurious Hurstwood she had known. She felt that something had changed. He was secretive, and he did not seem to trust her or share his feelings with her. She found herself asking him questions about little things. If she had loved him, she might have believed his answers. But since she did not, she came to her own unpleasant conclusions.

As for Hurstwood, he was fighting to overcome the difficulties of his changed situation. Hour after hour, and day after day, he compared what he had now with what he used to have. He was afraid that he might run into old friends. He realized that no one who had known him in Chicago would even think of visiting him now. These things had an impact on his good nature. His one hope was that things would change for the better as far as money was concerned. And at least he still had Carrie. He was gradually paying for his furniture. He was keeping his job. For now, Carrie would have to make do with the few things he could give her. He thought that he could keep up appearances until he made more money.

But he did not take into account what Carrie might want or think. She was young. She did not always share his mood.

Married life can occasionally be difficult, no matter how much people have in common. Sometimes, feelings clash. Even in loving families, little things can come out at such times. Afterward, it takes great love to erase what has been said. Without such love, the little problems grow.

CHAPTER 31

Seeing and Being Seen

Carrie, despite her initial disappointment, soon became fascinated by the city. For the first time in her life, she felt settled and socially acceptable. She had new furniture, a maid, and a piano, which she said she would like to learn to play. Her thoughts were merry and innocent. She could hear the wonderful sounds of ships' whistles from the harbor and the long, low cries of ferryboats in the fog. They were like messages from the marvelous sea. Carrie also wondered how ten families could live in the same apartment building without even knowing or caring about each other. Looking through her windows at the city and the river beyond kept her entertained for more than a year.

Hurstwood never told her about his difficulties. He continued to look self-confident, and he was attentive to her. Each evening, he arrived promptly to dinner. He enjoyed watching Carrie develop her cooking and homemaking skills. During the winter, it made sense to stay indoors. So they never talked about going out to the theater. Hurstwood pretended that he was reinvesting his money in order to develop his business. He spent little money on his own clothing. He did not often suggest that Carrie buy anything for herself.

Carrie accepted the situation, since she tended to be passive and receptive. Once in a while they would go to the theater together, but they never got to know anyone. Naturally, Hurstwood stopped treating Carrie with the fine, formal manners he used when he was first pursuing her. They had no misunderstandings or arguments. Since they had no money or social life, there was no reason for jealousy.

But after the first year, Hurstwood's business began to bring in a little more money. He started allowing himself to buy more clothes. He began to develop friendships through his work. He felt that occasionally he could stay away from home to have dinner with his new friends. The first time he did this, he sent a message saying that he would be home late. Carrie ate alone, and wished that it might not happen again.

When Hurstwood finally got home, Carrie asked, "Where were you, George?"

"Tied up at the office," he said pleasantly. "There were some accounts I had to straighten out."

"I'm sorry you couldn't get home," she said kindly. "I was planning to prepare such a nice dinner for you."

The second time, he also sent Carrie a message. But this time he waited until the last moment to send it.

The third time he completely forgot to tell Carrie. When he came in later that evening, Hurstwood explained, "I couldn't get home. I was so busy."

"Couldn't you have sent me word?" asked Carrie.

"I meant to," he said, "but I forgot it until it was too late to do any good."

"And I had such a good dinner!" said Carrie. But she was beginning to draw her own conclusions about what was going on.

Hurstwood drew different conclusions. He imagined that Carrie was content with her life as a homemaker. He thought that she was happy channeling her energies into household duties. And so he offered her only what he thought would make her happy—furniture, food, some necessary clothing. He stopped thinking about entertaining her, about taking her out into the shiny life of the city. Though he felt attracted to the world outside the home, he did not think that she would want to go along. Once he went to the theater alone. Another evening he joined a couple of his new friends in a game of poker.

Carrie began to sense that Hurstwood had changed somewhat. She was not at all jealous, because she didn't love him enough to be jealous. She understood that Hurstwood would want to go places and spend time with friends. She just didn't want to be neglected herself.

During their second year on Seventy-Eighth

Street, a very attractive twenty-three-year-old woman and her husband moved into the apartment across the hall. They seemed to be refined and fairly wealthy. Carrie felt that she might enjoy developing a friendship with them.

One morning Carrie came face-to-face with the young woman. She instantly liked her pretty and good-natured manner. The neighbor admired Carrie's innocent face.

That morning at the breakfast table, Carrie said to Hurstwood, "Someone over there plays the piano beautifully."

"Who is she?" asked Hurstwood.

"I don't know," said Carrie. "The name on the doorbell is Vance."

"Well, you never can tell what sort of people you're living next to in this town, can you?" cautioned Hurstwood.

"Just think," said Carrie. "I have been in this house with nine other families for over a year, and I don't know a soul."

"It's just as well," said Hurstwood. "You never know who you're going to get in with. Some of these people are pretty bad characters."

"I suppose so," said Carrie, agreeably.

Carrie and Mrs. Vance occasionally ran into each other in the halls. Eventually, they started to visit each other. Both apartments were nicely furnished. But the Vances' apartment was somewhat more luxurious.

One day, Mrs. Vance said to Carrie, "I want

you to come over this evening and meet my husband. He wants to meet you. You play cards, don't you?"

"A little," said Carrie.

"Well, we'll have a game of cards. If your husband is home, bring him over."

"He's not coming to dinner tonight," said Carrie.

"Well, when he does come in, we'll call him over."

That evening, Carrie met Mrs. Vance's husband, a large man who was a few years younger than Hurstwood. He wasn't very good-looking. But he kept his wife happy because he had money. He liked Carrie at first glance, and he was pleasant to her.

At last Hurstwood arrived.

"I am very glad to meet you," he said to Mrs. Vance. He showed the same grace and charm that appealed to Carrie when they first met. But it had been a long time since he had been so flattering and attentive to Carrie. She missed it, even though she did not realize it.

"Did you think your wife had run away?" said Mr. Vance, joking pleasantly with Hurstwood as he shook his hand.

"I was beginning to wonder whether she had found a better husband," responded Hurstwood.

As Hurstwood turned his attention to Mrs. Vance, Carrie compared herself to her new friend. She realized that she was not well dressed—at least, not nearly as well dressed as Mrs. Vance. She felt that her life was becoming stale. Her old sadness and longing returned. The possibilities that she was missing seemed almost to whisper to her. Her desires urged her to do something more with her life.

Hurstwood did not notice the shade of sadness which had settled in Carrie's eyes. He was not even aware that he himself had changed. And Carrie was so passive that she did not take action immediately. But she did find ways of placing herself in useful situations. That way, she could simply let the tide of change carry her along.

"Let's go to the theater this afternoon," Mrs. Vance suggested to Carrie one morning. Hurstwood and Vance had already gone their separate ways.

"All right," said Carrie. She noticed that Mrs. Vance seemed pampered and well-groomed. Her husband must love her dearly and grant her every wish. "When should we leave?"

"Let's go right away and walk down Broadway from Thirty-Fourth Street," said Mrs. Vance. "It's such an interesting walk."

"I'll be glad to go," said Carrie. "How much will we have to pay for seats?"

"Not more than a dollar," said Mrs. Vance.

At one o'clock, Mrs. Vance reappeared. She was dressed in a stunning outfit. She owned so many dainty things that Carrie didn't have—gold jewelry, an elegant green leather purse with her initials on it, a beautifully designed scarf. Carrie felt that she needed more and better clothes to keep up with this woman. She thought that people would look at Mrs. Vance instead of her simply because she had fancier clothing. And yet, Carrie herself had become quite attractive. She wore stylish clothing that was almost as fashionable as her friend's. But Carrie didn't see things that way. And so she became even more dissatisfied with her situation.

Before and after the matinee shows, Broadway was a showy parade. Women appeared in their very best hats, shoes, and gloves. They strolled down Broadway on their way to the fine shops and theaters. Men, too, paraded in the finest suits, shoes, and hats that they could afford. And they loved to watch and admire the women who walked by.

As they stepped along Broadway, Carrie noticed that Mrs. Vance stiffened as handsome men and elegantly dressed ladies glanced at her. It seemed proper and natural to stare at the beautiful people who swarmed by them. Men with perfect topcoats, high hats, and silver-headed walking sticks elbowed near. They stared at Carrie and looked her over admiringly. Ladies rustled by with their stiff, elegant dresses, fake smiles, and expensive perfume. Some of them wore heavy makeup, perfumed their hair, and looked at the men with large, misty, dreamy eyes.

Suddenly Carrie awoke to find herself on parade in a showplace. And what a showplace! Jewelry store windows gleamed everywhere. There were flower shops, fur stores, clothing stores, candy shops—one after the other. Fancy carriages waited for wealthy women to finish shopping in expensive showrooms. The whole street seemed so rich and showy. But Carrie felt that she was not part of it. She longed to look as beautiful, fashionable, and self-assured as Mrs. Vance. She imagined that other people noticed that she was less well dressed than her friend. It cut her to the quick. So she resolved that she would not come back here again until she looked better. If only she could feel the delight of parading here as an equal to these stylish people. Ah, then she would be happy!

CHAPTER 32

Sights and Insights

Whenever Carrie watched a play, she longed to be part of the scenes. She imagined how she would feel if she experienced in her life what the characters experienced onstage. Afterward, she would sit in her rocking chair and think about her one success onstage in Chicago. She lived as much in her thoughts about acting as she did in the realities of daily life.

Today the stroll down Broadway made her long for the pleasures and beauty that passed her by. It was as if a quiet song of longing had been set singing in her heart. Who were these hundreds and hundreds of rich, beautiful women? Where did they find such elegant dresses, wonderful fabrics, silver and gold jewelry? What kinds of carved furniture, decorated walls, elaborate draperies filled their mansions? She ached, knowing that she was not one of them. She, too, had dreamed a dream, but hers had not come true. How lonely she had been these past two years—and how unaware until now that she had not yet achieved what she had expected.

Carrie thought the play she saw that day was

extraordinarily beautiful. The characters were charming ladies and wealthy gentleman. They suffered the pain of love and jealousy in golden settings—in overstuffed chairs, surrounded by maids and butlers in uniforms. Grief and suffering can seem almost appealing under such ideal conditions. Carrie longed to be part of this world—to suffer in that world, rather than in her own. And if she couldn't really live in that world, at least she could act that way on the stage. She became lost in the world that she was watching onstage, and wished that she never had to return to her own.

After the play, the sights of Broadway convinced her that New York held other possibilities for her. Here was a world of pleasure and delight that she had never before imagined. Women were spending money as if they were pouring out water. Money flowed in every elegant shop that she passed. Flowers. Candy. Jewelry. She would not have really lived until she, too, could possess all this. And yet, she hardly had enough money to see a show once or twice a month. These thoughts kept coming back to Carrie. And like solid stone that is worn away by drops of water, eventually Carrie would have to give in.

That night, her pretty, cozy apartment suddenly seemed small and dull. Everyone else in the world enjoyed more luxuries than she. In her mind, Carrie kept seeing scenes from the play. She remembered one of the actresses, and could almost feel her grief. She, too, could act appealingly. There were places where she could have acted even better. Oh, if only she could have such a part, her life would be so much richer!

When Hurstwood came home, Carrie was sitting, rocking and thinking. She did not want to have anything interrupt her daydreams. So she said very little to him.

A few weeks later, Mrs. Vance invited Carrie to go to dinner and the theater with her and her husband. That evening, Carrie carefully put on her best outfit. She had been listening to Mrs. Vance's advice about fashions. Hurstwood had noticed that Carrie wanted more and more fine clothing. He didn't say anything to her about it yet. But because he was worried about money, he was not enthusiastic about her purchases, either. Since Hurstwood didn't compliment her on her new clothes, Carrie thought that he wasn't paying enough attention to her.

When Carrie arrived at the Vances' apartment, Mr. Vance seemed surprised that her husband wasn't with her.

"Better leave a little note for him, telling him where we are. He might turn up."

"I will," said Carrie, who had not thought of it before.

Then a strong, good-looking, clean-cut young man arrived.

"Mrs. Wheeler, let me introduce Mr. Ames, a cousin of mine," said Mrs. Vance. "You're going along with us, aren't you, Bob?"

"I'm very glad to meet you," said Ames, bowing politely to Carrie.

"Mr. Ames is in New York for a few days," explained Vance. "We're trying to show him around a little."

"Oh, are you?" said Carrie, taking another glance at the well-dressed young man.

"Yes. I've come in from Indianapolis for a week or so."

"I guess you find New York quite wonderful to see, don't you?" said Carrie.

He was extremely pleasant and without any pretensions. Carrie felt that it would be easy to talk to him.

"Come on, people," said Mrs. Vance, smiling. "Bob, you'll have to look after Mrs. Wheeler."

"I'll try to," said Bob, smiling shyly and edging closer to Carrie.

On the way to the restaurant, Ames sat next to Carrie. He felt that it was his duty to pay some attention to her. He thought that Carrie seemed too young and pretty to be married already. But he respected the fact that Carrie was married. Besides, he was interested in a pretty, unmarried young woman in Indianapolis.

"Were you born in New York?" Ames asked Carrie.

"Oh, no. I've only been here for two years."

"Oh, well, you've had time to see a great deal of it, anyhow."

"I don't seem to have," answered Carrie. "I

don't know much more about it than when I first came here."

"You're not from the West, are you?"

"Yes. I'm from Wisconsin," she answered.

"Well, it does seem as if most people in this town haven't been here so very long."

"What do you do for a living?" asked Carrie.

"I'm connected with an electrical company," said the youth.

When they reached Fifth Avenue, they stopped in front of a luxurious hotel, which was blazing with lights. There they entered the lavish restaurant. In all of Carrie's experience, she had never seen anything like this. Only the very wealthy could afford to dine here. In the past, Hurstwood would have come often to such a place. But he no longer had enough money to take Carrie out to dinner anywhere. Carrie had read in the newspapers about the dances, parties, and dinners that rich and famous people gave at this restaurant. Now, at last, she had really entered it. Here was the splendid dining room, all decorated and aglow, where the wealthy ate. The polished tables were shining, the glasses caught the light from the brilliant chandeliers, and the gold trim glowed on the walls. The ladies wore diamonds, jewels, and fine feathers. The tall mirrors reflected it all, a hundred times. Ah, how fortunate was Mrs. Vance—so young, beautiful, and well-off. What a wonderful thing it was to be rich!

Once seated, Carrie looked at the elegant

menu. There were dozens of dishes to choose from—all at ridiculously high prices. She was reminded of another menu, on a far different occasion—the first time that she sat with Drouet in a good restaurant in Chicago. It was like hearing a sad note from an old song. She recalled that other Carrie—poor, hungry, drifting, hopeless, wandering because she could not find work. And all Chicago was a cold and closed world. All this came back to her in a flash. And then it was gone.

Carrie looked around her in awe. So this was how rich people spent every day and evening of their lives. It must be like this everywhere. And she was not a part of any of it. In two long years, she had never even been in such a place as this.

Finally, Ames said to Carrie, "I sometimes think it is a shame for people to spend so much money this way."

Carrie was surprised by his seriousness. He seemed to be thinking about something that had never occurred to her. Interested, she answered, "Do you?"

"Yes," he said gently. "They pay so much more than these things are worth. They put on such a show."

"I don't know why people shouldn't spend money when they have it," said Mrs. Vance.

"It doesn't do any harm," added Vance.

Carrie wondered what other things Ames thought were right and wrong. She felt that she might approve of his ideas, even though she didn't understand them.

Turning to Carrie, Ames observed, "Look at that woman's dress over there."

"Where?" asked Carrie.

"Over there in the corner. Do you see that pin?"

"Isn't it large?" said Carrie.

"One of the largest clusters of jewels I have ever seen," said Ames.

Carrie felt that he was better educated than she—and that his mind was better and brighter. With his clear, innocent, natural look, this strong young man seemed far ahead of her. He seemed wiser than Hurstwood, brighter and more serious than Drouet. She felt the pain of not understanding things that he could grasp. And she felt that she wanted him to like her. But she was not a part of his life or the things that interested him.

The abundant food helped Ames express his ideas more strongly. "I wouldn't want to be rich," Ames told Carrie, later in the meal. "At least, not rich enough to spend my money this way."

"Oh, wouldn't you?" said Carrie.

"No," he said. "What good would it do? A man doesn't need this sort of thing to be happy."

Carrie had her doubts about this. But she thought about it, since the idea came from him. He was probably so strong that he didn't need anybody or anything to make him happy. There was something about him and his world that appealed to Carrie. He reminded her of the sorrows and sacrifices that she had seen in plays, but hadn't fully understood. He didn't care about being wealthy. And that made her feel less bitter about not being able to live in this world of luxury.

Later, during the show, Carrie asked Ames, "Don't you think it would be wonderful to be an actor?"

Ames answered, "Yes, at least to be a good actor. I think that the theater is a great thing."

This little approval made Carrie's heart start pounding. Ah, if only she could be an actress—a good one! This man was wise. He knew. And he approved of it. If she were a fine actress, men like Ames would approve of her.

After the show, it became clear that he was not going back to the Vances' apartment with them. Somehow, Carrie felt surprised—and disappointed. She didn't know whether she would ever see this man again. But what difference did it make? What difference could it make?

Hurstwood had gotten home before her and was already in bed. His clothes were scattered carelessly around the room. It seemed so unpleasant to her. Carrie came to the door, but then walked away. She did not want to go in yet. She wanted to think about everything she had seen and heard and felt this evening.

Back in the dining room, Carrie sat in her chair and rocked. She was beginning to see through a fog of longing and conflicting desires. She felt so much hope and pity, sorrow and pain. She was rocking, back and forth, and beginning to see.

CHAPTER 33

Moving Out

Ames moved out West, so Carrie did not see him anymore. But she kept thinking about him. And she saw the contrast between this man, who seemed ideal, and all other men—especially those men who were close to her.

As for Hurstwood, he constantly compared his old situation with his current one. In Chicago his career had been moving upward. But now the tide had turned. His money, his work, and his physical health were all changing for the worse. He spent his time thinking, thinking, thinking. He was becoming depressed. He read in the newspapers about the rich and famous people that he used to entertain in Chicago. But his new friends were neither rich nor famous. Gradually he lost his desire to welcome the people who stopped by his bar. After two years, his attitude began to affect his work. Business started to drop off. This irritated and worried him even more.

Hurstwood began to realize all the things that he had left behind in Chicago. His situation had not seemed so wonderful at the time. Then it seemed easy to be part of the center of money and social life. Now it seemed like a city with a wall around it. You could not get in. The people inside didn't care who you were. They were having so much fun that they didn't even notice the people who were locked out. Now he was on the outside.

One night Carrie mentioned a few little things that she wanted to buy. In response, Hurstwood confessed to her that the business was not doing as well as it had been before. For the first time, she suspected that he was trying to trick her. After all, he bought clothes for himself without consulting her. Maybe he was trying to keep her from spending money on herself. She didn't say anything. But she felt resentful. He was not paying attention to things that were important to her. She had to depend on the Vances for all her pleasures.

And then the Vances announced that they were moving out of the building. They were going away for the summer. When they returned, they were going to rent a fancier apartment downtown.

Carrie was genuinely sad. She had enjoyed spending time with Mrs. Vance. She didn't have any other friends. Again, she would be all alone. She became restless and dissatisfied—not exactly with Hurstwood, but with life. What did she have? Nothing except this little apartment. The Vances could travel and do the things worth doing. But here she was, bored with her life. What was the point of it all? What was she made to do in this life?

Hurstwood kept thinking about ways to increase his income and to reduce Carrie's desire to buy clothes. Finally one night he said to Carrie, "I don't think I'll ever be able to get anywhere working where I am now."

"What's the matter?" asked Carrie.

"Oh, my partner's stupid and greedy. He won't agree to spend any money on fixing up the bar. But the business won't ever make money unless we make some improvements."

"Can't you make him?" said Carrie.

"No. I've tried. I can see only one way to make more money. And that's to get a bar of my own."

"Why don't you?" said Carrie.

"Well, all my money is tied up right now in the old place. If I could save some money for a while, I think I would soon have enough to buy another bar. Then I'd have a place that would give us plenty of money."

"Can't we save?" asked Carrie.

"We could try," suggested Hurstwood. "I was thinking that we could move into a smaller apartment and spend less money for a year. I could add in the money I've invested in the old place. That would give me enough money to open a good bar. Then we could live any way you want."

"That would be all right with me," said Carrie. But even so, she felt bad to think that things had come to this. Moving to a smaller apartment made it sound as if they were poor.

Carrie began to see Hurstwood as a silent,

gloomy old man, rather than as a strong, carefree young man. She felt that she was tied to him as his wife. She would share whatever happened to him. But she began to feel that she had made a mistake. And she also remembered that he had practically forced her to run away with him.

Carrie was unhappy about the move. The new neighborhood did not appeal to her. There were no views of the river. The people here were poorer. Their apartment was smaller. She no longer had a maid.

Hurstwood was not pleased, either, about having to change their lifestyle. But he thought that there was nothing else he could do. He tried to point out positive things about the move. He told Carrie that after a year he would be able to take her out more often to dinner and the theater. This change was for a short time only. But he started focusing more and more just on survival. He wanted to be alone with his newspapers and his own thoughts. His love for Carrie no longer brought him pleasure.

Hurstwood's gloomy attitude bothered his business partner, as well. He wanted to get Hurstwood out of the business. One day he told Hurstwood that they were going to lose their lease soon. What would become of the saloon?

"Do you think it would be worthwhile to open up a bar somewhere else in the neighborhood?" Hurstwood asked.

"What would be the use?" replied his partner.

"We couldn't get another corner property around here."

"Do you think we could make money somewhere else?" asked Hurstwood.

"I wouldn't try it," his partner responded.

But closing the bar meant that Hurstwood would lose his thousand-dollar investment in the business. He could never save another thousand dollars in time to buy another bar. He realized that his partner just wanted to end their relationship, and would soon open another bar by himself. He saw that he would be in serious financial difficulty unless something else turned up. He looked around for other opportunities, but he found nothing. He no longer had thirteen hundred dollars to buy part of a business. He was so depressed that he made a bad impression on other people.

A month later, his partner said to Hurstwood, pretending to be concerned, "So, I guess this is the end."

"Well, if it is, it is," answered Hurstwood, without expression. He would not give his partner the satisfaction of knowing how worried he was.

Now Hurstwood saw that he needed to say something to Carrie.

"You know," he said, "my investment in the saloon has turned out to be a terrible deal."

"How is that?" asked Carrie in astonishment.

"Well, we've lost our lease. The business may come to an end."

"Can't you start somewhere else?"

"There doesn't seem to be another place. And my partner doesn't want to move somewhere else."

"Do you lose all the money that you put in?"

"Yes," said Hurstwood, trying not to show his feelings.

"Oh, isn't that wrong?" said Carrie.

"It's just a trick," said Hurstwood. "After a while, they'll open another place there, all right."

Carrie looked at him. She could tell from the way he looked what it meant. It was serious, very serious.

"Do you think you can get another business?" she asked, timidly.

Hurstwood thought a while. There was no use in pretending anymore about having money and investments.

Carrie could see now that he had nothing. He was broke.

"I don't know," he said solemnly. "I can try."

░ CHAPTER 34 ░

The Costs of Living

It took Carrie several days to realize fully that losing the business meant that they would be struggling just to survive. Her thoughts went back to her early days in Chicago, the Hansons and their apartment, her attempt to find work. Her heart protested. It was terrible! Everything about poverty was terrible. She wished she knew a way out. Her recent experiences with the Vances' glamorous lifestyle made it impossible to accept her current situation. She had been taught how to dress and what to do. But she did not have enough money to do either. Poverty threatened to seize her and take from her the world of wealth.

Ames, too, had gone. But the ideals he had brought into her life remained. He had said that riches were not everything. That there was much more in the world than she knew. That the stage was good. He was a strong man and true. She could hardly bear to compare him to Hurstwood and Drouet.

During his last days at the saloon, Hurstwood took some time off and hunted for work. If he didn't find something soon, he would have to start spending the little money he had saved. And then he would have nothing to reinvest in a business of his own. He would have to get a job working for someone else. It was depressing.

He tracked down business opportunities that advertised in the newspapers. But everything he found in his line of work was either too expensive or too unappealing. He read about other people's worries—a failed business, a starving family, a man dying of starvation out on the streets. One day he read the headline: "80,000 People Out of Employment in New York This Winter."

"Eighty thousand!" he thought. "What an awful thing that is."

For the first time in his life, he understood and felt other people's hardship. These articles darkened his mood, like gray clouds gathering on a clear day. He tried to shake them off, to forget about these troubles and keep going. Sometimes he would try to reassure himself by thinking, "What's the use of worrying? I'm not out of work yet. I've still got six weeks more at the bar. Even if worst comes to worst, I've got enough money saved up to live on for six months."

Occasionally as he worried about his future, his thoughts turned back to his past—to his wife and family. For three years he had avoided thinking about Julia. He hated her, and he could get along without her. Let her go. He would be fine. But now that he was not doing so well, he began to wonder what she was doing and how his children were getting along. In his mind he could see them living comfortably in his nice house and spending everything he had earned.

"By golly! It's wrong that they should have it all," he thought.

The only way he could live with himself was to try to justify what he had done. After all, what had he done that was so bad? Why should he be shut out this way and have all these problems piled up on him? It seemed only yesterday that he was comfortable and wealthy. But now everything had been taken from him.

Looking back on the situation that led up to the theft, he thought, "She didn't deserve what she got out of me, that's for sure. I didn't do anything all that bad, if people only knew."

One afternoon he stopped at a business that was advertised in the paper. But it was such a cheap-looking bar that he couldn't even bear to go inside.

Then he looked at another saloon that was in much better condition. He talked with the owner for almost an hour. Finally, Hurstwood asked, "Well, now, just how much money would it take to buy half the business?" He had in mind a limit of seven hundred dollars.

"Three thousand," answered the man.

Hurstwood's jaw fell. "Cash?" he said, shocked.

"Cash."

He pretended to need time to think it over and hurried away.

The afternoon was gray and cold. A bitter winter wind was blowing. Totally depressed, he came home early. Carrie was getting ready to start dinner. He struck a match and lit the gas for the stove. It was the first time that he had helped with the household chores. But it seemed to justify his being at home, rather than at work. Then he sat down and started reading the evening newspaper.

Carrie saw that he was in bad shape. The lines on his face were deeper. His gloomy expression made him look unpleasant, almost threatening.

Carrie called him when the dinner was ready.

He did not answer, but just kept on reading.

"Won't you eat now?" she asked, feeling miserable herself.

He picked at his food, saying nothing.

"It's been gloomy today, hasn't it?" Carrie said, trying to get him to talk.

"Yes," he said.

"You're still sure that you'll have to close the bar?" Carrie asked.

"Of course we are," he answered, with a sharp edge to his voice.

"Well, you don't need to talk to me like that," Carrie responded angrily.

He thought about saying more, but let it go at that. Instead, he picked up his paper.

Carrie stood up from the table, barely containing her anger.

Hurstwood saw that she was hurt. "Don't go away like that. Sit back down and finish your dinner."

She left the room without answering.

He looked at the paper for a few moments. Then he got up and put on his coat.

"I'm going downtown, Carrie," he said. "I'm in a bad mood tonight."

She did not answer.

"Don't be angry," he said. "It will be all right tomorrow."

He looked at her. But she paid no attention to him, and continued washing her dishes.

"Goodbye!" he said finally, and went out.

As the last day of business approached, Hurstwood could no longer hide his feelings. And Carrie began to wonder where she was drifting. They talked even less than usual. Hurstwood didn't dislike Carrie. He just found it almost impossible to have a friendly conversation with her, or anyone. But Carrie became less and less interested in him. She was beginning to avoid him. Hurstwood noticed this, and it made it even harder for him to approach her.

At last the final day came. The sun shone. Hurstwood felt relieved. It was as if a load were about to be taken off his back. Maybe things weren't as terrible as they seemed, after all. He joked with Carrie, "Well, today's my last day on earth."

Carrie smiled at his humor.

"I'll finish up things at the bar," he said after

breakfast. "Then I'll start looking around. Tomorrow I'll spend the whole day looking for a job. I think I can get something, now that I have this other business off my hands."

He had disliked many things about the bar. But now that it was closing, he felt sad. He wished that things had been different.

Carrie prepared a nice dinner for him. But when he came home, Hurstwood was in a serious and thoughtful mood.

"Well?" asked Carrie, curious.

"I'm out of that," he answered, taking off his coat.

She looked at him and wondered what his financial situation was now.

"Will you have enough money to buy into another business?" asked Carrie.

"No," he said. "I'll have to get a job and save up."

"It would be nice if you could get another saloon," said Carrie, feeling both anxious and hopeful.

"I guess I'll be able to," he said, thinking it over.

For the next few days, he went out looking for an investment opportunity. Finally he realized that he would not have enough money to buy a share of a business, fix up a new place, and still have enough to live on. When he thought about it clearly, he knew that he needed to find other work now. Then he could save up enough money to invest in a business later on.

But what was it that he wanted to do? Manage a place? He didn't have enough money to buy his way into a bar. And he couldn't use his connections to find a position. Anyone he knew from Chicago would know what had happened out there. He didn't have any experience working in any other kind of business.

Besides, how would he go about getting a job? He couldn't bear to think about having to go up to an employer, wait outside the office door, and announce that he was looking for work. His clothing was still good, and people assumed that he was wealthy, not unemployed. At forty-three, he was no longer young. He wasn't used to exercise, and walking wasn't easy. His legs were tired, his shoulders ached, and his feet hurt from going all over the city looking for work.

He stepped into a hotel lobby to shield himself from the cold and weariness of walking the streets. He used to look down on people who sat around in hotel lobbies because they had no place else to go. But here he was, even though he might meet someone who knew him. To think that he had come to this!

"I can't go on like this," he said to himself. "I need to think of some place I might find work and then go apply for a job."

It occurred to him that he might be able to find a job as a bartender. But then he decided against the idea. Just a bartender—he, the ex-manager!

It became boring just to sit in the hotel lobby.

So at four o'clock he went home. He tried to look businesslike as he went into the apartment. But he was glad to sink into a rocking chair and read the newspaper.

As she prepared dinner, Carrie mentioned to him, "The man was here today to collect the rent."

"Oh, was he?" said Hurstwood.

He frowned as he remembered that this was the day that the rent was due. He fished down into his pocket for his wallet. This was the first time that he had to pay out when no money was coming in. He looked at the fat, green roll of dollar bills. He was like a sick man, looking at the one thing that might save his life. Then he counted out the money and gave it to Carrie.

He buried himself in his newspaper and read. What a relief it was not to be walking and thinking. The news stories took his mind off his troubles, at least a little. Here was a young, attractive woman suing her rich, fat, candy-making husband for divorce. Here was another item about a ship that wrecked itself in the ice and snow. A long, bright column told about all the goings-on in the world of the theater—the shows, the actors, the managers. He read about millionaires leaving early for their winter vacations or their hunting trips. And so he read, read, read—rocking near the warm radiator and waiting for dinner to be served.

CHAPTER 35

Cold Reality

The next morning Hurstwood waded through the help wanted ads in the newspapers. He had the whole day in front of him—a long day for him to discover something. He looked over ads for bakers, cooks, tailors, drivers. Only two things caught his eye—a salesman for a whiskey distributor and a cashier for a wholesale furniture store.

He decided to follow up the first ad right away. Because he was so well dressed, the manager greeted him warmly. He thought that Hurstwood must be one of his out-of-town customers.

Then Hurstwood said, "You advertised for a salesman?"

"Oh," the man answered with surprise. "Yes. Yes, I did."

"I thought I'd drop in," said Hurstwood, with dignity. "I've had some experience in that field."

"Oh, have you?" said the man.

"Well, yes. I've managed several liquor establishments in my time. Recently I was part-owner of a saloon at Warren and Hudson Streets."

"I see," said the man. "We did want a sales-man. But I don't think you'd really be interested in the job."

"I see," said Hurstwood. "Well, I'm not in a position to choose my work right now. If the job's available, I'd be happy to take it."

The man wanted someone young, active, and glad to work hard for little money. He did not like Hurstwood at all. He was an old man. And he seemed to think that he was better than his employer.

Finally the man said, "We'd be glad to consider your application. Why don't you send us references from your last few employers?"

"I will," said Hurstwood. But he knew that he could not.

Then he left and looked at the furniture store. It was small. The men inside were not busy. Probably they were not well paid. Maybe they were really looking for a woman. He walked by the store, glanced at it, and then decided not to go in.

Hurstwood was tired. The sky was gray, and the wind was blowing cold. He decided to go into a hotel lobby and sit for a while. Inside, it was warm and bright. He probably would not run into anyone he knew. He sank into one of the plush sofas in front of the large windows. He looked out onto Broadway and sat, thinking. Things didn't seem so bad in here. He still had a few hundred dollars in his wallet.

But he had escaped the weariness of the streets only to enter the boredom of the hotel lobby. The minutes seemed to go very slowly. He watched the hotel guests and the people passing by on Broadway. He saw how happy all the young men seemed, how pretty the women looked. They all wore such fine clothes. They all seemed to be focused on going somewhere.

It was still a little early, but he decided to go back to the apartment. At least there he was on his own property. He could sit in his rocking chair and read his newspapers. He could shut out this busy, exciting scene.

When he got home, he felt that he needed to pretend to be making some progress.

"I've been talking with a wholesale liquor company," he said to Carrie. "I may have to do some traveling."

"Wouldn't that be nice!" said Carrie with enthusiasm.

"It wouldn't be such a bad thing," he answered.

Then he lit the gas, and sat down near the radiator. When he read the newspaper, his troubles seemed to disappear.

But the next day was even worse. Now he couldn't even think of where to go. None of the ads in the paper appealed to him.

Carrie reminded him that she needed her weekly allowance to pay for the household expenses. He sighed as he pulled out his wallet. He dreaded this paying out, paying out, with nothing coming in. He knew it couldn't go on like this forever.

Although he said nothing, Carrie felt that he was upset. She wondered if soon he might find it distressing to pay her.

"But it's not my fault," she thought to herself. "Why should I be made to worry?"

Finally Hurstwood went out. When he reached the Grand Hotel on Broadway, he was cold and tired. He went into their barbershop in order to justify his sitting inside the hotel.

With nothing to do, he went home again early. He continued this routine for several days. Each day, he felt the pain of needing to hunt for a job. Each day, disgust, depression, and shame drove him into a hotel lobby to sit and rest.

Late one afternoon, the snow began to fall. The next morning it was still coming down, the wind had increased, and the newspapers announced a blizzard.

"I guess I won't try to go out today," he said to Carrie at breakfast. "It's going to be awful bad, so the papers say."

All day and all night it snowed. Hurstwood sat and read by his radiator in the corner. He made himself comfortable and warmed his feet. The storm made him feel that he didn't need to look for work.

Carrie observed how comfortable he seemed. But she doubted that he was as contented as he pretended to be.

Hurstwood, however, read on and on. He did not pay much attention to Carrie. She did her household chores and said little to disturb him.

The next day it was still snowing. The day after it was bitter cold. Instead of going out to look for work, Hurstwood offered to run some errands for Carrie. It made him feel as if he weren't totally useless.

On the fourth day, the sky had cleared, but the streets were sloppy from the snow. He put off leaving the house until noon. Finally he went to look at a saloon that had been advertised in the paper. But by the time he reached the Broadway Central Hotel, he had changed his mind.

"What's the use?" he thought, looking at the slop and snow. "I don't have enough money to buy a part of the saloon. It's a thousand to one that nothing will come of it."

So instead of going further, he went into the hotel lobby. He sat down inside and waited again, wondering what he could do.

A well-dressed man entered the lobby. He recognized a familiar face and came over to greet him. When he realized it was Hurstwood, he wished he could have avoided him. But it was too late.

"Why, hello, Cargill," said Hurstwood, ashamed to be seen by someone who knew him from Chicago. "How are you?"

"Very well," replied Cargill, trying to find something to talk about. "You're doing well, I suppose?"

"Excellent," Hurstwood answered.

"Glad to hear it."

They looked at each other, both rather embarrassed.

"Well, I need to go meet a friend upstairs," Cargill said abruptly. "So I'll leave you. Goodbye!"

Hurstwood nodded. Humiliated, he then left the lobby. He tried to think of some place to go or something to do. The weather was so bad that he wanted only to be inside. He felt as if he were catching a cold. This was no day to be out. Even though it was still early, he would just go home.

That night he had a fever. The next day, he sat around helplessly while Carrie waited on him. Carrie noticed that his hair was uncombed, and he looked old and worn-out. Carrie wanted to be good-natured and sympathetic. But something about the man put her off.

"You'd better sleep alone tonight," she said. "You'll feel better."

"All right," he said.

He sat hunched up near the radiator, reading. Carrie went out to the front room, where it was not as warm. She sat by the window and cried. Was this really the life she was meant to have? To live cooped up in a small apartment with someone who was out of work, did nothing, and showed no interest in her? She was merely a servant to him now, nothing more.

"What a life! What a life!" Carrie thought, hopelessly.

After a few days, Hurstwood again went out to look for work. But after he met another of his old friends, he decided not to spend any more time sitting around hotel lobbies. So every day he came home early. Finally, he stopped even pretending that he was going somewhere. Winter was no time to look for a job.

Now that he was at home, he watched how Carrie did the housework. Once when Carrie asked for her weekly allowance, he said, "Do you think we live as cheaply as we could?"

"I do the best I can," said Carrie.

Then one day he asked her how much she paid for meat. He thought it was expensive. So the next time she needed meat, he offered to go buy it for her. Little by little, he made all the purchases for the household. Eventually she lost her weekly allowance. And he started buying less and less. One day he came home with half as much meat as usual. "We never seem to eat that much of it," he explained.

Carrie was miserable. Oh, how this man had changed! Day after day, here he sat, reading his papers. Nothing in the world outside the apartment appealed to him. She couldn't help looking at him with scorn.

Hurstwood could not see his way out of this situation. So he just stopped caring. Every month he took more out of his savings. Now, he had only five hundred dollars left. He hugged this money, almost feeling that he could hold out that way indefinitely.

Now that he was sitting around the house all day, he decided that he might as well wear his old clothes. Then he put off going to the barbershop in order to save money. He began losing his self-respect.

And Carrie lost respect for him. She could not understand what had gotten into the man. He still had some money. He had one decent suit left. He was not bad-looking when he dressed up. She had had her own difficult struggle when she first came to Chicago. But she had never stopped trying. He never tried, though. He never even looked at the want ads anymore.

One evening, while watching her cook dinner, Hurstwood asked, "Why do you use so much butter?"

"To make it taste good, of course," she answered.

"Butter is so expensive these days," he suggested.

Finally her thoughts came out. "You wouldn't mind it if you were working," she responded.

He said nothing more, but left her to go read his newspaper. Still, her comment bothered him. It was the first cutting remark that she had made.

That same evening, Carrie went off to the front room when it was time for bed. When Hurstwood went to bed, he discovered that Carrie wasn't there, as she usually was.

"That's funny," he said. "Maybe she's still sitting up, reading."

He didn't think anymore about the matter and fell asleep. The next morning, Carrie was not beside him. Neither of them mentioned this.

That evening, Carrie said, "I think I'll sleep alone tonight. I have a headache."

"All right," said Hurstwood.

The third night she went to her bed in the front room without explanation or apology.

This came as a blow to Hurstwood. But he never mentioned it.

"All right," he said to himself grimly. "Let her sleep alone."

CHAPTER 36

Nothing but Bluff

Mrs. Vance had not forgotten Carrie. But Carrie was ashamed of the way they were living now. So she never sent her their new address. Mrs. Vance wondered why she never heard anymore from Carrie. But she thought that she must have left New York. Eventually, she gave up on ever seeing her again. So she was surprised to run into her one day when she was downtown, shopping.

"Why, Mrs. Wheeler," said Mrs. Vance, looking Carrie over in a single glance. "Where have you been? Why haven't you been to see me? I've been wondering all this time what had become of you. Really, I . . ."

"I'm so glad to see you," said Carrie. She was pleased, but also embarrassed to see her old friend. "Why, I'm living downtown here. I've been meaning to come and see you. Where are you living now?"

Mrs. Vance gave her their new address, an even wealthier neighborhood than before. "Why don't you come and see me?"

"I will," said Carrie. "Really, I've been want-ing to come. I know I ought to. It's a shame. But you know . . ."

"What's your address?" asked Mrs. Vance.

Carrie told her and then added, "You must come down and see me sometime."

Mrs. Vance knew that it was a poorer location. She also noticed that Carrie's appearance was less elegant than before. "They must be hard up for money," she thought to herself.

When Carrie returned home, Hurstwood was sitting there, reading as usual. He hadn't shaved for at least four days.

"Oh," thought Carrie. "What if she were to come here and see him like this?"

Driven to desperation, she asked at dinner, "Did you ever hear anymore from that wholesale store?"

"No," he said. "They don't want an inexperi-enced man."

Carrie dropped the subject, feeling unable to say more.

After a while, she tried again to approach the topic. "I met Mrs. Vance this afternoon. She did look so nice."

"Well, she can afford to look nice. At least, as long as he puts up the money for it," answered Hurstwood. "He's got an easy job."

Hurstwood didn't look up from the paper. So he did not see that Carrie was looking at him with weariness and displeasure.

"She's too extravagant," said Hurstwood. "You'd need a lot of money to keep up with her."

"Mr. Vance doesn't seem to find it very hard."

Hurstwood understood that she was criticizing him. "He may not now. But his life isn't over yet. You can't tell what'll happen. He may fall on hard times just like anybody else."

Hurstwood enjoyed thinking that rich people might someday lose everything. He even expected it. Sitting in his apartment, he read about all the things that other people were doing. Sometimes his old independent, confident, undefeated attitude returned. He thought, "I can do something. I'm not down yet. There are a lot of things coming to me if I want to go after them." At these times he would get dressed up, shave, and go out. Not with any definite aim, though. He just felt like being outside and doing something.

And when Hurstwood left the apartment, his money left, too. He knew of several poker rooms downtown. It was a pleasant change to go there and see some of the people he knew.

He used to be a pretty good poker player. When he had more money to risk, he sometimes won a hundred dollars or more in a friendly card game. Now he thought about joining a game. "I might win a couple of hundred dollars. I'm not so out of practice."

The first time he played, he lost a little money. So for the rest of the afternoon, he played more cautiously.

But the next day he returned, looking to have fun as well as make some money. He joined a game where one man was coolly betting lots of money. Hurstwood thought the young fellow must be bluffing. He was probably just pretending to have a good hand of cards. Hurstwood was sure that he, too, could bluff. He thought he could deceive even a shrewd gambler. Besides, he had an excellent hand of cards. So he thought he had a good chance of winning the whole pile of money. Why not bet a few more dollars?

Soon Hurstwood's forehead was wet with worry. He was in deep now—very deep for him. He had already put sixty dollars of his good money into this game. Usually he was not a coward, but the thought of losing so much money weakened him. Finally he gave up. He couldn't trust that his cards were high enough. So he called the other man's bluff, and asked to see what cards he really had.

The young man spread out a perfect set of cards.

"I thought I had you," Hurstwood said, weakly.

The young man swept up all the money he had won. Hurstwood walked away. But before he left the building, he stopped to count his remaining cash. "Three hundred and forty dollars," he said. With their routine household expenses, and now with this loss, so much of his money had already gone. He decided that he would not gamble anymore.

When he came home that day, Hurstwood changed back into his old clothes.

"Why do you always put on those old clothes?" asked Carrie.

"What's the use of wearing my good ones around here?" he asked.

"Well, maybe you'd feel better." Then she added, "Besides, someone might stop by."

"Who?" he said.

"Well, Mrs. Vance," said Carrie. "She did say she'd come by someday."

"She sure has taken her time getting around to it, hasn't she?" said Hurstwood sarcastically. The way she spent money did not appeal to him.

Angered by the man's attitude, Carrie responded, "Well, maybe that's because I didn't want her to come."

"Even if she comes, she doesn't have to see me," he answered, resentfully.

Hurstwood's lack of pride and self-respect made Carrie almost hate him.

What added to her bitterness was that one day Mrs. Vance actually did stop by. Even worse, she arrived when Carrie was out. Hurstwood opened the door.

"How—how do you do?" he stammered.

Mrs. Vance could hardly believe her eyes. "Is your wife at home?" she asked.

"No," he said, "Carrie's out, but she'll be back soon."

Mrs. Vance realized how much things had

changed. "I can't stay. But please tell your wife that she must come over and see me."

"I will," said Hurstwood, intensely relieved that she was going. He was so ashamed that afterward he sat back down in his chair, and he thought.

When Carrie returned, Hurstwood told her that Mrs. Vance had stopped by.

"Did she see you?" she asked, showing her full despair.

This remark cut Hurstwood like a whip and made him resentful. "If she had eyes, she did. I opened the door."

"What did she have to say?" Carrie asked, nervously.

"Nothing," he answered. "She couldn't stay."

Finally letting out her feelings, Carrie exclaimed, "And she saw you looking like that!"

"What of it?" he said, becoming angry. "I didn't know she was coming, did I?"

"You knew she might," said Carrie. "I told you she said she was coming. I've asked you a dozen times to wear your other clothes. Oh, this is awful."

"Oh, just forget about it," he answered. "What difference does it make? You couldn't spend time with her, anyway. They've got too much money."

"Who said I wanted to?" said Carrie, fiercely.

"Well, you act like it, going on about the way I look. You'd think I'd committed—"

Carrie interrupted him. "It's true. I couldn't even if I wanted to. But whose fault is that? You feel like you can just sit around all day and talk about who I can spend my time with. So why don't you go out and look for work?"

This struck Hurstwood like a thunderbolt. "What's it to you?" he said, standing up, almost fiercely. "I pay the rent, don't I? I furnish the—"

"Yes, you pay the rent," said Carrie. "You talk as if there was nothing else in the world except this apartment to sit around in. You haven't done a thing for three months except sit around and interfere here. I'd like to know what you married me for?"

"I didn't marry you," he said, in a snarling tone.

"I'd like to know what you did, then, in Montreal?" she answered.

"Well, I didn't marry you," he answered. "You can get that out of your head. You talk as though you didn't know."

Carrie looked at him a moment, her eyes wide. She had believed that their marriage was legal and binding.

"What did you lie to me for, then?" she asked, fiercely. "Why did you force me to run away with you?"

Her voice became almost a sob.

"Force!" he said, his lip curled in anger. "As if I really had to force you."

Carrie broke down under the strain. Sobbing,

she turned and ran into the front room.

Hurstwood was feeling hot now, and shaken up. He looked around. Then he went for his clothes and dressed.

Carrie heard him leave the apartment. She thought, at first, that he might be leaving for good. She wasn't upset about losing him. But she was alarmed that she might be left without any money at all.

Hurstwood tried to protect himself from his own self-accusations, which told him that Carrie had been right. "Look for work!" he said to himself. "Look for work! She tells me to get out and look for work. And there stood Mrs. Vance, looking me over. I know what she was thinking." He remembered that he used to try to impress her, to look worthy of her. Now, to think that she had caught him looking like this.

"What the heck," he thought, trying to hide his own shame from himself. "I'm not so bad. I'm not down yet."

He decided to go to one of the finest hotels in New York and treat himself to dinner. He didn't worry that his shrinking savings did not allow such extravagance. Like an addict, he needed to do whatever he could to ease his pain. Anything to relieve his mental distress, to satisfy his craving for comfort. He must do it. No thoughts about tomorrow. He couldn't stand thinking about what would happen to him. He couldn't face the coming disaster, any more than people can face the certainty of death. It was clear that soon he would be without a single dollar. So he tried to shut that certainty completely out of his mind.

He sat reading at dinner, while he enjoyed the cocktails, the food, the music. Watching the well-dressed guests reminded him of the old days when he, too, had money.

The dinner was expensive. Afterward, he watched the guests leave for their evening's entertainment. He wondered where he should go. Not home. Carrie would be up. No, he would not go back there this evening. He would stay out late and enjoy himself. He would act like a man who was independent, not broke. He bought a cigar, and thought about how he used to spend the good old evenings in Chicago. He'd played many fine card games back then. And that brought his thoughts around to poker.

He thought about the sixty dollars he had lost the other day. "I just didn't play the game right. I shouldn't have weakened. I should have kept betting more money. I could have out-bluffed that other fellow. I was just out of practice, that's all."

He began to figure out how he might have won if only he had bluffed a little harder, a little longer. "I'll bet I could make some real money playing poker. I think I'll try my luck tonight." Suppose he did win a couple of hundred dollars? After all, lots of people made their living at poker. And it was a good living, too.

So off he went to a nearby poker room. He

felt as much like the old Hurstwood as he ever would again. Except that it was not really the old Hurstwood. It was only a man with a divided conscience, a man lured by the false hope of winning at poker.

At first, he won a few games and felt lucky. Then he lost a few games and became even more determined to win. He enjoyed taking risks. Once, when he was dealt a poor hand of cards, he decided to bet anyway and try to bluff the other players. He won.

Now he began to think that luck was with him. No one else had done as well as he. Then he was dealt only an average hand of cards. So he decided to try the same strategy a second time. He would bluff the other players again and win even more money. He didn't realize that the other players were observing him closely. By now they had learned the tricks that Hurstwood used. And some of them were holding better cards.

It got to the point where Hurstwood had bet seventy-five dollars. Another man called his bluff.

Hurstwood spread out his cards. They were worth nothing. He had lost all seventy-five dollars.

This bitter loss made him desperate. "Let's have another game," he said, grimly.

He played until after one o'clock in the morning. He did not win back his money.

Afterward, he went out onto the chill, bare streets. He was thinking about his money, not about his fight with Carrie. Back in his bedroom, he counted out his money. There was only a hundred and ninety dollars left.

In the morning, Carrie hardly spoke to him. So he felt that he had to go out again. He had treated her badly. But he couldn't afford to make up with her. Desperation seemed to seize him. So for the next two days, he went out and lived like a gentleman. At least, he lived the way he thought a gentleman would—which meant spending money. But that only made things worse. Finally, he had to face the cold, bitter reality.

The third morning, Carrie reminded him that the rent was due that day.

"It is?" said Hurstwood, frowning.

"Yes. Today is the first of the month," answered Carrie.

In despair, he reached for his wallet. "It seems an awful lot to pay for rent," he said.

He was down to his last hundred dollars.

CHAPTER 37

Getting in the Stage Door

Hurstwood's way of handling his money had carried them only until June. With only one hundred dollars left, he needed to let Carrie know that a disaster was approaching.

One day he brought up the subject. "I don't know," he said. "It seems to take an awful lot of money for us to live."

"It doesn't seem to me that we spend very much," responded Carrie.

"My money is nearly gone," he said. "And I hardly know where it went."

"All seven hundred dollars?" asked Carrie.

"All but a hundred."

He looked so gloomy that it scared her. She saw that she had been drifting all this time. Her life didn't seem to be going anywhere.

"Well, George," she exclaimed, "why don't you go out and look for a job? Surely you can find something."

"I have looked," he said. "You can't just make people give you a job."

She stared at him and asked, "Well, what do you think you will do? A hundred dollars won't last long."

"I don't know," he said. "All I can do is look."

Carrie became frightened by Hurstwood's announcement. She wondered what she could do. She had often thought about acting as a way to get the things she longed for. Maybe the stage could be her door to entering that golden world she dreamed of. In Chicago, she had acted only when there was no other option. Here, too, it might be the only way to meet a desperate need. Something had to be done if he did not get work soon. She would have to go out once again and try to do battle, alone.

But how could she find a job as an actress? There must be people who would listen to her and try her out—men who might give her an opportunity.

The next morning at the breakfast table, Carrie finally asked, innocently, "How do people get on the stage, George?"

"I don't know," he said. "They probably have agents."

"Regular people who get you a job?"

"You're not still thinking about being an actress, are you?" he asked.

"No," she answered. "I was just wondering."

Something bothered him about this idea. Carrie seemed too simple, too passive to be a great actress. He thought she didn't have enough intelligence. But that was because he did not understand that a person might have emotional intelligence. Besides, if she tried to get on the stage, she might fall into the hands of some cheap theater manager. And then she'd become just like the rest of *them*. He had a good idea about what *they* ended up doing. Carrie was pretty. She would get along all right. And then where would that leave him?

"I'd get that idea out of my head, if I were you. It's a lot more difficult than you think."

"You said I did real well in Chicago," she answered. She felt that he was insulting her acting ability.

"You did," he answered. "But Chicago isn't New York, not by a long shot."

Carrie did not even answer this comment. It hurt her too much.

"The stage," he went on, "is all right if you can get to be one of the big stars. But it takes a long time to get there, if you can get there at all. And if you can't, it has nothing to offer."

"Oh, I don't know," said Carrie, becoming angry.

Suddenly he saw what might happen. She would get on the stage in some cheap way. And then she would abandon him.

"Well, I do," he answered. "If I were you, I wouldn't think of it. It's not much of a profession for a woman."

"It's better than going hungry," said Carrie. "If you don't want me to do that, why don't you get work yourself?"

He had no answer for this. "Oh, just forget about it," he responded.

So Carrie secretly made up her mind to try, anyway. She didn't care what he thought. She was not going to be dragged into poverty or something even worse just to please him. She could act. She would find something, and then she would work her way to the top. What would he say then? She imagined herself appearing in a fine show on Broadway. It didn't matter whether she was the star or not. How wonderful it would be just to have a part, get a decent salary, and wear the kind of clothes she liked. She would have enough money to go here and there as she pleased. The contrast with Hurstwood's dreary situation made the picture in her mind even more vivid and appealing.

Surprisingly, Hurstwood, too, started to think about this possibility. When his money ran out, he would need someone to support him. Why couldn't Carrie help him a little, just until he got a job for himself?

One day he approached Carrie with this idea in mind. "You know, if only I can get through the summer, I think I'll be all right. I'm starting to hear from some of my old friends again," he lied. "They've suggested some business opportunities."

Carrie believed the entire story. She sincerely wished he could get through the summer. He looked so hopeless.

"How much money have you left?"

"Only fifty dollars."

"Oh, mercy," she exclaimed. "What will we do? It's only twenty days until the rent will be due again."

"Maybe you could get something in the theater?" Hurstwood suggested, without looking at Carrie.

"Maybe I could," said Carrie, glad that someone approved of the idea.

"I'll take any job I can get," he offered. "I'm sure I can get something."

So Carrie cleaned up the dishes. Then she picked up the paper to find an ad for a theatrical agent. She wrote down the names and addresses of three agents: Mrs. Bermudez, Marcus Jenks, and Percy Weil. She paused only a moment, and then put on the best outfit that she had. She moved toward the door. "I might as well go right away," she said, without looking back.

Hurstwood felt a little ashamed as he watched her leave. He was losing his sense of pride. He sat for a while, and then it became too much. He got up and put on his hat.

"I guess I'll go out," he said to himself. He was headed nowhere in particular, but somehow he felt that he must go.

Carrie went first to Mrs. Bermudez. In the waiting area were several people—men—who said nothing and did nothing. Finally a large middle-aged woman came out of the office. She seemed alert and good-natured. At least she was smiling.

She told two women that she would be getting in touch with them in the next few weeks, and showed them to the door.

Then she turned to Carrie, with sharp eyes and a serious, shrewd expression.

"Well, young woman," she said, "what can I do for you?"

"Well," said Carrie, not knowing how to begin, "do you get acting jobs for people?"

"Yes."

"Could you get me one?"

"Have you ever had any experience?"

"A very little," said Carrie.

"Whom did you perform with?"

"Oh, with no one," said Carrie. "It was just a little show that—"

"Oh, I see," said the woman, interrupting her. "No, I don't know of anything now."

Carrie's face showed her disappointment.

"You'll need to get some experience in New York," suggested Mrs. Bermudez. "We'll take your name, though."

She had a similar experience in Mr. Jenks's office. But he finished by suggesting, "Maybe you could perform in some small local theater. Or maybe you could get a program with your name on it. Then I might be able to do something."

In the third office, Percy Weil asked, "What sort of work do you want to do?"

"Oh, I'd like to get a part in a play," said Carrie.

"Well," said the man, "it'll cost you something to do that."

"How much?" said Carrie. She had not thought of this before.

"Well, that's up to you," he answered shrewdly.

"Oh," she said, not quite sure what he meant.

The agent saw that she was innocent and inexperienced. He knew how anxious some young women were to get on the stage. So he continued, "You'll need to pay a fifty-dollar deposit at least. No agent would bother working for you for less than that."

"I see," said Carrie, and walked out.

She thought about this offer. She had some jewelry—a diamond ring, a pin, and a few other pieces. A pawnbroker would give her fifty dollars for them. But maybe the agent would just take her money and not give her anything.

Hurstwood was already home. "Well?" he asked, when Carrie returned.

"I didn't find out anything today," she said, taking off her gloves. "They all want money to get you a job."

"How much?" asked Hurstwood.

"Fifty dollars."

"They don't want anything else, do they?"

"Oh, who knows? You can never tell whether they'd ever get you anything after you paid them."

"Well, I wouldn't put up fifty on that basis," said Hurstwood. He acted as if he had the money, as if it were his decision.

"I don't know," said Carrie. "I think I'll try

some of the theater managers."

When Hurstwood heard this, he was frightened to death. He rocked back and forth in his chair, and chewed his finger. But maybe this plan made sense, after all, under such extreme circumstances. Later on, he would do better.

CHAPTER 38

A Woman's Role

Finding a part as a chorus girl was as difficult as finding a job in any other field. Many young women were able to stand in a line and look pretty. So there were many applicants for only a few jobs. It didn't matter how good the women thought they were. They were all treated the same.

All the managers were too busy to see Carrie. Or she needed to have an appointment first. Or else she needed to write the manager and ask him to see her. The manager acted like a little king, who ruled over his theater and the young women he hired.

At the end of the day, Carrie came home. She felt weary and humiliated.

"I didn't get to see anyone," Carrie told Hurstwood. "I just walked, and walked, and waited around."

Hurstwood only looked at her.

"I suppose you have to have some friends before you can get in," she added, in despair.

Hurstwood understood. But the way he looked at things from his rocking chair, Carrie's situation didn't seem as bitter as his own. After all, she could rest now. Tomorrow was another day.

Tomorrow came, and the next, and the next.

One day, Carrie was able to see the manager at the Casino. He was a large man, dressed in expensive, showy clothes. He judged women the way another person might look at a racehorse. One of the theater owners had said that the chorus girls weren't pretty enough. But Carrie was pretty and graceful. Maybe they could use her, even if she didn't have any experience.

"Come around at the beginning of next week," he said. "I may make some changes then."

The beginning of next week seemed far away. And the beginning of next month, when the rent was due, was getting closer. Carrie began to worry as she had never worried before.

One morning she finally asked Hurstwood, "Do you really look for anything when you go out?"

"Of course I do," he answered, annoyed by what she was suggesting.

"I'd take anything right now," she said in despair. "It will soon be the first of the month again, and the rent will be due."

Hurstwood stopped reading his paper and changed his clothes. He would go and see if he couldn't get a job somewhere, even as a bartender.

But after one or two rejections, he stopped even pretending to be confident. He noticed that even his best clothes were looking old. This was a bitter thought. "It's no use," he thought. "I might as well go on back home."

On Monday, Carrie went back to the Casino.

"Did I tell you to come by today?" asked the manager, looking her over as she stood in front of him.

"You said the first of the week," said Carrie, embarrassed.

"Ever had any experience?" he asked again, almost severely.

Carrie admitted that she had none.

He looked her over again as he shuffled some papers. He liked the looks of this pretty, worried-looking young woman. "Come over to the theater tomorrow morning."

Carrie's heart raced. She could see that he wanted her. "I will," she said eagerly.

As she turned to go, she wondered, "Will he really put me to work? Could this really be true?"

But a sharp voice washed away her fears. "Be sure you're there promptly," the manager added roughly. "You'll be dropped if you're not."

Carrie hurried away. She wouldn't have to nag Hurstwood about his laziness. For now she had a job. She had a job!

But then, she began to wonder what was really going on. It was strange that she could find a job in only a few weeks, when Hurstwood had found nothing after several months. He just seemed to hang around the apartment, doing nothing. "Why doesn't he get a job?" she asked herself. "If I can get one, surely he should be able to, too. It wasn't very hard for me." Of course, she forgot that being young and pretty might have made it easier for her.

"Well?" said Hurstwood, when she returned.

"I have a job."

"What sort of job?" he asked, relieved. Maybe now he, too, might be able to get something.

"In the chorus," she answered.

"Is it the Casino show you told me about?"

"Yes," she answered. "I begin rehearsing tomorrow."

"Do you know how much you'll make?"

"No, I didn't want to ask," said Carrie.

Hurstwood shaved that afternoon. "Tomorrow," he thought, "I'll look for a job myself." He started feeling hopeful again.

The next morning, Carrie arrived on time. The theater awed and delighted her. It was a center of brightness and pleasure. How hard she would try to be worthy of it. People came here in their fine clothing and fancy carriages. And now she, too, was a part of it. Oh, if only she could stay here, how happy she would be!

"What is your name?" said the manager, who was running the rehearsal.

"Madenda," she replied, remembering the name that Drouet had selected in Chicago. "Carrie Madenda."

"Well, now, Miss Madenda," he said, "you go over there." He pointed to a position in the chorus line of young women.

This manager was much harsher and more

temperamental than the one back in Chicago. He was sometimes almost brutally rough. He looked down on these young women, especially those who still had any dignity or innocence. When they made a mistake, he shouted at them and tried to humiliate them into following his orders. Carrie pitied them. And she trembled in fear that he would yell at her.

At one point, she was so anxious to do everything right that she danced a little too stiffly. Suddenly, she heard the manager angrily call out a name.

"Mason," said the voice. "Miss Mason!"

She looked around to see who it could be. The woman behind Carrie gave her a gentle shove. But Carrie did not understand.

"You, you!" shouted the manager. "Can't you hear?"

"Oh," said Carrie, shrinking, and blushing in embarrassment.

"Isn't your name Mason?" asked the manager.

"No, sir," said Carrie. "It's Madenda."

"Well, what's the matter with your feet? Can't you dance?"

"Yes, sir," said Carrie. Long ago she had learned to dance.

"Why don't you do it then? Don't go shuffling along as if you were dead. I've got to have dancers with life in them!"

Carrie's cheek burned with shame. Her lips trembled a little.

"Yes, sir," she said.

After three hours of constant, intense rehearsing, Carrie was worn out. But she was too excited to notice. The possibility of becoming free of financial cares kept her going. She planned to go home and practice her moves just the way she had been directed. She would not make any mistakes if she could help it.

But when it was time for dinner, she had to stop practicing and prepare the meal. She was annoyed. Would she have to go to work and also do all the housekeeping? "After the show starts, I won't do it anymore," she thought. "He can get his meals on his own."

But the reality of the theater wasn't as wonderful as it had first appeared. Her salary was less than she had expected. Of course, everyone treated the leading ladies and gentlemen with respect. They were the high and mighty stars. But she, a lowly chorus girl, was nothing—absolutely nothing at all.

At home, Hurstwood seemed to have nothing to do. She began to think that he was waiting for her to do everything for him. Now that she had a way to support herself, this irritated her. He seemed to be depending on her little income to meet all their needs.

He just sat and read his paper, not paying any attention to her. Then one day he mentioned calmly that he had bought some butter. "I thought maybe you might want to bake us a cake."

Such a suggestion astonished her. Now that

she was becoming more independent, she had the courage to notice what he was doing. She wanted to tell him how she felt. But something in the man's manner still kept her in awe of him.

After the first week's rehearsal, Hurstwood said, "We're really going to have to cut back on what we spend. You won't get paid for another week or so, will you?"

"No," said Carrie, who was stirring a pan at the stove.

"I've only got enough money to pay the rent, with thirteen dollars left over," he added.

"So that's his plan," she thought to herself. "I'll have to use my money now to pay for everything we need." But she had hoped to buy a few things for herself. After all, she needed clothes. Her hat was old.

"But how could my salary pay for everything?" she thought. "I can't do it alone. Why doesn't he get a job?"

Opening night arrived. Hurstwood did not think of going to see the first performance. It would only be a waste of money. Carrie had such a small part. She was nothing.

As in Chicago, at first Carrie was seized with stage fright. But her part was so small that she realized it did not matter how she did. She was happy that she was one of twelve women who wore pretty golden skirts that came to an inch above the knee. She marched and danced and sang with the rest of the chorus line. It was a big hit. But Carrie thought that some of the women with big roles did not act very well. "I could do better than that," Carrie thought to herself.

Afterward, the manager scolded several of the chorus girls. But since he said nothing to her, Carrie imagined that she had been satisfactory. She dressed quickly and left the theater. Outside, some elegant young men in fine clothing were waiting. They looked her over closely. One of them called out to her, "You're not going home alone, are you?"

Carrie merely walked even faster until she was back in the apartment.

At the end of the week, Carrie tried to get Hurstwood to start looking again for work. She objected to giving up her own money. Yet she was beginning to feel that she would have to do so, anyway. "Did you hear anything more about those jobs you were looking at?" she asked.

"No," he answered, "those people are not quite ready to hire. I think they'll have a job for me soon, though."

Hurstwood felt that Carrie was becoming impatient. So he cleverly decided to appeal to her good nature. He was a little ashamed about taking advantage of her. But he justified himself by thinking that he really would go out and get a job soon.

"If I could only hold out a little longer, I think I could get a good job. One person said he'll hire me next month."

Carrie listened, a little suspicious.

"Would you mind helping me out until then?" he appealed. "I think I'll be all right in a few weeks."

Carrie agreed, feeling that there was nothing else she could do.

"We can get by if we're careful with our money. I'll pay you back, of course."

Carrie felt mean, making him appeal to her so humbly. But she resented not being able to keep all the money for herself.

Finally she said, "Oh, all right. I'll help you. But why don't you just take anything, George? At least for now. What difference does the kind of job make? Maybe, after a while, you'll be able to get something better."

Relieved, but stung by her comment, he said he would try. "I'll take anything I can find. Even if it means digging ditches. At least nobody would know me there."

"Oh, you needn't do that," said Carrie, pitying the man. "But there must be other things."

"I'll get something!" he said, taking on the appearance of being determined.

Then he went back to his newspaper.

CHAPTER 39

Going Out with Others

Hurstwood decided that this was not the day to go looking for a job. And each day after that was not the day, either.

During the next month, Carrie's desire for clothes and jewelry grew. The more she realized that she could not use her money to buy nice things for herself, the more she wanted what she couldn't have. And the more she wanted to have nice things, the more she wished that she didn't have Hurstwood in her way.

When Hurstwood was down to his last ten dollars, he decided to tell Carrie that he had no more money. That way, he could still keep a little cash for himself and not be completely dependent on Carrie.

"I've got some money there in my purse," Carrie responded.

She hardly noticed that this was becoming their new routine. Soon Hurstwood helped himself to a few dollars whenever he needed to buy something. Afterward, he always left the packages on the table, together with the change. That way, she could check to see that he hadn't kept any money for himself.

Carrie began to feel sorry for him. After all, he was only asking her for something to eat. Maybe she had been too hard on him. He might still be able to get a job. He really wasn't a bad person.

But one night, Carrie noticed that one of the other chorus girls was wearing a pretty new outfit. "She can afford to dress well," thought Carrie. "And so could I, if only I could keep the money I'm making. I don't have a decent thing to wear."

She looked at her feet. "I think I'll at least buy a new pair of shoes on Saturday. I don't care what comes of it."

Another young woman in the chorus line, whose name was Lola Osborne, seemed especially sweet and kind. She was experienced and independent, but generous with other people. She admired Carrie very much, without feeling threatened by her.

One day when they were getting ready to go onstage, Lola started a conversation with Carrie. "They say this show is going on the road next month. Do you think you'll go with it?"

"I don't know," said Carrie. "I guess so, if they'll take me."

"Oh, they'll take you. But I wouldn't go. They won't pay you any more. And it will cost you everything you make just to live. I never leave New York. There are too many shows going on here."

"Can you always get in another show?"

"I always have. There's one that's going to open at the Broadway Theater later this month. I'm going to try and get in that one."

"Do they all pay about the same?" she asked.

"Yes. Sometimes you get a little more. But this show doesn't pay very much."

"I get twelve dollars," said Carrie.

"That's all?" said the girl. "They pay me fifteen, and you do more work than I do. I wouldn't put up with that, if I were you. They're just giving you less because they think you don't know any better. You ought to be making fifteen. You do fine, and the manager knows it. You'll get more in the next show if you want it."

"Do you suppose I could make more money up at the Broadway?"

"Of course you can," answered the girl. "You come with me when I go. I'll do the talking."

Carrie was glad to hear that it wasn't so very difficult, after all, to get a job in a show. If she could always get work this way, then she didn't have to worry about her future.

But the next morning, she was again faced with her dreary home life. Her household chores took up all her spare time, while Hurstwood just sat there and did nothing. Maybe she would be able to earn enough money to buy food and pay their rent. But there would be nothing left over.

To relieve her sense of hopelessness, she bought a pair of shoes and a few other things. Suddenly, a week before the rent was due, Carrie realized that they were going to run short of money.

Looking in her purse, Carrie exclaimed, "I don't think that I'll have enough to pay for food and the rent. Do you think that job you looked at will come through?"

"I think so," answered Hurstwood. Then he added, "Don't worry. Maybe the grocery store will wait to get paid. We've been going there long enough that they should trust us for a week or two."

"He tells me not to worry," thought Carrie. "But if he worried a little more, he wouldn't just sit there and wait for me to bring home some money. He'd find a job. How could any man go seven months without finding work?"

Hurstwood found it easy to talk to the store owner. He agreed to let Hurstwood wait to pay until the end of every week, instead of each time he bought something. That way, Hurstwood had enough money to pay the rent on time. Then when it was time to pay the grocery bill, he simply borrowed money from his personal cash reserve. As soon as Carrie got paid, he took her money and replaced the amount he had spent of his own ten dollars. Then each week he delayed paying the grocery bill by one more day. Gradually he owed more and more money. It was the game of a desperate man.

Carrie found it depressing to see him always sitting around in his sloppy clothes. He was always at home, and he was always gloomy. She started looking for relief from the misery and boredom that had taken over her apartment. During the day, she spent time either performing or rehearsing. Otherwise, she visited one or two of the other chorus girls.

One day she visited Lola Osborne in the small, but comfortable room that she rented.

"Isn't your home in New York?" Carrie asked.

"Yes, but I can't get along with my family. They always expect me to do what they want. Do you live with your family?"

Carrie was ashamed to say that she was married. After all, she had told Lola that she needed to earn more money. She had confessed that she was anxious about her future. How could she tell her friend that she was married? How could she admit that her husband wasn't doing anything to support her?

"Yes. I live with some relatives," Carrie finally answered.

Lola assumed that Carrie could spend her time however she wanted. And Carrie started spending more time with her. She began coming home later and later. Sometimes she came home so late that she hardly had time to fix dinner for Hurstwood before she had to leave again for the evening performance.

Hurstwood noticed this. But he was in no position to argue with her, though once he asked her what she did all afternoon. But she felt he was trying to limit her freedom. So she did not tell him about Lola.

Hurstwood let it go. He was too depressed to do anything. He simply let Carrie drift out of his life. It was the same way that he let every opportunity pass him by. Still, he could not help clinging to her, helplessly. But his weak demands irritated Carrie, and only widened the distance between them.

One day, the manager asked the director of the chorus line, "Who is that fourth girl there on the right—the one turning this way right now?" He had noticed how the young woman tossed her head to one side and held her arms as if ready for action. She moved in a special and pleasing way, so naturally and without self-consciousness.

"Oh," said the director, "that's Miss Madenda."

"She's good-looking. Why don't you let her be at the front of that line?"

"I will," said the man.

"Good. She'll look better out front than the woman you've got there now."

"All right. I will do that," said the director.

A few days later, the manager said to the chorus director, "That girl knows how to carry herself." He would have enjoyed spending some time with Carrie. But he made it a rule never to have anything to do with the chorus girls.

So he told the director to put her at the front of a line of women, who were dressed in beautiful white costumes with silver trim. As the leader of that chorus line, Carrie wore a stunning outfit with even more silver on it. She was pleased to be promoted to this important position. She was especially pleased that her salary was now raised from twelve to eighteen dollars.

Hurstwood heard nothing about this, though.

"I'm not going to give him the rest of my money," thought Carrie. "I do enough as it is. Instead, I'll just buy myself something to wear."

So she began buying things for herself, without thinking about the consequences. But when she went to buy an expensive new blouse, she found out that her small salary would not pay for very much. She thought about how much she could buy, if only she could use all of it on herself. She imagined spending all of her money on clothes and other things that she liked. But she forgot that, if she were alone, she would also have to pay for her own room and food.

Carrie realized that she would have to spend more than just her raise if she wanted to buy this blouse. She would also have to use some of the household money. She knew that she was going too far. But she loved fine clothing more than anything else.

The next day, Hurstwood asked for money to pay the grocery store bill. Carrie looked in her purse. It was clear that there would not be enough money to pay for all their expenses that week.

Hurstwood said nothing. He had noticed that she was buying new things, neglecting the household chores, staying away all afternoon. He felt that something was about to happen.

All at once, Carrie said, "I don't see what I'm going to do. I can't pay for everything. I don't earn enough."

She was challenging Hurstwood directly. He had to respond.

"I don't want you to do it all," he said, trying to stay calm. "I only want a little help until I can get a job."

"Oh, sure," answered Carrie. "That's what you always say."

"But I've tried to find work!" he exclaimed. "What do you want me to do?"

"You couldn't have tried all that hard," she responded. "I was able to get a job."

"Well, I did try," he said, becoming angry. "So don't throw your success in my face. All I'm asking for is a little help until I can get a job. I'm not down yet. I'll be all right. You'll see."

He tried to speak steadily, but his voice trembled a little.

Carrie's anger melted instantly. She felt ashamed that she had almost made him cry.

"Well," she said, "here's the money." She emptied her purse out onto the table. "I don't have quite enough to pay it all. But if they can wait until Saturday, I'll have some more money then."

"I only want enough to pay the grocery bill," said Hurstwood sadly. "You keep the rest."

But he thought to himself, "She must be mak ing more money than she's telling me. How else could she buy all those things? I don't care. Let her keep her money. I'll get another job one of these days. And then she can go to the devil."

Carrie put back some money and went to make dinner. She felt that she needed to make up to him for her little show of anger. But after a while she thought, "I don't care how he feels. Somebody needs to tell him to get out there and find a job. It isn't right that I have to support him."

A few days later, when Carrie was visiting Lola, several lively young men stopped by. They were Lola's friends, and they invited Carrie to join them for an afternoon drive in Central Park.

"I can't," said Carrie.

"Oh, come on," urged Lola. "What else do you have to do?"

"I have to be home by five," said Carrie.

"What for?"

"Oh, to make dinner."

"But they'll take us to dinner," said Lola.

"Oh, no," said Carrie. "I can't go."

Besides, after her experiences with Drouet and Hurstwood, these younger men seemed silly. She felt older than they, even though she was really the same age. Even so, their youthful energy and enthusiasm did appeal to her.

"Oh, do come. They're really nice fellows. We'll get you back in time."

Carrie thought a while, and at last agreed.

"Now, remember. I've got to be back by four-thirty," she said.

This information went in one of Lola's ears and out the other.

"Oh, we'll be right back, Miss Madenda," said one of the fellows, bowing. "You don't think we'd keep you past your deadline, now, do you?"

"Well, I don't know," said Carrie, smiling.

So they went off for a drive. Carrie was awed by the show of wealth in Central Park—the elaborate clothing, the elegant carriages, the beauty of it all. And so for a while she forgot about her own troubles. She even forgot about Hurstwood.

But back in the apartment, he was waiting for Carrie to make his dinner. He waited until four, then five, then six o'clock. Finally he got up out of his chair. "I guess she isn't coming home," he said, grimly. "She's got something going for herself, now. And I'm going to be left out of it."

By the time Carrie noticed that it was getting late, it was almost five o'clock. By then, their carriage was at the far end of the park. It was too late to go home and come back in time for their performance that night. She thought of Hurstwood. Never before had she missed dinner without an excuse. But there was nothing to do about that now. So she agreed to join her companions for dinner.

Once in the restaurant, Carrie painfully remembered that other dinner with the Vances. Mrs. Vance never called her again after the time she had come to the apartment and seen Hurstwood. That made Carrie think about Ames. He spent time with better people than these friends of hers. He had such high ideals. He had said, "It's fine to be a good actress."

What sort of an actress was she?

"What are you thinking about, Miss Madenda?" asked one of the young men, who was quite interested in her. "Come on, now. Let's see if I can guess."

"Oh, no," said Carrie. "Don't try."

She stopped thinking about Ames, at least for now, and joined the lively talk at the table. Then the young man asked her to join him again after her performance.

"No," she said, "I can't. I have a previous engagement."

"Oh, come on now, Miss Madenda," begged the young man.

"No," said Carrie, "I can't. You've been so kind, but you'll have to excuse me."

The young man looked exceedingly disappointed.

"Cheer up, old man," whispered his companion. "After the show, we'll stop by the theater, anyhow. She may change her mind."

CHAPTER 40

Striking Out on One's Own

Carrie came home directly after the show. The next morning, she felt she should apologize.

"I couldn't get home yesterday afternoon," she said.

"Ah, Carrie," Hurstwood answered, "what's the use of saying that? I don't care what you do. But you don't need to lie to me about it."

"But I couldn't get home," Carrie protested, becoming angry. Then she saw that he looked as if he had already made up his mind. So she exclaimed, "Oh, all right! I don't care."

And from then on, she did care less and less about her home life. They could find no common ground for talking to one another. Carrie continued to do the household chores. She let Hurstwood ask her for money to pay their expenses.

He hated to ask her, though. So he put off paying the bills. He decided to stock up on groceries so that he would not have to buy anything else for a while. So he ran up a large bill at the grocery store. But it was a bill that he never paid off.

Instead, he just stopped going to that store and switched to a different one. He did the same thing wherever he shopped. And so he drifted further and further into a situation that could have only one ending.

September went by. Carrie asked about the job he had mentioned. But Hurstwood simply replied, "The position won't be available until October, now."

Carrie became disgusted with the man. She spent less time at home, and more time with her friends. She put the little money she gained from her promotion into clothes.

Then Carrie's show announced that it was going to leave New York. So Carrie went with Lola to apply for a job at another theater.

"Ever had any experience?" asked the manager.

"I'm in the chorus line at the Casino now."

"Oh, you are?" he said. He offered her a job for two dollars more than she had been earning.

Carrie was delighted. She began to feel that she had a place in the world. People seemed to recognize her ability.

But as things became better outside the apartment, they seemed to become even worse inside. Now it was nothing more than a place for Hurstwood to sit. He spent all day in his rocking chair, sitting and rocking, rocking and reading.

October went by, and then November. Before Hurstwood knew it, it was the dead of winter. And there he sat.

He knew that Carrie was doing better. Her clothes were better, even elegant now. His clothes were worn thin, a poor man's clothes. He had no appetite. He ate little and became thin. He didn't even bother pretending to Carrie anymore that he would have a job offer soon. He just folded his hands and waited—for what, he didn't know.

Finally, the owner of the grocery store stopped by the apartment. He came to collect the money that Hurstwood owed him. It was two months overdue. The grocer said that he needed the money right away.

Carrie was not totally surprised. But she was quite upset.

Hurstwood felt annoyed. He told the grocer, "Well, it's no use telling me you need it now. I won't have the money until Saturday."

After the man left, Carrie asked Hurstwood, "How are we going to pay it?" She was shocked at how much money they owed. "I can't do it just on my salary."

"Well, you don't have to," he said. "He can't have what we can't give him. He'll just have to wait."

"I don't see how we ran up that big a bill," said Carrie, vaguely suspicious.

"Well, we did," answered Hurstwood, angrily. "Do you think I ate it all myself? You talk as if I stole something."

"Well, I shouldn't have to pay for it all myself. I've got more than I can pay for as it is."

Carrie went out. And there Hurstwood sat. Never before had Carrie accused him of stealing— or almost accused him. Before long, he'd have to put up with even worse things from her. Besides, he'd been managing the groceries this way so that he wouldn't have to ask her for money. And he'd eaten very little himself—almost nothing. He was sick of it all. He really had to do something now.

So he looked in the newspaper. In nearby Brooklyn, seven thousand trolley workers had gone out on strike. They wanted to be guaranteed more hours of work and higher wages. The workers hoped to force their employers to go along with their demands. After all, it was cold out, and thousands of people used the trolleys every day.

Hurstwood sympathized with the workers' demands. They seemed fair. But he thought that they were foolish to strike in such cold weather. "They'll never win. They don't have any money. The police will protect the companies, not the strikers. They've got to. The public needs to ride the trolleys."

He didn't think that the big companies were right to take advantage of the workers. But the employers had more money, public support, and police protection.

Then he noticed want ads for people who were willing to drive the trolleys during the strike. They would have to walk past the striking workers. But they were guaranteed protection. Still, men who took jobs away from the strikers were called "scabs" and other insulting names. Striking workers hated them for undermining their position. Sometimes they were so angry that they became violent.

But Hurstwood thought that the companies were powerful enough to protect the "scabs." He thought, "They've got the police on their side. Those men on strike can't do anything to hurt them."

Suddenly he got up from his rocking chair. "Damn it all! I'm not down yet," he said.

He looked out the window onto the cold street below. Gradually, an idea came into his mind. "I'll go over to Brooklyn and get a job. Why not? Anyone can."

For several hours he weighed the pros and cons.

He might get hurt. But the companies had the police on their side. Anyone who worked for them during the strike would be protected.

He didn't know how to drive a trolley. But he could apply to be a conductor, instead.

Suppose they were hiring only drivers? They'd have to take anybody.

The next morning he put on his best clothes, which were already looking worn. He packed himself a lunch.

"Where are you going?" Carrie asked, curious about this new activity.

"Over to Brooklyn," he answered. "I think I can get work over there."

"On the trolley lines?" said Carrie, surprised.

"Yes," he replied.

"Aren't you afraid?" she asked.

"What of?" he answered. "The police are protecting them."

"The paper said four men were hurt yesterday."

"Well, you can't believe everything you read in the papers. They'll get the trolleys running, that's for sure."

He was looking more determined, though grim. Something of the old Hurstwood had returned. Still, it was just the shadow of his former strength. Carrie felt sorry for him. Outside, a cold wind was blowing around a few flakes of snow.

Once Hurstwood crossed the water into Brooklyn, no trolleys were running. So he had to walk a long way until he reached the office of the Brooklyn City Railroad Company. On his way there, he saw groups of men hanging around street corners and nearby saloons. He noticed their cold and gloomy faces. They looked poor and desperate. These striking trolley workers were in a kind of war with their employers.

Across the street from the office, the strikers stood around, watching. Hurstwood made his way over to the steps that led up to the office.

A police officer stopped him. "What are you looking for?" he asked.

"I want to see if I can get a job."

He let Hurstwood enter the office. The police

officer's heart was with the strikers, and he hated this "scab." But he felt that it was important to keep order. It was his duty to protect this man. But it was his duty only when he was commanded to do so.

When Hurstwood entered the office, he asked the clerk if he was hiring.

"What are you—a driver?" asked the clerk.

"No. I'm not anything," said Hurstwood. He wasn't embarrassed to say this. He knew that the company needed people to work for them during the strike. If this one wouldn't hire him, another one would.

"Well, we prefer experienced drivers, of course," said the man. He paused. Then he said, "Still, I guess you can learn. What is your name?"

"Wheeler," said Hurstwood.

"Go over to the yard and see the foreman. He'll show you what to do."

Hurstwood left the office and started walking toward the trolley yard.

The police officer watched him and thought, "There's another one who wants to try it. I have a feeling he'll be in for more than he'd like." He had been in strikes before.

CHAPTER 41

Some Strike,
Others Are Struck

Hurstwood waited for his instructions.

There were other men waiting—desperate, worn, hungry-looking men. They talked about the trouble they might run into from striking workers.

"The man who just came back from a run told me that they hit him in the ear with a rock," said one.

"I read in the paper that they're going to call out the civil defense troops," said another.

"Well, one of those fellows must have had a hell of a time," someone added. "They broke his trolley's windows. Then they pulled him off the car and into the street before the police could stop 'em."

"Yes, but there are more police around today," another one added.

Hurstwood listened without paying much attention. These men just seemed scared.

He overheard two other men talking. One said, "I had a job in a paper factory until I was laid off in October."

"I lost my job when the factory closed," said the other. "I don't blame these fellows for striking. They have their rights. But I still need to find some kind of work."

"Same here. If I could have kept a job near my home, I wouldn't be over here takin' chances like these."

"It's hell these days, ain't it? A poor man ain't nowhere. You could starve, by golly, right in the streets. And there ain't nobody would help you."

Hurstwood somehow felt a little superior to these two men—a little better off. He was still remembering the old days, when he had been successful.

The instructor called Hurstwood. He climbed into the trolley and listened as the man showed him how to operate the car. He'd seen drivers work before. He was sure he could do as well, with just a little practice.

He waited and waited, while the man talked on.

"Now you take it," the instructor said, finally.

But Hurstwood found that it was harder than he had imagined. He would have driven through the rear fence if the instructor hadn't grabbed one of the levers in time.

One o'clock came. He was still practicing. He began to feel hungry. It was snowing steadily now, and he was cold. He was getting tired of driving back and forth on the same short practice track.

Finally he was able to stop for lunch. He went into the nearby car barn and sat on a step. By now, the lunch he had packed was dry, and there was no water. He swallowed the bread and looked around. It was so dull, so miserable, so disagreeable. Not because it was bitter, but because it was hard.

After lunch, he spent most of the afternoon waiting around for his turn to practice some more.

At five-thirty, he realized that it wasn't worth going home that night. It would take him two and a half hours of cold walking and riding just to get home. Then he would have to leave by four-thirty the next morning in order to report by seven. He still had a little of Carrie's money. He had intended to use it to pay the heating bill. But he realized that he could use it to buy dinner at a cheap local restaurant. But where could he afford to sleep?

He decided to ask the foreman. "Isn't there some place I can stay around here tonight? If I have to go back to New York, I'm afraid I won't—"

"There are some cots upstairs," interrupted the man, "if you want one of them."

Hurstwood slept in his clothes. He tried to keep the dirty blanket away from his face. But he was so weary that he finally dozed off. It was so cold that the blanket seemed more and more comfortable. Finally he pulled it up around his neck and slept. He dreamed that he was back in Chicago, in his own comfortable home. He had been talking with his daughter about a trip she was planning. When he awoke, he was struck by the cold, bitter reality.

He went outside and found a barrel that had once been used to hold water for horses to drink. He washed his face with the ice-cold water. The foreman saw Hurstwood and suggested that he get some breakfast.

Hurstwood hesitated. Finally he asked, with difficulty, "Could you let me have a meal ticket since I don't have enough money to pay for it?"

"Here you are," said the man, handing him one.

He ate a poor breakfast of cheap meat and bad coffee. Afterward, his trolley was ready. He climbed into the car and waited for his instructions. He was nervous, but relieved. Anything was better than waiting in that barn.

Until now, the strike had been fairly peaceful. The striking workers had stopped a few cars and argued with the drivers. But only five or six men had been seriously injured.

Now things were becoming more violent. The strikers were becoming restless from doing nothing all day. They were becoming angry as they watched the companies, backed by the police, break the strike and win the battle. The strikers started attacking cars and men, tearing up the tracks, even firing guns. There were street fights and violent mobs. Civil troops were called in.

Hurstwood knew nothing of these changes.

The foreman told him to keep going, no matter what. "Don't stop for anyone who doesn't look like a real passenger. Whatever you do, don't stop for a crowd."

Then the conductor gave Hurstwood the signal to start the trolley. Two large, strong policemen climbed up beside him on the steering platform, one on each side.

"Run your car out," called the foreman, waving him forward. The conductor, also inexperienced, jumped up behind him and rang the bell twice as a signal to start. Hurstwood turned the lever and ran the car out into the street.

For the first part of the trip, there were few houses and people. They ran along smoothly. Hurstwood thought that the situation was not so unpleasant, after all. But he was becoming chilled by the cold wind on the open platform.

Suddenly a curve appeared ahead of him. Hurstwood almost lost control of the trolley.

Around the bend there were more people. A boy yelled angrily at Hurstwood, "Scab! Scab!"

Hurstwood tried not to think about the insult. He expected to get comments like that, and probably many more of them, too.

A little farther on, a man stood beside the track and signaled Hurstwood to stop the car.

"Ignore him," said one of the police officers. "He's up to some kind of trick."

The officer was right. As they passed by without stopping, the man shook his fist. "You damn coward!" he yelled.

Some other strikers, standing beside the man, threw angry insults after the speeding trolley.

Hurstwood felt the sting of their words. The

real thing was a little worse than he had thought it would be.

A few blocks farther on, he saw a pile of stones blocking the track.

Hurstwood stopped the car just before it. A crowd surrounded the trolley.

One of the men tried to talk him out of driving the car. In a pleasant, friendly voice, he urged Hurstwood not to undermine their strike. "Come off the car, Pal. You don't want to take food out of another man's mouth, do you?"

Hurstwood kept his hands on the controls, not sure what to do.

One of the police officers yelled to the crowd, "Stand back. Clear the way, now. Give the man a chance to do his work."

The man, who seemed to be the leader, ignored the policeman and continued talking to Hurstwood. "Listen, Pal. We're all working men, just like you. If you had been treated the way we've been, you wouldn't want someone to come in and take your job, would you? You wouldn't want someone to take away your rights, would you?"

Then the policemen jumped off the trolley and into the crowd. They began shoving and yelling, "Stand back, now! Get the hell out of here!"

"Don't shove me," said one of the strikers, holding his ground. "I'm not doing anything."

One of the officers swung his club, threatening to hit the man.

Another striker pushed his friend away. But he started cursing at the policeman.

The officer's club hit him on the forehead. The striker blinked, wobbled, and staggered backward.

Another striker's fist struck the officer's neck.

Furious, the policeman swung his club wildly in all directions. His partner did not try to calm the crowd. Instead, he started cursing back at the strikers. The strikers backed away from the clubs, but continued to stand nearby and jeer.

Finally, Hurstwood and the conductor joined the two officers on the ground. They picked the stones off the track, while the crowd continued to yell curses and threats.

"You scab, you!"

"You coward!"

"Steal a man's job, will you?"

"Rob the poor, will you, you thief?"

"We'll get you yet. You just wait!"

"You're the leeches that keep the poor people down!"

"May God starve you yet," yelled a woman at one of the policemen. "You hardhearted, murdering devil—hitting my son over the head with your club!"

But the officer ignored her and climbed back onto the front of the trolley.

Now that they had cleared away the stones, Hurstwood prepared to start the trolley. Suddenly rocks and stones flew through the window. One struck the edge of Hurstwood's head.

One of the officers grabbed the handle and started the trolley.

Hurstwood then took back the controls. Stones and curses were still raining on them as they sped away.

Hurstwood stared straight ahead. It was an amazing experience for him. He had read about strikes before. But the reality seemed something entirely different. He was not a coward. He had already suffered so much that he made up his mind to keep going.

In the heart of the business district, no one attacked the trolley. They simply stared at its broken windows and at Hurstwood, who was not wearing the uniform of the regular drivers. One of the officers stopped to report what had happened. He called for more policemen to clear out the crowd that was waiting for them to return on their next run.

On the route back, people watched, yelled, and cursed. But no one attacked them. Hurstwood was relieved when he saw the trolley barn. "Well," he thought, "I came out of that run all right."

After a break, Hurstwood was called out to make another run. A new team of officers was aboard. Feeling slightly more confident and less fearful, he sped along the less busy streets. The weather was raw, with snow flurries and a gusty wind. His clothing was not made for standing on an open trolley platform. He shivered, stamped his feet, and beat his arms as he had seen other drivers do in the past. Grim and sour, he said nothing. But he thought that it was a tough thing to have come to this. Still, Carrie's insult made him keep going. He was not down so low that he needed to take that kind of remark from her. He could do something—even this—for a little while. It would get better. He could start saving up some money.

A boy threw a lump of dirt at him, which hit him on the arm. It stung. And it made him angrier than anything else that had happened that day.

On one of the corners, an ex-driver called peacefully to him, "Won't you stop driving, Pal, and be a man? Remember, we're just fighting for a decent day's wages, that's all. We've got families to support."

Something about the voice appealed to Hurstwood. But he pretended not to see him. He kept his eyes straight ahead and sped away.

Then he drove up to a crowd that had blocked the tracks with an old telephone pole.

"Get that thing off the track!" shouted the two policemen.

"Get it off yourself!" the crowd yelled back.

The two policemen got down, and Hurstwood started to follow. But they told him to stay on the trolley so that none of the strikers ran away with it.

The same man who had spoken to him earlier was trying again to convince him not to break the strike. "Come down, Pal, and be a man. Don't fight the poor. Leave that to the big corporations."

As before, Hurstwood pretended not to hear him.

"Come on. You don't want to fight poor men, do you? Don't fight at all," he kept urging.

A third officer arrived. Someone had called for more officers. Hurstwood looked around, fearful, but determined.

Then a man grabbed him by the coat. "Get off the car!" the man yelled, trying to pull Hurstwood off the trolley.

"Let go of me," Hurstwood snarled, savagely.

"I'll show you—you scab!" cried a young man, jumping onto the car and swinging at Hurstwood. The fist struck him in the shoulder.

A policeman came to his rescue, cursing the man and pushing him away.

Hurstwood began wondering if he had made a bad decision. Things were becoming serious. People were yelling at him. A girl was making faces.

But then more police officers arrived and cleared the track.

"Get the trolley out of here, quick," the officer told him.

Again he sped away.

Toward the end of the run, about a mile from the lot, they entered an extremely poor neighborhood. Hurstwood wanted to run through it quickly, but again the track was blocked. He saw men carrying something out to it.

"There they are again!" exclaimed one policeman.

"I'll let them have it this time," said the other,

who was running out of patience.

As before, the crowd was yelling and cursing. But this time, the mob started throwing things at the trolley. Some windows were smashed. Hurstwood just missed being hit by a stone.

Both policemen jumped out and ran toward the crowd. The mob responded by running toward the car. A young woman almost hit Hurstwood with a rough stick. Her companions jumped on the car and pulled Hurstwood to the ground.

"Let go of me," he said, falling on his side.

"You leech," he heard someone say. Kicks and blows rained on him. He seemed to be suffocating.

Finally, the police officers were able to drag him away from the mob. He felt as if he would faint from exhaustion. Something was wet on his chin. He put up his hand and felt, then looked. It was red. He had been cut.

There were more police officers, and they were arresting anyone who tried to charge past them.

Then an ambulance arrived.

"Come on, now, if you want to take your car," said one of the officers.

Hurstwood was very cold and frightened. "Where's the conductor?" he asked.

"Oh, he's over there," answered the policeman, pointing toward the ambulance.

Hurstwood stepped nervously onto the trolley. Just then, there was a gun shot. Something stung his shoulder.

"Who fired that?" he heard an officer shout.

"By God! Who did that?"

Both policemen left him to look for the person who fired the shot.

"This is too much for me," said Hurstwood, trembling. He got off the trolley and walked nervously to the corner. Then he hurried down a side street.

"Whew!" he said, gasping.

A little girl saw him. "You'd better sneak away quietly," she called.

He walked toward home in a blinding snowstorm. He crossed the river back into New York. Then he continued on foot until he reached the apartment. He entered and found that it was warm. Carrie was out. He struck a match, lit the gas, and found something to eat. He checked his shoulder and his chin. He had been only slightly cut.

"Well," he thought, "there are some pretty rough things going on over there in Brooklyn."

Finally he sat down in his comfortable rocking chair. It was a wonderful relief. With a sigh, he picked up the evening newspaper. The headline read: "Strike Spreading in Brooklyn: Rioting Breaks Out in All Parts of the City."

He made himself very comfortable and continued. It was the one article he read with intense interest.

CHAPTER 42

Dollars and Change

The night that Hurstwood spent in the trolley barn in Brooklyn, Carrie performed on Broadway. The line of chorus girls was parading in front of the star of the show, a comedian. He was playing the role of an emperor. They were the beautiful and exotic women in his harem.

Suddenly he decided to add a comment that was not in the script. The audience chuckled when he demanded of the woman in front of him, "Well, who are you?"

Carrie just happened to be the woman who was curtsying to him right at that moment. The comedian did not expect an answer, since none of the chorus girls had speaking parts. But Carrie's experience and belief in herself made her daring. So she sweetly curtsied again and answered spontaneously, "I am yours truly."

Something in the way she said it made the audience laugh.

"I thought your name was Smith," he replied, making sure that he got the last laugh.

Afterward, Carrie was worried that she would get in trouble for adding lines. After all, it was strictly against the rules. But when the comedian saw how intelligent she seemed and how much the audience liked her response, he said, "You can leave that in from now on. Don't add any more, though."

"Thank you," said Carrie, humbly.

All the chorus girls knew that Carrie had gotten her first lucky break. Carrie hugged herself, knowing that something good would soon come of it.

But the next day, her mood changed. When she came home after rehearsal, Hurstwood's gloomy presence made her long to end their distressing relationship. She asked what he had been doing, but all he said was, "They're not running any cars without police. They don't want to hire anybody just now—not until next week."

Hurstwood said nothing else. So Carrie assumed that nothing more had happened—certainly nothing that would justify his quitting the job. It seemed to her that he simply did not want to work.

The next week came, but Carrie saw no change. Hurstwood seemed more passive and distant than ever. He hardly spoke to her anymore.

All day long, Hurstwood read and read. Sometimes he would stare at an article in the paper. But he would be thinking of something else. The first time this happened, he was reading about a party at one of the clubs he had belonged to back in Chicago. While he sat there, staring at the paper, he thought he heard the old voices and the clink of glasses.

"You're a fine fellow, Hurstwood," he thought he heard his friend say. He saw himself at the party, once again well dressed, good-natured, and smiling—delighting his friends with his entertaining stories.

Suddenly he looked up. He was back in his apartment in New York. But the room was so still that it seemed ghostlike. The first time this happened, it seemed strange to him. But the more it happened, the less strange it seemed.

The storeowners that had trusted him and let him pay on credit now started showing up at the apartment. They asked for the money that he owed them. At first he made up excuses. Later he didn't even try to explain, or else he pretended to be out.

Carrie was doing well in the chorus line. Even though she was timid, she knew that she could not let down the other members of the chorus. By now she had more experience than some of the other chorus girls. And she was too experienced to be excited or distracted by men's flirtatious and flattering comments. She had learned that men can change and fail. At this point in her life, only a kind, sincere, truly superior man could impress her. Only a man of genius—a man like Ames.

Lola Osborne, Carrie's friend, noticed that Carrie was a rising star. Lola also realized that she could never make it in the theater on her own. So she decided to attach herself to Carrie, clinging like a little kitten with its soft little claws.

One day she said to Carrie, "I know where I could get the loveliest apartment, cheap. It's too big for me, but it would be just right for two people. If we shared it, we'd each have to pay only half the rent."

"Well, I'm not sure whether I want to change," said Carrie. But she was already beginning to feel as though she had to be free. If she didn't have to support Hurstwood, then she'd have much more money for herself. If she left him, then he'd have to take care of himself. But he had become so strange lately that she was afraid that he might not let her leave. He might even hunt her down after the show and stalk her. That would be embarrassing and even frightening.

But then one of the actresses announced that she was leaving the show. She had a small part as a timid sweetheart. Carrie was selected to replace her.

"How much are you going to get?" asked Lola, when she heard the good news.

"I didn't think to ask," said Carrie.

"Well, find out. Goodness, you'll never get anything if you don't ask. Tell them you must have at least forty dollars."

"Oh, that's too much. I couldn't," said Carrie. "Sure you can!" exclaimed Lola. "At least ask 'em for it."

Later the manager told her what clothes she would need for the part. Knowing that she would need to buy these out of her own money, Carrie asked how much she would be paid.

"Thirty-five dollars," he replied.

Carrie was too delighted and amazed to think of asking for more. She almost hugged Lola, who clung to her even harder.

"They ought to pay you more," said Lola, "especially when you've got to buy your own clothes for the part."

Carrie had saved nothing for such an emergency. Where to get the money? Soon the rent would be due. She needed to buy the clothes if she wanted to keep the speaking role. "I never use the apartment," Carrie thought. "I won't pay the rent anymore. I'm not going to give up my money this time. I'll move."

Lola then said to Carrie, "Come share an apartment with me. We can have the loveliest place. It won't cost you hardly anything that way."

"I'd like to," Carrie admitted.

"Oh, do," urged Lola. "We'll have such a good time."

Carrie thought a while. "All right. I will," she said.

At the same time, Hurstwood had come up with his own idea about how to deal with the rent. The apartment cost so much money. "It's hard on her," he thought. "We could get a cheaper place."

So the next day at breakfast, Hurstwood suggested to Carrie, "I should think we could get a smaller place. We don't need four rooms."

"Oh, I don't know," she answered cautiously. She was worried that this meant he was becoming more determined to stay with her.

"There must be places around here where we could get just a couple of rooms. That would work out just as well for us."

Her heart protested. "Never!" she thought. To think of being in only two rooms with him! She decided to spend almost all her money on clothes. That way, there would not be enough money to move. She did so that very day. Now she had no choice. She would have to leave.

She visited her friend and announced, "Lola, I think I'll come. Can we rent it right away?"

"Certainly," cried Lola. "That's great!"

Carrie paid her half of the rent. But then she confided, "Now I've only got just enough to get by till the end of the week."

"Oh, I've got some," said Lola. "I've got twenty-five dollars, if you need it."

"No, thanks," said Carrie. "I guess I'll be all right."

They decided to move Friday, which was two days away. But now that everything was settled, Carrie felt like a criminal. She realized that Hurstwood was not really worthless, lazy, or unpleasant. There was something pathetic about him. He had been run down and beaten by things beyond his control. Perhaps he couldn't help it, after all. He had done well in Chicago. She remembered how strong and elegant he had seemed back then. Had it been all his fault? But now his eyes were vague, his face lined, his hair graying. He rocked in his chair and read his paper, unaware of what was about to happen to him.

Carrie knew that the end was near. She felt sorry for him now, and wanted to do as much for him as she could. She asked Hurstwood to buy some fancy food for dinner. She gave him a much larger bill than he needed. He looked in wonder at all the money. When he came back from the store, he put the change on the table.

"You'd better keep it," Carrie told him. "We'll need some other things."

"No," he said, with a sort of pride, "you keep it."

"Oh, go on and keep it," she replied, rather shaken by his trying to keep his dignity. "There'll be other things."

He wondered about this, not knowing how pathetic he seemed to her. But he noticed her kindness, and that made him think better of her. "Carrie's good-natured, anyhow," he thought.

Carrie felt bad about leaving Hurstwood, just as she had felt bad about leaving Drouet. Not that she had any choice about leaving. Still she did not want to hurt anyone who had been good to her.

The next day, she went to see Lola, who was busy packing.

"Would you mind lending me the twenty-five dollars you mentioned?"

"Why, no," said Lola, going for her purse.

"I want to get some other things," said Carrie.

On Friday morning, the sky was bright blue and the sun poured down its golden light. Carrie opened the windows of their apartment and felt the warm south wind blowing.

"It's lovely out today," she remarked.

"Is it?" said Hurstwood.

After breakfast, Hurstwood changed into his other clothes.

"Will you be back for lunch?" asked Carrie nervously.

"No," he said.

Hurstwood left the apartment and started walking toward the Harlem River. He tramped through the streets, looking at all the new buildings that had gone up in the old neighborhoods, making them so much better. By one o'clock, he reached the river. There it was—shining brightly in the clear light, winding its way between trees and hills. He stood looking at it, and then followed it for a while. At four o'clock he turned to go home. He was hungry and looked forward to eating in the warm room.

When he reached the apartment at five-thirty, it was dark. Even if Carrie did come home, dinner would be late. So he lit the gas and decided to fix something for himself.

But there was something strange about the apartment. Something was missing. What was it? He looked around the room, and then saw an envelope near his rocking chair.

He felt a chill settle over him as he opened the envelope. Inside were some soft dollar bills. He crunched the money in one hand, and read the note.

Dear George,
I'm going away. I'm not coming back anymore. It's no use trying to stay in the apartment. I can't do it. I wouldn't mind helping you, if I could. But I can't pay the rent and support both of us. I need the little bit of money I make to pay for my clothes. I'm leaving you twenty dollars. It's all I have just now. You can do whatever you like with the furniture. I won't need it.

Carrie

He dropped the note and looked quietly around the room. Now he knew what was missing. The little clock, which was hers, was gone. Then he went into the front room, his bedroom, the living room. Gone were a few silver ornaments, the lace tablecloth, her suitcase. He opened the drawers. There was nothing of hers. Back in his own room hung his old clothes, just as he had left them. Nothing else was gone.

He stood a few moments, staring at the floor. The silence became overwhelming. The apartment seemed empty. He forgot that he was hungry. It seemed too late to eat.

Suddenly he noticed that the money was still in his hand.

"I'll find a way out of this," he said to himself.

Then the intense loneliness of his situation flooded him.

"Left me!" he muttered. "Left me!"

The place had been so comfortable. He had spent so many days there, warm and safe. Now it was just a memory. In front of him was something much colder. He sank down in his chair, resting his chin in his hand.

"She didn't have to go away," he thought, rocking in his chair. "I'd have found a job."

Then he added clearly, out loud, "I tried, didn't I?"

At midnight he was still rocking, staring at the floor.

CHAPTER 43

Smiles and Frowns

Now that she had moved into her comfortable room, Carrie wondered how Hurstwood had taken her departure. At first she half expected to find him waiting for her outside the theater door. But after a few days, she still had heard nothing from him and stopped worrying that he would try to bother her. Soon she forgot all about him. Now she was free of the gloom that had been weighing her down.

The showy world of her new profession completely absorbed her. She read the newspapers and theatrical magazines, and longed to have her name mentioned. A desire to become famous took hold of her.

The Sunday before she started her new role, Carrie saw a small notice in one of the magazines.

The part of the country maiden in *The Wives of Abdul* will no longer be played by Inez Carew. It will now be performed by Carrie Madenda. Miss Madenda seems to be one of the brightest members of the chorus at the Broadway.

Carrie hugged herself with delight. Oh, wasn't it just fine! At last! The first, the long hoped-for, the delightful notice! And they called her bright. She showed it to Lola.

Lola was pleased for her friend. "You'll see," she said. "Soon they'll put in your picture, too. You act better than most of the people who get their pictures in now."

Carrie felt deeply grateful for this. She almost loved Lola for the encouragement and praise she gave her. It was so helpful to her—almost necessary.

After appearing in her new part, she received another positive review. She was thrilled. She began to think that the world was noticing her.

Her first week's salary of thirty-five dollars seemed like an enormous amount of money. She gave Lola back the money she had borrowed and paid her share of the rent. She made the next payment on the clothes she had bought. The next week she had even more money, since she had already repaid Lola. It seemed ridiculous. She had so much money left over to spend on herself.

"You'd better save a little for the summer," cautioned Lola. "The show will probably close in May."

Carrie agreed. After years of trying to get by on so little money, now she had a regular paycheck and a purse bursting with good, green dollar bills. No one was dependent on her. She began buying pretty clothes, eating well, and decorating her room. She enjoyed going out with Lola on carriage rides, to after-theater restaurants, for strolls along Broadway. Soon friends began to gather around her.

A young man in their show became interested in her. One midnight, after their performance, he invited her to a restaurant for an after-theater snack. But she found him too awkward, too conceited. He did not talk of anything that lifted Carrie above the common level of clothes and material success. After dinner, he smiled at her, very warmly and pleasantly.

"Do you have to go straight home?" he asked. "Yes," she answered, understanding what he meant.

"She's not as innocent as she looks," he thought. This made him even more interested in her.

At last her picture appeared in the paper. The caption read, "Miss Carrie Madenda, one of the favorites in *The Wives of Abdul* chorus line." She thought of buying a few extra copies of the paper. But then she remembered that there was no one she knew well enough to send them to. It seemed that only Lola, in all the world, was really interested in her success.

The city was a cold place socially. Carrie began to feel that her little amount of money brought her nothing. The world of wealth and fame was as far away as ever. People seemed to be out for their own pleasure. They didn't care what happened to anyone else. Everyone approached her with easy laughter. But she felt that they were not acting out of warm, caring, true friendship.

The opera announced that it was closing in May. Carrie wondered whether she should travel with the show next season. But Lola advised her to stay in New York.

"But what if I can't get anything else around here?"

"We can get along," Lola said. "I always have. Besides, when you leave New York, they forget all about you."

Carrie met with the manager of the summer show at the Casino. He had never heard of her. But then she showed him the reviews that mentioned her, her picture in the paper, and the program that listed her as an actress with a part.

He decided to give her a non-speaking part for thirty dollars. Because she was pretty, the men who made up the ads for the show included Carrie's photo in their announcements. She was delighted with the announcements. But when she saw that she had nothing to say or do onstage, she frowned in disappointment.

The man who wrote the show saw how gloomy she looked, and told the manager that he wanted to cut out the part. But then at the dress rehearsal, he decided that her sad expression made her part look even funnier. So the manager told Carrie to frown even more, and to keep her mournful expression through the entire show.

At the opening performance, Carrie frowned and frowned through the first act. But the audience was watching the stars and did not notice her.

During the second act, the audience became bored during a long conversation between the lead actors. They started looking around the stage and spotted Carrie. There she was—wearing a gray suit, looking sweet and gentle, but frowning. She just stood there, frowning at the stars of the show. The audience began to smile, then giggle. The gentlemen in the front rows thought she looked like a delicious young thing. They would have loved to take away that frown with their kisses. All the men desired her. She was wonderful.

By the next act, Carrie was the most interesting part of the play. Nothing was as entertaining as Carrie's teasing, charming, delightful expression. The more the audience watched her, the more they showed their delight. She was a hit.

The reviews in the papers praised Carrie's humorous performance. One critic wrote, "Miss Madenda does one of the most delightful bits of character work ever seen on the Casino stage. The audience has chosen Miss Madenda as their favorite. She easily held their attention and brought their applause."

Another critic wrote, "If you wish to be merry, see Carrie frown."

Even the author of the show was pleased.

The next day, the manager congratulated her. "You seem to have taken the town by storm. This is delightful. I am glad for both of us." Then he explained that the author was writing a little song for her. "He would like you to sing it next week."

"Oh, I can't sing," replied Carrie.

"It isn't anything difficult. He said that it's very simple and would be just right for you."

"Well, of course, I wouldn't mind trying," said Carrie.

Then the manager put a new contract in front of Carrie. "We want to be fair about your salary, of course. Your old contract was for only thirty dollars a week for the next three months. How would it be if we made it, say, one hundred and fifty dollars a week? And for twelve months instead of three?"

"Oh, that would be fine," said Carrie, hardly believing her ears.

"Then why don't you just sign this."

The new contract looked the same as the old one, except that the numbers were different. With a trembling hand, she signed her name.

"One hundred and fifty a week!" she thought. She couldn't really understand what it meant to have that much money. It was only a number. But it was a shimmering, glittering number that opened a world of possibilities to her.

Meanwhile, in a dark, dreary, dirty hotel, Hurstwood read the newspaper reviews. At first he didn't realize who this Carrie Madenda really was. Then suddenly it became clear.

"I guess she's struck it rich," he thought. He remembered his old world—the shiny world of the theater, with its bright lights, fine carriages, beautiful flowers. Ah, now she was inside the walled city of wealth and fame. Its splendid gates had opened, letting her in from the cold, gloomy world outside. She was far away from him now—just like every other famous person he had known.

"Well, let her have her fame and fortune," he said grimly. "I won't bother her."

His pride was bent and worn, but still unbroken.

CHAPTER 44

What Money Can't Buy

The next day Carrie was taken to a different dressing room. She was delighted to find that it was much nicer than the one she used to share with the other chorus girls. She was no longer told, but asked what to do—and asked politely. The other cast members looked at her with envy. The actors that used to look down on her smiled now, as if to say, "We've always liked you and been your friends." The audience applauded for her. But she felt a little guilty. Maybe she wasn't worthy of all this? It never occurred to her to be proud or conceited. She was the same as she had always been. The manager called a carriage to take her home after the performance. But she still went back with Lola to the small place they shared.

Somehow, a man named Mr. Withers found out where she lived and showed up one afternoon.

"Excuse me for asking," he said politely. "But have you thought about living somewhere else?"

"No, I hadn't," Carrie replied.

"Well, I represent the Wellington Hotel. You

may have read about it?"

Carrie knew that it was one of the newest and most impressive hotels on Broadway. She had heard that it had a splendid restaurant.

"Indeed," continued Mr. Withers. "We have some very elegant rooms that we would like you to look at. Our apartments are perfect in every detail."

Carrie wondered if he thought she was a millionaire.

"What are your rates?" she asked.

"Our regular rates are three to fifty dollars a day."

"Goodness!" interrupted Carrie. "I couldn't afford to pay that much."

"But let me explain. We do have special rates. It is good publicity to have a well-known actress, like you, stay at our hotel."

Carrie flushed with pride and embarrassment.

Mr. Withers bowed politely, and then continued, "You see, that brings us more business. So I want to arrange for you to stop by the Wellington and take a look. We will give you your choice of nice, bright, outside rooms—the very best rooms that we have."

Carrie tried to interrupt, but he did not give her a chance. "Please don't worry about the rates. We really don't even need to discuss them. Anything will do for now—anything you think you could afford to pay."

"You're very kind," said Carrie, touched by his

graciousness. "I would very much like to come. I would want to pay what is right, however. I wouldn't want to—"

"You don't need to worry about that at all," interrupted Mr. Withers. "If three dollars a day is satisfactory to you, it will be fine with us. So you'll allow me to show you the rooms?"

"I'd be glad to," said Carrie. But then suddenly she remembered Lola.

"I have a roommate," she added, "who will have to go wherever I do. I forgot about that."

"Yes, of course," said Mr. Withers. "It is up to you to decide who you want with you. Everything can be arranged however you wish."

Lola was delighted to hear Carrie's news. That afternoon Mr. Withers showed them an elegant and beautifully decorated apartment. The living room had a piano, several huge rocking chairs, and some paintings on the walls. Normally such an apartment would cost a hundred dollars a week.

"Oh, lovely!" exclaimed Lola, walking around.

"It is so comfortable," said Carrie. She lifted a lace curtain on one of the windows and looked down onto crowded Broadway.

"Do you find these satisfactory?" asked Mr. Withers.

"Oh, very," answered Carrie.

"Well, then, they are ready for you whenever you would like to move in."

Carrie looked at the elegant carpet in the hallway, the marble in the showy lobby. She had often dreamed of living in a place like this.

They moved in the next day.

After her matinee performance the next Wednesday, there was a knock at her door. It was Mrs. Vance.

"Why, look at you!" exclaimed Mrs. Vance. "How in the world did this happen?"

Carrie laughed. Her friend did not seem at all embarrassed. It was as though their long separation was just an accident.

"I don't know," said Carrie. Mrs. Vance was so lovely and good-natured that Carrie stopped feeling awkward about seeing her.

"Well, you know, I saw your picture in the Sunday paper. But your name confused me. It looked just like you, though. So I decided that I would have to come and see for myself. I was never more surprised in my life. How are you, anyway?"

"Oh, very well," answered Carrie. "How have you been?"

"Fine. But you are quite a success! All the papers are talking about you. You must be just too proud to breathe. I was almost afraid to come back here this afternoon."

"Oh, nonsense," said Carrie, embarrassed. "You know I'd always be glad to see you."

"Well, anyhow, why don't you join me for lunch? Where are you staying?"

"At the Wellington," said Carrie. She felt a touch of pride in giving her new address.

"Oh, are you?" exclaimed the other, impressed.

Mrs. Vance could not help wondering what had happened to Hurstwood. But she did not ask. No doubt, Carrie had left him.

"I'm afraid I don't have enough time to join you today. I have to be back here for the evening performance."

Mrs. Vance thought that Carrie was even more appealing, now that she was so successful. "Well, then, let me know when you can come visit—if you can at all."

"Why, anytime you like," said Carrie.

"Well, tomorrow then. I'm living at the Chelsea now."

"Moved again?" exclaimed Carrie, laughing.

"Yes. You know I can't stay more than six months in the same place. I just have to move. I'll see you tomorrow, then, at five-thirty."

"I won't forget," said Carrie.

It occurred to her that now she was just as good as Mrs. Vance—perhaps even better. Mrs. Vance had seemed so interested in her. For once, Carrie felt that she was the one looking down on other people—not the other way around.

Carrie never grew tired of flattery. Now that she had money and fame, men found her even more attractive. They sent her fan mail, telling her how much they adored her and begging her to go out with them. Wealthy gentlemen told her how wonderful—and how rich—they were. Carrie understood, though, that they were interested only in her fame and fortune. And that made her even less interested in going out with them.

One day she read a letter, which said:

> I have a million dollars. I could give you every luxury. You could have anything you wish. I'm not saying this because I want to speak of my money. But I love you, and I want to satisfy your every desire. I am writing out of love. Won't you please give me a half-hour to show you how much I love you?

"Look at this," she laughed, showing the letter to Lola. "This man says 'I am writing out of love.' Imagine! Aren't men silly?"

"He must have lots of money, the way he talks," said Lola.

"That's what they all say," said Carrie.

"Why don't you see him," suggested Lola, "and hear what he has to say?"

"I will not," said Carrie. "I know what he'd say. I don't want to meet anybody that way."

Lola grinned. "He couldn't hurt you. You might even have some fun with him."

Carrie shook her head "no."

"You certainly have some strange ideas," said her friend.

For the next week, the world seemed to know and trust Carrie, even though she had not yet been paid her new, higher salary. Everyone seemed satisfied that she was a rising star. The doors of fine places opened for her. She did not even need to ask. She was welcome anytime to visit Mrs. Vance's elegant apartment at the Chelsea. Men sent her flowers, love notes, offers of money. Each day her dreams and her desires grew and multiplied. Soon she imagined that she had much, much more than even her one-hundred-and-fifty-dollar salary could buy.

Finally payday arrived. The cashier smiled and greeted her politely when she went to collect the money. "Ah, yes," said the cashier. "Miss Madenda—one hundred and fifty dollars. The show seems to have become quite a success."

As she walked away, Carrie heard the cashier greet the next person, an unimportant dancer in the chorus line.

"How much?" the cashier demanded, sharply. She noticed his change in tone. It reminded her of her job at the shoe factory. There the foreman handed her an envelope as though she were a slave or a beggar. She worked so hard there, and still earned only four dollars and fifty cents a week. Right now in Chicago, the same factory would be filled with poor, plainly dressed young women, working in long lines at clattering machines. At noon they would have a half-hour to eat a miserable lunch. They would have to accept very little money for work that was a hundred times harder than what she was doing now. Oh, it was so easy now! The world was so rosy and bright.

A hundred and fifty dollars! She was thrilled. As she walked back to her hotel, she wondered how she would spend it all. She thought about what she had and what she wanted. And then she realized. To move higher or do something better would take even more money. She must have more—much more.

Then other people started making demands on her. She was asked to perform without pay for a benefit show to raise money for charities. A young author asked her to produce a play he had written. A critic wrote a review saying that he liked Carrie. But then he added that she was successful only because she was pretty, good-natured, and lucky. This stung her. Since it was summer, there were few shows onstage and little to do for entertainment. The rich had left the city on vacation. Carrie realized that the door to life's perfect happiness was not yet open to her.

"I don't know," she said to Lola one day, sitting at one of the windows which looked down onto Broadway. "I get lonely. Don't you?"

"No," said Lola, "not very often. But that's because you won't go anywhere. That's what's the matter with you."

"Where can I go?"

"Why, there are lots of places," replied Lola. She thought about all her dates with carefree young men. "You won't go out with anybody."

"I don't want to go out with those people who write to me. I know what kind of men they are."

"Well, you shouldn't be lonely," said Lola, thinking of Carrie's success. "There are lots of people who would give anything to have what you have."

Carrie looked out again at the crowds wandering down Broadway.

"I don't know," she said. Without realizing it, she was already starting to become restless and dissatisfied.

CHAPTER 45

How Much Can
a Person Stand?

Hurstwood sat in his cheap hotel room. Seventy dollars was all there was between him and nothing. He had sold his furniture and used the money to pay the rent, which was now fifty cents a day. He spent the summer and fall in the hotel, reading. But now his money was slipping away. To make his money last longer, he finally moved to a cheaper hotel. There he paid only thirty-five cents a day.

When all except twenty dollars of his money had gone, he moved to a boarding house in the Bowery district, one of the poorest parts of the city. Here his room cost only fifteen cents a night. During the day, he sat in a bare living room, shared by all the residents, and dreamed of his old life in Chicago. As the present became darker and drearier, the past seemed brighter and more real. In his mind, he was back at Fitzgerald and Moy's, entertaining his old friends. Sometimes when he spoke in his daydreams, he actually moved his lips. Once he imagined that he had been telling a joke. Without realizing it, he said the punch line out loud. "Why don't you jump, you bloody fool?" he said, not only in his dream, but in reality, as well. "Jump!" he repeated. An old man sitting nearby looked up and glared at him. Hurstwood felt ashamed. But, without meaning to do so, he still sometimes talked out loud when he was day-dreaming.

He saw reminders of Carrie everywhere—reviews and pictures in the papers, a pretty poster with her looking sweet and dainty. Each one made her seem more distant. She was entering a world of wealth and pleasure, a world that was moving far-ther and farther away from him. He looked at his own shabby clothes and resented her success. But he also found it comforting to know that she was still nearby. As long as he knew where she was, he was not quite alone.

But one day he noticed that a different show was playing at the Casino. Carrie had left the city! Shaken up, he almost had to admit that somehow he was depending on her being nearby. Now she was gone. Goodness knows when she would be back. Terrified, he counted his remaining money. There were only ten dollars left.

He looked around at the other men in the boarding house. How did they manage? They did-n't seem to do anything. Probably they begged for money. Back in Chicago, he often gave dimes to beggars. He had seen other men asking for money on the streets. Maybe he could get some that way. He was horrified by the thought, but desperate.

Finally, he came to his last fifty cents. He knew he had to do something. But as he walked around, looking for something to do, another day went by. So now he was down to his last twenty cents. There was not even enough money to buy food the next day.

He called up all his courage and walked into the Broadway Central Hotel. Hurstwood went up to one of the hotel managers and looked him straight in the eye.

"Could you give me some work to do for a few days?" he asked. "I'm in a position where I have to find a job right away."

The manager looked him over. It was clear that he had no money at all.

"I came here," explained Hurstwood, nervously, "because I, too, was once a manager. I've had some bad luck, but I'm not here to tell you that. I want some work, if only for a week."

The man saw the gleam of desperation in the ex-manager's eyes. "What hotel did you manage?" he asked.

"It wasn't a hotel," said Hurstwood. "For fifteen years I was manager of Fitzgerald and Moy's saloon in Chicago."

"Well, why did you leave?" asked the hotel man. At the moment, Hurstwood certainly did not look as if he had ever been a successful manager.

"Well, it was my own foolishness. There's no need to go into it. You could find out if you wanted to. The point is, I'm broke. And I haven't had anything to eat yet today."

The hotel manager did not know what to do with this worn-out man. And yet, Hurstwood seemed so sincere, intelligent, and desperate that he wanted to do something to help him.

He called the head porter and told him to find Hurstwood something to do. He asked the cook to give him something to eat. And then he let him sleep in the attic of the hotel.

For several months Hurstwood endured it all. He ate whatever the cook gave him; he let the clerks and porters and janitors tell him what to do. They did not like his superior manner and his gloomy way of keeping to himself. So they made the situation unpleasant for him. For all this hard work, he was given only a few dollars a week. But he accepted this, and tried to save as much as possible.

One day in February, he was sent out on an errand through the cold, snowy streets. He came back chilled, wet, and exhausted. The next day he tried to lift a heavy box, but could not.

"What's the matter, there?" asked the head porter. "Can't you handle it?"

Hurstwood was straining to lift it, but now he gave up. "No," he said, weakly.

The man looked at him and saw that he was deathly pale. "Not sick, are you?" he asked.

"I think I am," answered Hurstwood.

"Well, you'd better go sit down, then."

The next day, he could not even get up. He had a high fever, was very weak, and could hardly breathe. The hotel doctor looked at him. "Better send him to Bellevue Hospital," he recommended. "He's got pneumonia."

Hurstwood did not leave the hospital until May.

By then he was thin, pale, and weak. He had been given some old clothes and a few cents in change.

"What can a man do?" he said. "I can't starve."

He saw a well-dressed man strolling toward him. Hurstwood worked up his courage and asked him directly, "Would you mind giving me ten cents? I'm in a position where I must ask some-one."

Without looking at him, the man fished in his pocket and handed him a dime.

"Thank you kindly," said Hurstwood, softly. But the other man ignored him.

He was ashamed of his situation. But he was relieved that this had worked. So he decided to try to get another twenty-five cents and then stop. That would be just enough to pay for that night's dinner and room. He looked at the people on the street, and tried to identify the ones that might give him some money. Finally he found someone to ask. But that person refused. Hurstwood was so shocked and hurt by this that it took him an hour to try again. This time he was given a nickel. By working carefully, he was able to get another twenty cents. But it took a long time, and it was painful.

The next day, he tried again to ask for money. He saw a man arrested for begging, which made his task even more stressful and unpleasant. But he kept on trying. In a vague way he thought that somehow things would get better.

One morning he was relieved to see an announcement that Miss Carrie Madenda was returning to the Casino. How successful she was! How much money she must have! He was so weak and hungry now that he finally said, "All right. I'll go and ask her for a little help. She won't refuse me a few dollars."

That evening he stood like a shadow by the stage door of the theater. One person after another passed him. Almost all were well dressed. Almost all ignored him.

Suddenly a carriage arrived, and the driver jumped out to open the door. Before Hurstwood could act, two ladies hurried by and disappeared into the theater. He thought that one was Carrie. But she seemed so elegant, so distant that he was not sure. Since no one else arrived, he concluded that it was Carrie. But if she had come in a carriage, she would also leave in a carriage. He would never be able to catch up with her that night.

"But I've got to get something tonight," he thought, as he walked out onto the street.

At the same time, another man walked out onto the corner where Broadway and Fifth Avenue meet. This man had once been a soldier, and then became poor and outcast. Now he had just enough money to support himself. He decided that he wanted to help people who were homeless. So every night he stood on this corner and asked people passing by for money. He used their charity to pay for a bed for every person who came to him that night for help.

One by one, men in worn and faded clothing came up to him. In the glare of the bright lights on Broadway, some of their faces looked dry and chalky. Other faces were red, puffy, and covered with blotches.

Soon a small group of people had gathered around the man, who was known as "the captain." He told the men, "Well, line up here. I'll see what I can do. I haven't a cent myself."

They fell into a sort of broken, ragged line, and waited. Then the people leaving the theaters came over to see what was going on.

The captain turned to the crowd. "Now, then, gentlemen, these men are without beds. They have to have a place to sleep tonight. They can't lie out in the streets. I need twelve cents to put one of them to bed. Who will give it to me?"

No reply.

"Well, we'll have to wait here, boys, until someone does. Twelve cents isn't so very much for one man."

A young man came forward. "Here's fifteen. It's all I can afford."

"All right. Now I have fifteen." He took one of the homeless men by the shoulder and led him a few feet away. "Now stand over here."

Then he came back to his place and began again.

"I have three cents left. These men must be put to bed somehow. There are," he said, counting out loud, "one, two, three, four, five, six, seven, eight, nine, ten, eleven, twelve men. Nine cents more will give the next man a good, comfortable bed for the night. I go there myself and make sure that's how the money is spent. Who will give me nine cents?"

This time a middle-aged man handed him a nickel.

"Now, I have eight cents. Four more will give this man a bed. Come, gentlemen. We are making very slow progress this evening. You all have good beds. Now how about these men?"

Another bystander placed a coin in his hand.

"That," said the captain, looking at the coin, "pays for two beds for two men. And it gives me five cents toward the next one. Who will give me seven cents more?"

"I will," said a voice.

Walking away from the Casino, Hurstwood just happened to walk by this scene. He was completely depressed, desperately hungry, extremely weary. He felt defeated. He had no food and no bed. He saw a line of men, and he recognized that they were like him. They, too, were drifting in their minds and on the streets. With surprise and relief, he heard a man repeat the words, "These men must have a bed." He watched as another man came out from the shadows and stood at the end of the line. So he decided to do the same thing. Why fight it? He was weary tonight. At least this was one way out of his difficulty. Tomorrow, maybe, he could do better.

Standing, waiting, Hurstwood became so weary that he was afraid he would drop from exhaustion. At last his turn came. The man ahead of him had already been paid for. Now Hurstwood was first in line, and the captain was trying to help him.

"Twelve cents, gentlemen—twelve cents puts this man to bed. He wouldn't stand here in the cold if he had anyplace else to go."

Hurstwood felt disgusted and ashamed. But hunger and weakness made him swallow his pride.

"Here you are," said a stranger, handing money to the captain.

Then the captain put a kind hand on the ex-manager's shoulder. "Line up over there," he said.

Hurstwood joined the line of the successful. The strain of uncertainty had been lifted, so now he could breathe more easily. Maybe the world was not quite so bad a place when there was such a good man in it.

A cab stopped, and a gentleman in a tuxedo handed a bill to the captain.

"That fixes up nine men for the night," said the captain. "Now, then, there are only seven men left. I need twelve cents."

Money came slowly as fewer people passed by

on Broadway.

But the captain was determined. He talked on, as though he could not fail.

"Come on, now. I can't stay out here all night. These men are getting tired and cold. Someone give me four cents."

A clock struck eleven. The theater lights were turned off.

By eleven-thirty, he was down to the last two men.

"Come, now," he urged. "Eighteen cents will fix us all up for the night. Eighteen cents. I have six. Somebody give me the money. Remember, I can't go home myself until I take these men down and put them to bed. Eighteen cents."

No one responded.

But the captain would not leave until all the men had beds.

Hurstwood tried not to groan. He was so weak that he could hardly stand.

At last a gentleman walked down the street, with an elegantly dressed lady gracefully holding onto his arm. Hurstwood stared wearily. He remembered the time when he used to walk down the street with his own wife, on their way home from the theater. The lady in fine clothing reminded him of Carrie in her new world of luxury.

The lady looked at the men, and sent her husband over with a bill.

"Thanks," said the captain. "Now we have some money for tomorrow night."

He lined up the last two men.

"One hundred and thirty-seven," he counted. He walked to the front of the line and led the men through the streets. After a long, weary, midnight march, at last they came to a boarding house. It looked closed for the night. But the landlord was expecting the captain and his men.

At last the doors swung open, and they were invited in. The captain watched, waiting to be sure that every single man was taken care of. Then he stepped back into the night to make his way to his own home.

Hurstwood struggled up the stairs. His legs ached as he finally sat down on the miserable bed in his small, dark room. "I can't stand much more of this," he said. "I've got to eat, or I'll die."

CHAPTER 46

Drifting in Different Directions

After her performance one evening, Carrie heard a familiar voice outside her dressing room door.

"Come on, now. I want to see Miss Madenda."

There was a knock at the door. Carrie opened it.

"Well, well!" exclaimed Drouet. "I knew it was you the moment I saw you."

Carrie stepped back, expecting to have an awkward, or even an angry conversation with him.

"So aren't you going to shake hands with me?" he said cheerfully.

Carrie smiled at his good-natured energy. He was older. But he still wore the same fine clothes, the same lively expression.

"Say, you do great in your role. I knew you would. I saw your name on the program. But I didn't know it was you until you came onstage. Then I remembered. That's the name you used out in Chicago, isn't it?"

"Yes," answered Carrie, a little dazed by the man's self-confidence. He seemed to expect that now they could go back to their old relationship.

"So, how have you been, anyway?"

"Oh, very well," said Carrie. "How have you been?"

"Me? Oh, fine. I'm in charge of a branch office here in New York, now."

"How nice!"

"Well, when did you start performing onstage, anyhow?" asked Drouet.

"About three years ago," said Carrie.

"Well, I knew you could do it. I always said you could act, didn't I?"

Carrie smiled. "Yes, you did," she said.

"Well, you do look great," he said. "Say, how about going out to dinner with me? I want to have a good talk with you."

"No, no," said Carrie. "I can't. Please don't ask me anymore."

Carrie noticed that his face fell. Maybe he was beginning to realize that things had changed. Still, he had always liked her, and he deserved to be treated kindly. Feeling guilty, she invited him to join her for lunch the next day.

"All right," said Drouet, brightening. "Where are you staying?"

"At the Waldorf," she answered. It was the newest, most fashionable hotel in New York City.

Carrie was not looking forward to having lunch with Drouet. But the next day, she saw that he was as nice-looking and pleasant as ever. And since he was still self-centered, he started by talking about his own career.

"I'm going to have a business of my own pretty soon," he told her. "I can get backing for two hundred thousand dollars."

Carrie listened good-naturedly.

"Say," he said, suddenly, "where is Hurstwood now?"

Embarrassed, Carrie flushed a little.

"I guess he's here in New York," she said. "I haven't seen him for some time."

Drouet was relieved that Carrie had gotten rid of Hurstwood. "It certainly was a mistake to do what he did," he said.

"Did what?" asked Carrie. She had no idea what Drouet was talking about.

"Oh, you know," replied Drouet, assuming that she knew what had happened before Hurstwood left Chicago.

"No, I don't," Carrie answered. "What do you mean?"

"Why that incident in Chicago—the time he left."

"I don't know what you are talking about," said Carrie.

"You're kidding!" exclaimed Drouet. He couldn't believe that Carrie didn't know. "You knew that he took ten thousand dollars with him when he left, didn't you?"

"What!" gasped Carrie, shocked. "You're not saying that he stole money, are you?"

Drouet, puzzled by her surprise, said, "But you knew that, didn't you?"

"Why, no," said Carrie. "Of course I didn't."

"Well, that's strange," said Drouet. "He did, you know. It was in all the newspapers."

"How much did you say he took?" said Carrie.

"Ten thousand dollars. I heard he sent most of it back afterward, though."

Carrie now saw everything in a new light. She remembered little things from the years since Hurstwood had forced her to run away with him. Now she understood why these things had happened. She also imagined that he had taken the money because of her. Instead of hating him, she felt sadness and pity for him. Poor fellow! What a thing to have had hanging over his head all this time.

During dinner, Drouet imagined that he was winning over Carrie. Maybe it would not be so difficult to enter her life again. Ah, what a prize! How beautiful, how elegant, how famous she was! She was the most desirable thing in his life right now.

"Do you remember how nervous you were that night at the Avery Theater, back in Chicago?" he asked.

Carrie smiled as she thought about it.

"I never saw anybody act better than you did then, Cad." Then he added a tone of sorrow to his voice. "Back then, I really thought that you and I were going to get along fine."

"You must not talk like that," said Carrie. She added a touch of coldness to her voice.

"Won't you let me tell you how much—"

"No," she interrupted, standing up from the

table. "I have to get ready for my performance tonight. I'll have to leave you."

"Oh, stay a little longer," begged Drouet. "You've got plenty of time."

"No," said Carrie, gently. She walked to the elevator and stepped inside.

"But when can I see you again?" asked Drouet.

"Oh, sometime, possibly," said Carrie. "I'll be here all summer. Goodnight!"

The elevator door closed.

Drouet walked sadly down the hall. He felt again all his old longing for her, now that she was so far away. But then he realized that the old days were gone for good. "She's not so great," he said. But in his heart, he did not believe this.

That was the same night that Carrie and Lola took a carriage to the theater and hurried in through the stage entrance. Carrie had passed Hurstwood, who was standing near the door. But she had not noticed him in the shadows.

The next night, though, she walked to the theater. Hurstwood was waiting for her. He was thinner than ever. At first she did not recognize the shabby, worn-out man in front of her. She was frightened when this hungry stranger walked up close to her.

"Carrie," he half-whispered, "can I have a few words with you?"

Suddenly she recognized him. She felt shock and pity. Still, she remembered what Drouet had said about his stealing the money.

"Why, George," she said, "what's the matter with you?"

"I've been sick," he answered. "I just got out of the hospital. For God's sake, let me have a little money, will you?"

"Of course," said Carrie. She opened her purse and pulled out all the money in it—a total of nine dollars. "Here. It's all I have with me."

"All right," he answered, softly. He almost resented her pity. Her luck had been so much better than his. "I'll give it back to you someday."

People walking by stared at Carrie. She knew that it would be bad publicity to spend any more time with this worn and broken man. Hurstwood realized this, too.

"Better go on in," he said. "I won't bother you anymore."

She tried to answer. But he turned and walked away, dragging his feet.

In June, the show left New York to play in London for the summer. Carrie was so busy getting ready for the trip that she forgot all about Hurstwood.

Hurstwood drifted through the long summer and fall. A small job as a janitor helped him for a month. Then begging, sometimes going hungry, sometimes sleeping in the park, he managed for a few more days. A few charities also helped. For weeks, in the dead of winter, he wandered around the city, begging. He did not know that Carrie had come back to New York and was now appearing on Broadway in a new play.

About this time, Ames returned to New York and opened a research laboratory. One afternoon Carrie ran into him at the Vances' apartment. But she was less interested in him than before. Now she had wealth and fame. She thought he would approve of her success. But he was disappointed that she had settled for acting in comedies. He thought she could do far better than that.

They stopped talking for a moment to listen to some music playing in the background.

"I don't know what it is about music," Carrie began. "But it always makes me feel as if I wanted something—as if I—"

"Yes," he said. "I know how you feel. But you shouldn't be sad. The world is full of things we desire. But, unfortunately, we can each live only one life in it. It doesn't do us any good to want what we cannot have, what we cannot be."

Carrie was thrilled that he seemed to take her so seriously.

"You know," he continued, "you are the kind of person who would do well in drama. That's where you belong—not in comedy."

"Why?" she asked. He was so unpretentious and so honest that, once again, she wanted to meet his high expectations of her.

"You seem to feel so much sympathy for others."

For the moment, Carrie stopped feeling lonely. Here was praise that was intelligent and thoughtful.

Ames seemed to appreciate her for who she really was.

"There is something about your mouth that makes you look like you're about to cry," he continued. "And there's a shadow around your eyes that gives them depth. It makes your face look sad and wistful."

Carrie looked directly at him. This was what her heart craved.

"You see, your face naturally expresses longing. It expresses a feeling that other people have inside. Looking at you is like listening to a sad song."

She was pleased that he talked to her this way. She longed to live up to his standards. He reminded her that she was drifting away from the old ideal that she had felt after her first performance in Chicago. Why had she lost it?

"People are always struggling to express their feelings," he went on. "But most people cannot. So they depend on others to express how they feel. Your face expresses their feelings of longing and desire."

She took this as a compliment. But then he added, "So that puts the burden of responsibility on you. You've done nothing to earn this face you have. You paid nothing for this gift. But since you have it, you must do something worthwhile with it."

"But what?" asked Carrie.

"Leave comedy, and act in dramatic plays. You have so much sympathy and such a beautiful voice.

Make them valuable to others. It will make your powers last longer."

"What do you mean?" she asked anxiously. He made it seem that all her success in comedy was worth nothing.

"You have this special quality in your face and in your nature. You don't have to use it to help other people. You can live alone, with the goal of satisfying only yourself. But then the look will leave your eyes. Your mouth will change. Your power to act will disappear."

Carrie felt slightly guilty, as if she had neglected something.

"If I were you," he said, "I'd change."

Carrie felt upset and troubled by his warnings. She worried about it for days, while sitting in her rocking chair.

Eventually she said to Lola, "I don't think I'll stay in comedy much longer."

"Oh, really? Why not?" Lola asked.

"I think," Carrie said, "I can do better in a serious play."

"What put that idea in your head?"

"Oh, nothing," she answered, sadly. "I've always thought so."

She sat there and grieved—longing, but doing nothing. It seemed like such a long way to this better thing, this distant ideal. And what she had now seemed so comfortable.

CHAPTER 47

The Pursuit of Happiness

When Hurstwood was unable to get enough money by begging, there were two charities that offered him some help. At the Sisters of Mercy mission house, he could get a free lunch. But first he had to stand in line with hundreds of other people. Even in the coldest weather, he had to wait patiently—often for hours—until it was his turn to go inside and eat. He also had to stand in line when he went to the back door of Fleischmann's bakery. There he could join about three hundred other people who were given a free loaf of bread every midnight. Otherwise, unless the weather was too harsh, he spent all day sitting on park benches or wandering aimlessly.

Life had always before seemed precious to him. But now Hurstwood was so weak that he could find little on earth worth living for. By January, he admitted to himself that his life was over. Each day he tried to find an old newspaper lying around. He looked inside to see if there were any chance that Carrie had come back to New York. But his eyes were beginning to hurt so much that he finally had to give up trying to read the newspaper. He had become so weak that all he could do was sleep—at least, whenever he had enough money to pay for a room.

His appearance had become so miserable that people turned away from him whenever he came near them. Police told him to hurry along. Restaurants kicked him out as soon as he finished eating. Boarding houses sent him away as soon as he stopped paying his rent. It became more and more difficult to get anything from anybody.

When a person walked by him on the street, he begged, "Give me a little something, will you? For God's sake, do. I'm starving."

But people refused over and over, and then hurried to get away from him.

Once a man answered, "Oh, go away. You're no good. I'm not giving you anything."

Hurstwood put his freezing hands back into his pockets. Tears came to his eyes.

"That's right," he said. "I'm no good now. I used to be all right. I used to have money."

With death in his heart, he thought about how other people had turned on the gas in their rooms and died. Why shouldn't he? But then he remembered that he didn't even have enough money to pay for a room.

Then he met a wealthy-looking gentleman, coming out of a barbershop.

"Would you mind giving me a little something?" Hurstwood asked this man boldly.

The gentleman looked him over and fished for a dime. Nothing but quarters were in his pocket. So he handed him one, just to get rid of him. "Go away, now."

Seeing the large, bright coin made Hurstwood feel a little better. So, for the moment, he stopped thinking about death. It was only when he got nothing but insults that death seemed better than life.

One day, in the middle of winter, it was bitterly cold. His feet were wet from the snow and slush. He started wandering. He stopped in front of the window of a fancy restaurant. Through the large plate glass windows, he saw red and gold decorations, white linen tablecloths, shining glassware, bright smiles on the faces of the people dining comfortably inside.

His mind was weak. But in his hunger he mumbled, sarcastically, "That's right. Go ahead and eat. You're the only people around here who want any food."

He wandered along Broadway. Police officers watched him closely, to make sure that he did not beg.

"What's the use?" he thought. "It's all over. I'm giving up."

Then he noticed that the wet snow seemed to glow from a reflected light. A brilliant sign lit up the sidewalk. He looked up and stared at the sign over the theater. It read, "Carrie Madenda—now playing at the Casino Theater." A large poster, framed in gold, showed a life-size picture of Carrie.

Something about it caught his attention. But he was so run-down that his mind was not very clear.

He went into the theater and told the attendant, "I want to see Miss Madenda."

The attendant shoved him away, saying, "Get out of here."

Hurstwood was too weak to resist. Still, he tried to explain, "You see, I'm really all right. I just want to see Miss Madenda. I—"

The man gave him a final push and closed the door. Hurstwood slipped and fell in the snow. He was hurt and ashamed. He began to cry and curse. "Damn you! I—I—I once used to hire people like you!"

Suddenly he felt a fierce anger against Carrie. "She owes me something to eat," he muttered. "She owes it to me."

But then he forgot what he was thinking about. Hopelessly, he turned back onto Broadway. He continued to drag his cold, wet feet through the snowy sidewalk—begging, crying, losing his thoughts, as his mind continued to decay.

That afternoon, throughout the city, the wind whipped the heavy snow. Night had already begun to fall. Along Broadway, business people and travelers with warm overcoats and umbrellas walked quickly toward their comfortable hotels.

In the Bowery district, men hunched down into their ragged clothes, pulled their thin hats over their ears, and waited.

In her luxurious apartment at the Waldorf,

Carrie was sitting, reading a book that Ames had recommended. Becoming weary, she yawned and walked over to the window. Looking out at all the cold, wet people passing by, she said to Lola, "Isn't it bad out there?"

Lola walked over to see and said, "I hope it keeps snowing so that we can go for a sleigh ride."

"Oh, dear," responded Carrie. "That's all you ever think of. Don't you even feel sorry for all those people who don't have anything to eat and nowhere to go tonight?"

"Of course I do," answered Lola. "But what can I do about it? I don't have anything."

Carrie smiled. "Even if you had, you still wouldn't care."

"I would, too," said Lola. "But when I was poor, people never gave me anything."

"Isn't it just awful?" said Carrie, gazing out at the winter storm.

Lola saw a ragged man stumble out of the Casino Theater, then slip and fall down in the snow. He started crying and cursing. Lola laughed. "Why look at that man over there! Don't men look silly when they fall?"

Carrie didn't bother looking. She simply said, "We'll have to take a carriage tonight."

At the same time, Mr. Charles Drouet had just entered the lobby of the Imperial Hotel. The bad weather increased his desire for indoor pleasures—a good dinner, an evening with a young woman, a show at the theater. A friend of his saw him, and asked if he had any plans for the evening.

"Why don't you come along with me?" said Drouet. "I can introduce you to something really terrific."

"Who is it?" asked his friend.

"Oh, just a couple of girls from around here. We could have a great time."

"Well, why don't you go get them, and we'll take 'em out to dinner?"

"Sure," said Drouet. "Wait'll I go upstairs and change my clothes."

"Well, I'll be in the barbershop," said the other. "I want to get a shave."

"All right," said Drouet, eagerly. He walked to the elevator in his fine new shoes. The traveling salesman was still as light on his feet as ever.

On the same snowy evening, a train was speeding into New York City from Chicago. A family of three—a young woman, her husband, and her mother—sat in an elegant train car, waiting for dinner.

The beautiful young woman, bored with the game they were playing, pushed away her cards. She announced, "I don't believe I want to play anymore."

Marrying a wealthy man had made her feel proud of herself and scornful of others.

Her husband, also dressed in expensive clothing, tried to keep her entertained. "Shall we go to dinner, then, Jessica?"

Jessica looked at the jewel-faced watch he had given her. "Oh, not yet," she answered. "I don't want to play anymore, though." She touched her lovely black hair.

Her husband gazed at her. Such beauty, even though it was cold, fascinated him.

"Jessica," said her mother, "check that pin on your blouse. It looks as if it might be coming loose."

Mrs. Hurstwood was pleased that her daughter still obeyed her. She was also pleased with her own clothing and jewelry. Such fine tailoring and elegant materials made her look much younger than she really was. She settled comfortably in her seat and smiled. It was so nice to be the mother-in-law of a rich young man. She herself had looked into his financial situation and encouraged her daughter to go out with him.

"Well, we won't have to put up with this cold weather for much longer," said the young man. "In two weeks we'll be in Rome."

At that moment, another young man walked down the aisle past them. He, too, was from Chicago, the son of a very wealthy banker. For some time he had been looking over this same beautiful, cold young woman. He boldly glanced over at her. She noticed. So, just to tease him, she turned her pretty face the other way. Jessica was not satisfied to be the modest wife of a wealthy man. She had far too much pride.

At this moment in the Bowery, Hurstwood stood in the wind and snow, waiting for an old boarding house to open its doors. Finally he was allowed to go inside, pay his fifteen-cent rent, and wearily drag himself to his room. The room was dingy—wooden, dusty, hard. There was a small gas burner in the corner.

He cleared his throat and locked the door.

Slowly he took off his coat, which was still soaking wet. He tucked it carefully along the small opening under the door. Then he neatly arranged his vest in the same place. He gently placed his old, wet, worn-out hat on the table. Then he pulled off his shoes and lay down on the bed.

He lay there, thinking, for a while. Then he got up and stood, calmly, in the dark. After a few moments, he turned on the gas. But he did not light it. For a while he stood there, hidden by the night, while the fumes gradually filled the room. Breathing in the gas, he finally fumbled for the bed.

"What's the use?" he said, weakly, as he lay down to rest.

Now Carrie had everything that she had thought she desired. She had her gowns and her carriage, her furniture and her bank account. She had friends—or at least people who would bow and smile and notice her success. For these she had once craved. There was applause, and there was publicity—things that had once seemed so far away and so necessary. But now all these things seemed unimportant and meaningless.

She had beauty, too.

And yet she was lonely. When she wasn't working, all she did was sit in her rocking chair, singing and dreaming.

Chicago had offered her more loveliness than she had ever known. She had been lured by fine clothing and elegant surroundings. These things seemed to make people happy. She, too, had been drawn to them—to Chicago and New York, to Drouet and Hurstwood, to the world of fashion and the world of theater. It was not that she needed these things. But she longed for the beauty and happiness that she thought they could give her.

Carrie heard no more from Drouet. She was not even aware of Hurstwood's death. There was a time when she thought that these men could guide her into the world of comfort and success. But she had learned that in their worlds, as in hers, she would not find happiness.

She had pursued beauty and success, but without thinking and understanding. Now, sitting alone, she was disillusioned. And yet, she still longed for something better. She was still waiting for the day when her dreams would become reality. Ames had shown her that there was something even better than those things she had now. But even if she reached that ideal, there would be another goal beyond that—and another and another.

Oh, Carrie, Carrie! Your heart will never be satisfied. It will forever be lured by beauty—pursuing it blindly and without reason. When your feet are weary and your life seems hopeless, your heart will ache, and your longings will return. Know, then, that you will never have too much. Nor will you ever have enough. In your rocking chair, by your window, you will long, alone. In your rocking chair, by your window, you will dream of a happiness that you may never feel.

About the Author

Like many writers, Theodore Dreiser decided to write about what he knew well. Many people and events in *Sister Carrie* are based on the author's own experience. In fact, Dreiser even had to change specific names and places so that the real-life people he wrote about would not sue him!

Theodore Dreiser was born on August 27, 1871, in Terre Haute, Indiana. His family was not wealthy, or even financially secure. Dreiser's own father managed a cotton mill. But when the mill burned down, suddenly he was out of work. The family quickly became poor. Most of Dreiser's brothers and sisters—he was the ninth of ten children—left home when they were still young. Like the main character in *Sister Carrie*, Dreiser's older sisters lived with men who never married them. One of his sisters became an unwed mother. Like Drouet and Hurstwood, two of Dreiser's brothers wasted their lives. One of them drank and gambled. The other wrote songs and introduced Dreiser to the world of popular entertainment. This brother was charming and generous, became financially successful, and often helped out his family when they needed money. But he soon spent all his money on women and clothes. He died at the age of only forty-eight, poor and alone.

Carrie herself was probably based on Dreiser's sister Emma. Emma left home to live with an architect. Later she left the architect to elope with the manager of a fancy saloon in Chicago. Like Hurstwood, this man was already married. And, like Hurstwood, he also stole money from his employer and ran away to Canada with another woman. Later, he and Emma moved to New York City, where he was unable to find work. Eventually, Emma, like Carrie, had to sneak away from him in order to lead a more secure life.

Dreiser himself was deeply affected by his father's loss of work, status, and financial stability. As a child, Dreiser often had nothing but fried mush to eat for dinner, and many nights he slept without heat. His family had to move often. His schoolwork suffered. But Dreiser educated himself by reading widely and observing other people closely. While he was still a teenager, Dreiser left home to try to build a successful life for himself in Chicago. But, like Carrie, he could find only dreary, low-paying jobs. He then spent a year at Indiana University, where he developed a love of writing and a fascination with observing the social lives of his classmates. After a year, he again looked for work, but found nothing suitable. He ended up living among homeless people on the streets of Chicago. Frightened, alone, and desperate, Dreiser had to steal $25 so that he could buy a coat to keep from freezing to death during that harsh Chicago winter.

In 1892, Dreiser finally found a job as a newspaper reporter. Through his work, he was able to observe city life up close. He wrote about all aspects of the city—from brutal domestic murders to celebrity interviews. He even reported a streetcar strike—and later used his observations to describe Hurstwood's experience as a strikebreaker. In Dreiser's work as a newspaper drama critic, he also had a chance to get to know the world of the theater—information that he later used in describing Carrie's experiences.

For one assignment, Dreiser was asked to cover a story about a contest that gave the twenty most popular Missouri schoolteachers a free trip to the Chicago World's Fair. On the train ride from St. Louis to Chicago, Dreiser met Sara White, one of the winners. They married and, in 1894, moved to New York City, where Dreiser earned a good salary as an editor. There—like Hurstwood, Drouet, and Carrie—Dreiser dressed in flashy clothing, dined in expensive restaurants, and lived in elegant apartments.

How did Dreiser shift from reporting newsworthy events to creating fictional characters? For some time, a friend had been encouraging Dreiser to try writing fiction. But Dreiser had no idea what to write. So one day, sitting in front of a blank sheet of paper, Dreiser decided to start just by writing down a title—"Sister Carrie." But what kind of character might Sister Carrie be? Dreiser thought about all the people he had known and observed in the course of his life—the sisters and brothers he had loved, the homeless people he had met, the newspaper stories he had covered, the celebrities he had interviewed. Then, like a good newspaper reporter, he recorded the facts—in vivid, realistic detail.

During Dreiser's time, however, some people did not want to read about real-life problems. They thought that popular fiction should only entertain, not inform the reader. So when Dreiser submitted a draft of *Sister Carrie* to Harper and Brothers publishing company, it was quickly rejected. But Dreiser did not give up. Instead, with his wife's help, Dreiser took out many of the more shocking details. He then submitted the revised *Sister Carrie* to Doubleday, Page and Company. Since Frank Doubleday, the head publisher, was about to leave on vacation, he asked Frank Norris, one of his editors, to look over the manuscript for him.

Norris, who was himself a young novelist, appreciated the value of the book and recommended that his company publish it. But upon returning from vacation, Frank Doubleday's wife happened to see a copy of the manuscript—just as it was about to be printed. She was horrified. Why wasn't Carrie punished for her "immoral" behavior? How could she be rewarded with fame and fortune after leading such a "sinful" life? Doubleday tried to stop publication of the book. But the publishing company had a binding contract with Dreiser. So on November 8, 1900, Doubleday agreed to print the book—but only 1,000 copies, which they then refused to market or distribute. Only about 456 copies were sold, for which Dreiser received $68.40 in royalties. He became so discouraged that he gave up writing fiction for ten years.

However, Frank Norris made sure that 127 copies were sent to reviewers, some of whom were well-known writers and influential critics. Many praised the book for its powerful realism. A British publisher printed a shortened edition in 1901, which became popular in England. Then, in 1907, partly at his own expense, Dreiser reprinted *Sister Carrie* in America. Finally, in 1912, Harper's, the publisher who had first rejected his manuscript, printed 10,000 copies. By then, Dreiser had published two other novels, was becoming better known as a writer, and had started writing fiction full-time. During his lifetime, Dreiser wrote a variety of works—including poetry, plays, essays, an autobiography, and seven novels. One of these, *An American Tragedy*, was turned into a movie. In 1952, a film version was also made of *Sister Carrie*.

Sister Carrie is considered an American literary classic. It was one of the first American novels to record accurate details about life in the city, the devastating effects of poverty, the harsh experiences of immigrants, and the brutal hardships suffered by working-class people. Unlike most earlier writers, Dreiser did not pass moral judgment on the personal lives of single women and their relationships with men. He even suggested that many women, like Carrie, were forced to compromise themselves in order to survive. In 1900, many people considered such behavior shocking and obscene. Some people tried to make sure that no one read what Dreiser had written. But Dreiser insisted on telling the truth about what he had observed and experienced. He believed that the public had a right to know the true story about life in the city, and judge it for themselves.

Many people respected and admired Dreiser for keeping his integrity as a writer. In fact, another famous author, Sinclair Lewis, said that he owed his own success to Dreiser. When Lewis won the Nobel Prize for Literature in 1930, he said, "Dreiser, more than any other man, is marching alone. . . . He has cleared the trail . . . in American fiction to honesty, boldness and passion of life. Without his pioneering, I doubt if any of us could, unless we liked to be sent to jail, seek to express life, beauty and terror." It took great courage and determination for Dreiser to write with such power, openness, and truth. Finally, a year before his death in 1945, Dreiser, too, was recognized for his contribution to American literature, when the American Academy of Arts and Letters awarded him the Merit Medal for Fiction.

About the Book

Some fictional characters are true heroes. We admire their good qualities and look up to them as positive role models. Some characters are true villains. We hate them because they do evil things and are motivated by all the wrong reasons. But the characters in *Sister Carrie* are neither all good nor all evil. Theodore Dreiser was one of the first American writers to create characters with a realistic blend of good and bad human qualities. Instead of judging his characters, he simply describes the real-life problems that they face and the choices that they make. Then he lets the readers decide for themselves what they think about the characters, and what they might do in the same situations.

In *Sister Carrie*, we understand and care about the main character, Carrie. But Carrie is neither a hero nor a villain. She does not show us the "right" way to live our lives. Instead, she gives us a chance to learn from her mistakes. She shows what can happen when people devote their lives to getting material things, rather than giving to others. She shows what can happen when people let themselves be seduced by false friends and deceptive dreams. She shows what can happen when people blindly pursue happiness, without thinking carefully about the meaning and purpose of their lives.

Carrie leaves her childhood home in order to find freedom, excitement, money, beauty, success.

She thinks, mistakenly, that these things will bring her happiness. And she hopes to find them in the glamorous city of Chicago. Carrie is lured by the "wonderful city world of lights, sounds, and excitement." She is dazzled by department stores filled with pretty clothes and fine jewelry. She desperately seeks a good job in one of Chicago's "magnificent" buildings with "impressive signs." She longs to see one of the melodramatic—and rather silly—shows so popular at the time. She expects it to be "easy to break ties" with her childhood family, since "they could never offer her anything important."

However, Carrie cannot earn enough money to live on her own. She ends up moving into an ugly apartment with her unimaginative sister and her grim brother-in-law. Instead of being free to enjoy the excitement of living in a big city, Carrie feels trapped by the drudgery of living with her sister, far from Chicago's downtown business district. With little education and no experience, she must take a low-paying, backbreaking job as a "shop girl" in a factory. There Carrie feels harassed by men, and ashamed that she cannot dress as well as the wealthier women who pass her on her way to work. At this point in her life, Carrie has achieved her goal of working in a big city. Yet "she felt that she deserved more. And her heart protested."

Feeling discouraged and helpless, Carrie assumes that the only way she can escape her misery is to be rescued by Drouet, her "knight in shining armor." Instead of thinking carefully about her actions and their consequences, Carrie assumes that Drouet's "hopeful, carefree, easygoing" manner will "carry away all her problems." She feels flattered and reassured when Drouet offers to provide her with a cozy apartment, steak dinners at restaurants, and pretty clothes. At first she enjoys a "new feeling of freedom" and sees "possibilities in her future." But when Drouet takes her to the theater, Carrie discovers even more exciting, more beautiful worlds—both on the stage and in the audience. Once in a while, Carrie wonders whether it is wrong to live as Drouet's mistress. But Carrie believes that only material things—beautiful things—will make her "feel happy and safe." So she sets aside her questions about right and wrong.

Instead, Carrie focuses on what "everyone else" seems to have. She compares herself to the wealthiest women in Chicago, and wants to look like them and live like them. For example, Carrie wishes that Drouet would pay her compliments and spend all his money on buying her clothes and keeping her entertained—just like the husband of her upstairs neighbor, Mrs. Hale. Carrie then compares Drouet to Hurstwood. She is dazzled by Hurstwood and assumes that he is "the better man—stronger and higher." She feels that Hurstwood appreciates her and brings out the best in her. Although Carrie does not love Hurstwood, she does sympathize with his loneliness and misery. She is also attracted to his money, power, and strength. But in fact, Hurstwood turns out to be a liar, kidnapper, thief, gambler, and bigamist. He judges his worth by how much money he has. So when he is very wealthy, he refuses to share his money with those people who have nothing. And later, when he has no money himself, he feels so worthless that he ends his life.

Yet Carrie never seems to learn from her mistakes. She continues to pursue the same dreams, without questioning whether they are realistic or worth pursuing. As an actress, she achieves independence, glamour, beauty, fame, and fortune. But the more she has, the more she wants. She moves into a small apartment with Lola, and then a much fancier suite in a grand hotel on Broadway. Wealthy, attentive men flatter her, shower her with gifts, and offer to buy her anything she desires. "Carrie understood, though, that they were interested only in her fame and fortune. And that made her even less interested in going out with them." She still feels lonely and unappreciated. But how can others understand and appreciate her when Carrie is only acting out a part?

And although Carrie has become a famous actress, is she a "good" actress? When Carrie sees Ames after she has become wealthy and famous, she assumes that he will "approve of her success. But he was disappointed. . . . He thought she could do far better." Ames appreciates that Carrie understands and feels two emotions—sympathy for others, and longing for things. But he advises

Carrie that "The world is full of things we desire.
. . . It doesn't do us any good to want what we
cannot have, what we cannot be." Ames reminds
Carrie that she is "drifting away from the old ideal
that she had felt after her first performance in
Chicago. Why had she lost it?" Longing "to live
up to his standards," Carrie "grieved—longing,
but doing nothing. It seemed like such a long way
to this better thing, this distant ideal. And what
she had now seemed so comfortable."

Although Carrie feels sorry for other people, she
is so focused on satisfying her own desires that she
never reaches out to others. Instead, she keeps
reaching for more and more of the same material
things. She never questions her goals for the future;
she never feels satisfied with what she has in the present. By the end of the book, Carrie has "everything
that she had thought she desired. . . . But now all
these things seemed unimportant and meaningless."

Where has Carrie gone wrong? She has a
beautiful face and beautiful things. But Carrie does
not live a beautiful life because her life lacks goodness and meaning. Carrie has pursued her goals
"without thinking and understanding." She
expects to find lasting happiness through material
success, without questioning whether such hopes
are real or just illusions. She longs and longs for
things that she doesn't have, instead of enjoying
and appreciating what she does have. She never
thinks about whether what she wants is really
worth having. Her life is filled with things, but it

remains empty of love. Because she devotes her life to getting more and more for herself, Carrie never experiences the joy of giving and sharing with others. And so she will never "have enough." Instead, she will forever "dream of a happiness that [she] may never feel."

Unlike many novels, *Sister Carrie* does not have a happy ending. Unfortunately, Drouet has not changed, still choosing simply to flirt with women rather than make commitments to them. Tragically, Hurstwood gives up on his own future because he thinks that he is "nothing" without money. Sadly, Carrie continues to rock back and forth in her chair, dreaming of the future, but never really going forward.

Although we may choose not to follow Carrie's example, we can easily understand what she wants, how she feels, and why she makes her choices. Like Carrie, many of us long for freedom, excitement, money, beauty, success, and happiness. By reading Carrie's story, we can see where Carrie's life went wrong—and try not to make the same choices for ourselves. Unlike Carrie, we can try to give and accept love. We can help other people, instead of just using them. We can learn from the mistakes we have made in the past, and avoid repeating them in the future. We can look carefully at our dreams, and decide which ones are really worth pursuing. And by appreciating what we have right now instead of always longing for more, we may be able to dream about—and feel—true happiness.